THE SKELETON LAKE

THE JAKE SAWYER SERIES (BOOK 6)

ANDREW LOWE

GET A FREE JAKE SAWYER NOVELLA

Sign up for the no-spam newsletter and get a FREE copy of the Sawyer prequel novella **THE LONG DARK**.

Check the details at the end of this book.

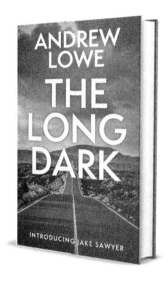

Email: andrew@andrewlowewriter.com
Web: andrewlowewriter.com
Twitter: @andylowe99

First published in 2021 by Redpoint Books
This edition April 2024
Cover photographs © Shutterstock
Cover by Book Cover Shop

ISBN: 978-1-9997290-0-4

For Tom and Josh

Though the mills of God grind slowly,
Yet they grind exceeding small;
Though with patience he stands waiting,
With exactness grinds he all.

— *HENRY WADSWORTH LONGFELLOW,*
'RETRIBUTION'

PROLOGUE

'Only me!'

Linda Keller bustled in through the sticky front door and dropped her keys into the Royal Doulton dish on the hall table.

She winced at the sitting room TV volume. *Dad's Army*. The chatter of dialogue, punctuated by bursts of studio laughter. Loud enough to be heard in the street.

'You need a new hearing aid battery, Charlie.'

Linda waddled down the hall, huffing and puffing. She was late fifties, hefty, short-legged. She hauled herself into the kitchen, set down a battered shoulder bag on the Formica table and transferred its contents to the fridge. Eggs, full-fat milk, chopped liver, butter, pâté.

'I got your duck spread.'

She scraped a half-eaten bowl of porridge into the pedal bin and added the bowl and spoon to a stack of soiled plates on the draining board.

'Oh, Charlie. You need to put these in soak. How many times do I have to tell you?' Linda glared at the dishes, hands on hips, then turned and walked back down the hall into the sitting room. 'I'll deal with them later.'

Charles Yates sat facing away from the door, in a high-backed armchair, in front of a boxy television set topped with two Doulton figurines: an old man in a floppy hat, holding a multicoloured bunch of balloons, and a young woman with a 1930s-style billowing skirt, her porcelain cheeks blotted with rouge. It was late afternoon, still light, but the heavy curtains were drawn, blocking the view out to the bungalow's modest back garden.

'What regiment is it?'

'Coldstream Guards, Grenadier Guards.'

The TV cast a cold light across the room, sending shadows dancing over the scruffy furnishings. Its glare reflected in a glass-fronted cabinet stuffed with ornaments and photos, most of them small and sepia, marooned in the centre of gaudy frames.

'But, Mum. It's such a silly colour.'

'Nonsense! Mr Mainwaring won't mind.'

Linda spotted the TV remote on the floor by the sofa. She smiled to herself, scooped it up, lowered the volume. 'I don't know how you can sleep through that racket. If you need an afternoon nap, you should use your bed, Charlie.'

'You don't think he looks silly, do you?'

Linda's nose twitched. The room smelt sour and unlaundered, with an earthy undertone of body odour, and a hint of something unfamiliar: florid, sickly.

'Is that your new aftershave?' She replaced the remote on the side table by Charles's armchair and hustled past the fold-out dining table, heading for the bedroom. 'If I'm honest, it's not very you. Maybe you'll get something nicer for your birthday next week. Eighty-five. You should have a party.' She muttered under her breath. 'Not that you've got anyone to invite.'

'That's very kind of you, Mrs Pike. But the ears wouldn't go under my helmet.'

Linda clunked her ankle on the side of the dining table and yelped with pain. 'Let's get these curtains open. It's like a funeral home in here.'

She turned, aimed at the window, caught a glint of liquid on the carpet in front of the armchair. She stepped forward, almost side-on to Charles, and saw his olive-green tea mug on the floor by the dresser.

'Oh, Charlie. You're off with the fairies, you really are. I bet there's more tea on the carpet than in your stomach.'

'I'm sure they're very cosy, but pantomime clothes are not good for discipline.'

Linda walked over to the curtains and pulled them apart.

Low sun, peering through the gap left by the open gate, revealing the side passage that led to the centre of Sheldon village.

She turned, bent down for the mug.

The liquid had spread over to the edge of the carpet and pooled at the base of the cabinet. Dark brown in the TV gloom, but now, in the sunlight: lighter, redder.

'There's six pounds of the best sausages. That's enough for the whole troop.'

Linda stared down at the liquid, baffled. She lifted her head and, for the first time, looked at Charles Yates. He was upright in his armchair, head tilted onto his shoulder. The white shirt beneath his cardigan was stained red, and he held one hand in his lap, with the other slumped at his side, half submerged in the puddle of blood that had gathered in the space between the seat and the arm.

'Rank, man. Rank!'

Linda cried out; a startled shout. She lunged forward, toward Charles, then recoiled. The sagging skin of his neck stretched like wet dough around a jagged slash wound

3

across his trachea. Again, she moved forward, hesitated, reached out to his face.

His eyes. Emptied. The balls punctured in their sockets. Lashes matted with jelly.

His cheeks. Slick with vitreous tears.

'Pardon? They were fresh this morning.'

Another cry, and a jolt of panic, sending Linda stumbling backwards, falling to the floor. She scrambled to get up again, her hand squelching in the saturated carpet.

She made it to her feet and pushed past the chair, down the hall, out through the sticky front door, where the shout rose to a scream.

PART ONE

SLIGHT RETURN

1

A silver Toyota bounced along a narrow dirt track, slow and steady, the driver clearly mindful of the car's suspension. It rolled to a halt in front of a single-storey grey-stone cottage set far back from the track, in the shadow of dense woodland.

A short stooped man got out of the car and pulled a large sports holdall from the boot. He hitched it across his back and hobbled up the path to the front door, his padded khaki jacket swallowed by the dusk light.

Music from within. Male singing, acoustic guitar.

Professor Donald Ainsworth opened the door and ducked in through the low opening, sidestepping to make room for the bag. He turned and looked back across the undulating fields, blotted with green now, impatient for spring. But in the far distance, the caps of the Furness Fells were still speckled in snow, and The Old Man, the alpha peak, kept watch over the darkening surface of Coniston Water.

Ainsworth took off his gloves and flattened his untidy hair over his bald patch.

'Hello?'

The door opened onto the central living area: cheap leather sofa, wall-mounted TV, wooden table and matching chairs, corner table with an old portable CD player. Stone floor, low ceiling, exposed brickwork walls. A wood burner stove blazed in a broad hearth beneath an iron mantel lined with candles, lantern and a mirror.

An enlarged photograph was tacked to the wall above the table: the mouth of a cave, set in the side of a tall crag, rising up from a verdant valley.

'I hope you bought the cinnamon bagels.'

Jake Sawyer emerged through a slim passage that linked to the back side of the cottage. He wore a full beard, and his coal-black hair was thick and wild. He was topless and barefoot, in shabby black jeans.

Ainsworth shook his head. 'No cinnamon. Had to bring sesame seed.'

Sawyer sighed. 'This is worse than Ocado.'

He paused the music and took a white shirt from the back of a chair, pushed his right arm through the sleeve. He turned to slide in his left arm, revealing his heavily muscled back, with a tattoo scored into the space between his shoulders: *Κατά τον δαίμονα εαυτού*.

'Is that Greek?' said Ainsworth.

'I got it in Paris. It means "true to his own spirit".' He faced Ainsworth, buttoning up the shirt, and gave a pained smile. 'I was eighteen.'

Ainsworth's eyes flashed across Sawyer's bare chest before he averted his gaze to the photo of the cave.

'I know. Dry skin patches. They're harder to explain. Could be related to a condition. I saw someone about it late last year. Haven't been able to follow up, though. Obviously.'

Ainsworth took a seat. 'If you're after a diagnosis, I don't do the body stuff.'

'Just the life of the mind.'

Ainsworth reached down and unzipped the bag. 'Arendt's great unfinished masterpiece. I'm a psychologist. That's more moral philosophy.'

'You're not really hirsute enough for this conversation, Donald. You need more beard to stroke. I had a copy of Arendt's other book, *The Human Condition*. I like that quote from Cato the Elder. "Never is he more active than when he does nothing, never is he less alone than when he is by himself."'

'So, you've been working on both body and mind?'

Sawyer inhaled, fixed Ainsworth with his glinting green eyes. 'You smell of the world.'

'The world?'

'The big room. Out there. Tobacco. Coffee.'

'I bought a flask. For the car.'

Sawyer eyed the bag. 'What's the drive? Three hours?'

Ainsworth spluttered. 'The way you drive, maybe.'

Sawyer swept a hand through his hair. 'As ever. I can't thank you enough. But I'll keep trying.'

Ainsworth took off his wire-framed glasses and wiped down the lenses. 'You should be more careful, Jake. I could have been anyone.'

'I heard your engine. I know it by now.'

Ainsworth took a few items out of the holdall and laid them on the table. 'I bought the books you wanted, and the CDs and DVDs. A few... burner phones.'

Sawyer smiled in approval. 'You're getting the lingo. And you're wondering why I'm listening to folk music.'

'Indeed. Sixties and seventies, too. And the contemporary albums for the iPod I got for you. Whatever happened to your nineties obsession?'

'It's my mum's taste. Psych rock, folk, Shocking Blue, Fairport Convention...'

Ainsworth studied one of the CDs. 'Brian Auger.'

Sawyer nodded. '"This Wheel's On Fire." Classic. Did you get the other stuff?'

'Yes. Jensen consulted. I told him it was for my own work. Security.'

'Thanks. You can't creep up on me now. How is Richard?'

Ainsworth frowned and scrubbed at his neat salt-and-pepper beard, barely a layer of stubble compared with Sawyer's. 'You told me you didn't want anything from the outside. Even if you begged.'

Sawyer's eyes wandered. 'Time to unlash me from the mast.'

'He's well. The book did okay. He's working on something new. I'm still studying criminal methods in the digital world.'

Sawyer took a shoebox from under the table. He removed the lid, glancing up at Ainsworth, checking his reaction. The cash was dwindling; just three rolls now. He peeled off a number of fifty-pound notes and handed them over. 'I went into the village.'

Ainsworth startled. 'What?'

'I needed to see a bit of life. I've been a few times now. Dropped in to the corner shop. It's the kind of place that sells everything from mops to toupees. There are a few things in there that I'd rather get for myself. Little comforts.'

'Did anyone notice you? Pay you attention?'

'No comedy double takes, no. I go when I need a shower. People steer clear. I've developed a convincing vagrant shuffle.'

'Sounds like a new dance craze.'

They laughed. Ainsworth took out two green plastic tumblers, a small bottle of Jameson and a large bottle of Diet Coke. He poured a whiskey for himself and a Coke for Sawyer. They clinked and drank.

Ainsworth winced as the spirit went down. 'There's a reward.'

'Crimestoppers?'

'Yes.'

Sawyer nodded. 'Farrell.'

Ainsworth took another sip, wiggled his tumbler in the air. 'This is a celebration, you know. It's my anniversary. Ten years of solo living.'

'So, tell me about her.'

'Huh?'

'You've met someone.'

Ainsworth set down his drink, held Sawyer's gaze. 'What do you mean?'

Sawyer took a slug of Coke. 'You used to grind your knuckles into your forehead, in a figure of eight. Self-soothing. But not the last couple of times you've visited. Your hair is neater, you've cultivated a nice grown-up beard. New jacket.'

Ainsworth smiled. 'I'm running a bridge group at the university. There's been a... connection with one of the politics lecturers. A strong player. Mid-forties.'

'Still got it.' Sawyer took another drink and sat back, studying Ainsworth. He stood up, walked to the window.

'I got the info on the business accounts you asked for,' said Ainsworth.

Sawyer pulled down the blind and clicked on a corner lamp. The room shimmered in the glow from the bulb. He crouched by the wood burner, opened the door and tossed a fresh log into the flames. He closed the door and stood upright. The firelight reared up behind, plunging him into silhouette.

'Again, thanks.'

'You already said that. I'm just returning the favour, Jake. You saved my sanity, with the Beck thing.'

Sawyer took his seat again. 'You've saved my life.'

A moment of silence, more serene than awkward.

'I bought the newspapers,' said Ainsworth, 'as usual. But I assume—'

'Including the one from the time I took my leave?'

'Yes.'

Another sip of Coke. 'Read me something. Just a few highlights.'

Ainsworth took a few copies of the *Derbyshire Times* out of the holdall. He pulled out an issue and read out loud from an article on page two. 'This is from a few days after you—'

'Who's the writer?'

'Dean Logan. *Fears grow for Hero Cop. Derbyshire police have expressed their concern for the welfare of Detective Inspector Jake Sawyer, following his self-discharge from Buxton's Cavendish Hospital on Tuesday.*' Ainsworth glanced up at Sawyer; he had his eyes closed, head resting against the wall. '"*We need to speak to DI Sawyer urgently," said Detective Superintendent Ivan Keating of Buxton's Major Investigation unit. "We believe he left the hospital after learning of a development in an internal enquiry regarding the death of a murder suspect in DI Sawyer's custody. DI Sawyer is a fine detective with an auspicious record, but he is not to be approached directly."* And then there's a bit of detail on numbers to call, et cetera.'

Sawyer slid the other copies of the newspaper towards him and browsed. 'What's the reward?'

'They started to offer that a month or so after you went missing. No figure specified.'

Sawyer stood up and continued to turn the pages while wriggling into a red-and-black striped woollen jumper.

'Dennis the Menace,' said Ainsworth.

Sawyer kept his eyes on the paper. 'Showing your age. I've also had Freddy Krueger. *Where's Wally?* is more appropriate to my situation, though.'

'That's the latest issue,' said Ainsworth, nodding at the newspaper. 'I read it when I stopped for coffee at Carlisle. Nasty case on the front page. Elderly chap. Murdered in his own home. Eighty-odd.'

Sawyer found the story. 'Eighty-four.' He frowned. 'Nothing stolen.'

Ainsworth winced back the last of his whiskey. 'So, any tenant issues?'

'I had to thaw out one of the water pipes last week.' He glanced up. 'Hairdryer.'

'Cold snap's over. Spring is—'

'Springing.' Sawyer closed the newspaper. 'How long have you had this place?'

Ainsworth narrowed his eyes. 'You asked me that last time.'

'Sorry. Memory's a bit scratchy. Must be the isolation. My brain pinballs around a lot.'

'This place is modest, I know. But it holds plenty of happy memories. Judith and I stayed here for a couple of summers when Lena was young. We bought it as a retreat, but only came out once more. I've been renting it out for six or seven years.'

'Do you use an agency for that?'

'No.'

Sawyer finished his drink, turned to stare into the fire. 'How's my brother?'

Ainsworth ran a cupped hand over his beard. 'You said you didn't want to know, unless there was an emergency.'

'I want to know.'

'He's in your old place, as far as I know. I checked, as you asked. Went to a conference in Manchester, few weeks ago.'

Sawyer leaned forward. 'And the place is in one piece?'

'Seemed fine to me. I parked just down the road, saw him at the window. He came out wearing walking boots, crossed the road and headed off towards Kinder Scout.'

'They will have questioned him. I would. Maybe put some surveillance on him. Any sign of anyone else?'

Ainsworth sighed. 'I don't know, Jake. I'm an academic, not a detective. Your old car is still there.' He moved to pour another shot of whiskey, changed his mind. 'Do you think he would have told them anything?'

'No. I transferred the deed digitally. No direct contact. I was hoping he could use it as a halfway house. And he doesn't have anything to tell them, anyway. Mike was always a terrible liar. When we were kids, he got into trouble for stealing one of my toys. A plush koala bear. He swore he hadn't touched it, but Mum knew. He had a major tell. The rising "no". Like a question. Too defensive.'

Sawyer took the remaining cash out of the box and replaced the lid.

'You'll like this,' said Ainsworth. 'Jensen told me he'd heard they had a detective trying to find you. Private. Apparently, he went to the Canary Islands. Lanzarote.'

Sawyer laughed. 'I mentioned it to Shepherd ages ago.'

'Your colleague? Why would he tell them that? I thought he—'

'So did I.' He turned back to the fire. 'He has a family.'

Ainsworth held the silence for a few seconds. 'How long, Jake?'

'For what?'

'Have you thought any more about this "plan"'?'

'I haven't thought about much else for the last five months.'

'So, how long are you going to stay like this?'

Sawyer inhaled through his nose, held the breath, let it out through his mouth. 'I'm ready.'

2

'How was your stay, A7781DT?'

Curtis Mavers scratched out his name with an ageing ballpoint and pushed the document back across the table. 'I'll be sure to leave you a five-star review, boss. There's a new website. *Rate my Prison*.'

The discharge officer, Hampton, frowned and tilted back his bald head, studying Mavers. 'Really?'

'Only messin'. Are we done? Time for bittersweet goodbyes?'

'I wouldn't get too emotional, lad. We'll probably see each other again soon. Seventy-five per cent of cons re-offend within nine years of release. Forty per cent in the first twelve months. I imagine it's higher for cons of your... ethnicity.'

Mavers gave a theatrical wince. 'If I'm struggling on the outside, boss, it'll be the thought of getting reacquainted with you that'll keep me going.'

Hampton's look hardened. 'That mouth will get you into trouble, one of these days.'

'You sound like my mum, boss.' He grinned. 'With respect.'

Hampton slipped the discharge form into a folder and took out a poorly photocopied checklist. 'Clothing all done. Not a lot of property, but it's all in your bag. Done your dabs.'

'And I am who you think I am?'

Hampton raised his eyes from the form, then looked back down again. 'Just a few quid in your spends account.'

'Can I use it to get a couple of Snickers? Didn't get breakfast.'

'Goes back into the kitty. You missed the deadline to transfer to an external account. Now, you've done just shy of three years of a five-year sentence. I'm serving you paperwork which clarifies your licence conditions.' He looked up, forced a smile. 'Are you fully aware of those?'

Mavers folded his beefy arms, exposing a forearm tattoo of a wolf with wild eyes, breathing flames from its open jaws. 'You mean, do I know what I'm supposed to do, who I'm supposed to see?'

'Exactly that.'

'Yes, boss. My assigned probation officer is a short bus ride from my approved address. My cousin's flat. That's where I'm staying until I get my own place.'

'And you need to be there at 9am tomorrow. Rock up at 9:01am, and you're back in here.'

Hampton handed over the paper and got to his feet; Mavers did likewise. He was tall and wide-shouldered, and seemed to sway in place, assessing his surroundings, poised to pounce. Hampton wasn't far off Mavers vertically, but in terms of comparative stature, he was more like a child.

'How are your role models, these days, A7781DT? Parents still alive?'

'Not anymore, boss. My mum was an English bank clerk. Dad built houses in his home town, Mandeville. She met him on holiday. I was made in Jamaica, born in the North of England.'

Hampton nodded, pondering. 'Here? Manchester?'

'Thankfully, no. Croxteth, Liverpool. Not the kind of place you'd choose to raise kids. Not many there have the luxury of choice, though.'

Hampton unlocked and opened the door by his desk and tilted his head for Mavers to lead the way. They walked through a musty entrance hall and stopped by a second officer stationed by a heavy external door. The officer checked Mavers's paperwork and opened the door.

Daylight. The chug of distant traffic.

Mavers smiled and held his arms out wide. 'Free at last!' He turned square to Hampton. 'This must be difficult for you, boss.'

'What do you mean?'

'I get to leave, but you're still stuck in this shithole.'

'I do go home every night, you know.'

Mavers glanced out of the open door. 'To Judy and the kids. Punching well above your weight there, boss.'

Hampton took a step forward, leaned in to rasp into Mavers's ear. 'It's time you were someone else's problem, A7781DT. Get a shift on. You don't want to keep your chauffeur waiting.'

'Chauffeur?'

'Somebody out there likes you. And they've sent a nice car to prove it.'

Mavers stepped outside, into the early morning chill. He stopped, closed his eyes, inhaled.

The second officer patted him on the shoulder. 'Off you fuck, son. Before I nick you for loitering.'

Mavers crossed the perimeter road and towards a line of parking bays. A stocky man emerged from a White Mercedes S-Class and opened the back door. Mavers approached him, ducking down to peer through the tinted windows. He smiled and eased onto the back seat, next to a grey-haired man in an expensive-looking charcoal suit. The driver closed the door behind him.

Mavers turned to his host. 'I can bus it to Piccadilly, Dale.'

The car drove off, sliding into the morning traffic on the southbound A56.

Dale Strickland took off his heavy-framed glasses and buffed up the lenses with his shirt cuff. 'Have a bounce, Curtis. I just had the seats reupholstered. Premium Nappa leather.' He replaced his glasses and ran his hand across the seat. 'Chrome-tanned. They only use the hides from young animals. Calves, lambs.'

'You a fuckin' Bond villain now, then?'

'Just enjoying the finer side of life. You're probably keen for some of that yourself, after three years of shitting in the corner.'

'A decent cup of tea would do me. How did you know when I was getting out?'

'I pretty much work with the man who let you out.' Strickland pushed a button and the back seat windows on either side lowered a few inches. 'Nothing personal, Curtis. You're just a bit... prison-fresh.'

'I heard you were Deputy Mayor, Dale. So when you say work "with", don't you mean work "for"?'

Strickland grinned. 'What are your plans?'

'Short term? Get back to the hood. Sort my benefits. Probation officer tomorrow morning. Up in Huyton.'

Strickland waved a hand. 'We can work that out.'

'Long term. I'm level now. Paid my debts on the inside.'

'By proxy.'

Mavers eyed him. 'Would have been nice to settle a few

affairs in person, but my circumstances forced me to use freelance talent.'

The car swept past the Gothic spires of Manchester Cathedral and dug into the commuter crawl at the edge of Deansgate. Dale opened a pull-down table cabinet in the back of the passenger seat and took out a bottle of Glenfiddich and two glasses. He poured two shots and handed one to Mavers. 'A man of your talents shouldn't be relying on state handouts. As part of my role, I've been working with Russell Hogan, the mayor of Greater Manchester, on an initiative to reduce drug-related deaths.'

Mavers stared into the glass, sloshed his Scotch around. 'I'd heard you were involved in handing out the drugs.'

'Curtis. I'm familiar with your background. I want to challenge and confront the kind of people responsible for what happened to your sister, and hundreds more like her. Drug use is a social problem. You don't make it go away by punishing the addicts, the victims. You need to go higher up the chain, take on the people who do the grooming and exploiting.' He leaned forward. 'Yes, I accept that I did some illegitimate business in that field. But it means that I know the culture. I understand it from both sides. I've established a charity as the public face of my drive for harm reduction, with branches in all of the boroughs.'

'So, you used to be a naughty boy but now you're the messiah.'

Strickland laughed. 'I wouldn't go that far. I just want to help the people who find themselves on the fringes, like Jayne Mavers. I pledged some of my salary to homeless and abuse charities when I ran for mayor, and I own a number of clubs that are giving young people somewhere to go, somewhere to meet. But now I've handed that off to another department, and I need someone to help me take on the pond scum in their big houses in Hale Barnes, watching 4K TVs in their indoor swimming pools, getting fatter on the suffering of people like your sister.'

Mavers sniffed at his drink. 'So, how do you get this done if you're not the top dog?'

'My position gives me access to certain details. People who the police leave alone, in exchange for drips of information. I'm not happy about that. And you shouldn't be either. You're in good shape, Curtis. You've used your time away well.' Dale gave Mavers's shoulder a squeeze. 'I can see you haven't gone soft on me.'

Mavers gazed out of the window. 'So we boot the current top dogs in the bollocks, disrupt their business. The numbers come down. Looks good for your boss.'

'Fuck my boss! It'll look good for me. And for you, this is a simple choice. Red pill or blue pill? We can either drop you at Piccadilly and you can continue on your merry way. Steady job stacking shelves at Aldi. Or we can keep driving for twenty minutes until we get to the apartment I've arranged for you in leafy Didsbury.'

Mavers ran his hand over the seat leather. He turned, clinked glasses with Strickland, knocked back his Scotch in one.

Strickland finished his glass, gestured to the driver in the rear-view mirror. The car turned into a side road, and pulled away from the city centre. 'There's another problem you might be able to help with.'

Mavers reached over to the bottle and poured himself another measure. 'Big problem?'

Strickland closed his eyes, sank back into the seat. 'More of a minor irritation, really. A stone in my shoe.'

Sawyer pounded his usual beat: a 10k loop around the less-travelled trails of Grizedale Forest. The Norway spruces glinted emerald green above; a sheltering canopy beneath the cloudless sky.

He wore cheap wired headphones, kept steady by his untamed hair. The music—Roísín Murphy, The Avalanches—came from an ancient iPod Mini, acquired by Ainsworth and filled to Sawyer's specification.

He kept his pace steady, taking care not to stumble on loose rocks or trailing stumps. For most, a twisted ankle out here would be a mishap; for him, it would be disastrous. Contact, attention, maybe of the medical type. A paper trail.

Remembered lines from Larkin cut through the kick drum pulse.

> *The trees are coming into leaf*
> *Like something almost being said*

Sawyer joined a rugged track that led down to the edge of Coniston village. He crunched through a bed of shallow bracken, and accelerated out onto the pavement that ran beside the western shore of the five-mile-long lake. He could join the farm road, which would double him back through the tarn and the approach to Ainsworth's cottage. Or he could drop into the convenience store, two doors down from the busy bistro.

He slowed, crossed the farm road, paused outside the store. He hitched his headphones around his neck, pulled up his hood and entered.

It was a medium-sized place, with three narrow aisles, well stocked with staples and short-stay items aimed at rental tourists and local campers.

Sawyer kept his head down, angled away from the counter at the far end, where the proprietor—a middle-aged man in a bright-red turban—served three male customers gathered in a line by a tall rack of impulse items.

He scooped up a variety multipack of Monster Munch, and sorted through a handful of coins for the exact amount: one pound fifty.

The men had taken a pink rubber ball from a box near the counter and were bouncing it off the floor to each other, laughing. The largest of the three put too much power into a bounce, and it ricocheted off the roof and into a tray of chocolate bars, scattering several to the floor.

'Please!' The proprietor hurried round from behind the counter. 'Don't do that.' He scooped up the bars and replaced them in the tray.

The big one looked at the other two, mock sheepish. 'Excuse me, mate. Have you just washed your hair?'

They collapsed with laughter, high-fiving each other.

Sawyer crouched and pretended to browse a low shelf, which allowed him to keep a view of the counter area. The men were white, mid-twenties, athletic; too cliquey and confident to be tourists. The big one took off a green Under

Armour baseball cap, rooted through a crop of greasy blond hair. The other two watched him as he pointed up to a shelf of cigarettes behind the counter.

'Give us a packet of Camels, mate.'

The proprietor turned and took down the cigarettes, placing them on the counter.

'Oh, and twenty B&H. King Size.'

Again, the man turned and retrieved the cigarettes, setting the gold pack on top of the Camels.

'Oh, and a packet of Marlboros.'

The proprietor hesitated, eyed the men in turn, then took down the cigarettes. 'You have money for this?'

One of the other two—shorter, heavier—spoke up. 'Tenner for the lot.'

'It's thirty-seven pounds and fifty pence.'

The big one pulled a crumpled banknote from his pocket. 'Alright. Fifteen. Come on, mate. Play the white man.'

They laughed again.

'Take it easy, lads.' Sawyer stepped up to the counter and set down a pound coin and a fifty pence piece. 'Just this. Thanks.'

The proprietor nodded and took the money.

The shorter one leaned into Sawyer's personal space. 'And who the fuck is this? Looks like an apprentice wizard.' Sawyer caught a sour whiff of unbrushed teeth and lager.

The third man—older than the other two, prematurely balding—shoved his friend aside to get a look at Sawyer. 'Woah! He must get his powers from Monster Munch.'

More laughs and high fives.

Sawyer avoided eye contact, turned and walked to the door.

'Tell you what, though,' said the short one. 'Nobody told me wizards stink of piss.'

Sawyer reached the door.

'Now, then.' The big man again, to the proprietor. 'Gunga Din. You've got two choices. You can let us have these fags for the reasonable sum of fifteen pounds. Or you can fuck off back to Bang-a-dish.'

Squealing, uproarious laughter.

Sawyer turned the handle and opened the door.

The proprietor stood his ground. 'Leave now. I'm selling you nothing. Leave my premises now, or I'll call the police.'

The big one leaned into the proprietor's face. 'Hey! They're not your police to call. Okay? This country is now back in the hands of the British. You had your day, setting up your shops, sending your money back home. Well, now the money's staying here where it belongs.'

Sawyer shut the door, closed his eyes.

Slow, measured breathing.

'Fair play, though,' said the older one. 'You seen the fucking piece back there? Dark, tall.'

'Don't speak about my daughter like that.'

'Probably has too much tikka masala, though,' said the big man. 'She needs prime British beef.'

The short one wheezed with laughter and wrapped an arm round the shoulders of the balding man. 'Better make sure you're not first in line, then, Ronnie.'

'Okay, pay attention,' said Sawyer, walking back to the counter and setting down his crisps. 'There's a lot to get through.'

The three men turned and glared at him. The big one leaned against the counter, while the other two took a step forward, chins up.

Sawyer held up a finger. 'Number one. Gunga Din is a fictional character from an 1890 poem by Rudyard Kipling, set in colonial India. It's about a water carrier who saves the life of a British soldier but is then shot and killed. I'm pretty sure Gunga Din was from a Muslim tribe. Since this man is wearing a traditional turban, I assume he's Sikh. You have the right country, though, but you're a few centuries out.'

The big man's hand went to the pocket of his jeans, hovered there.

'Two. I assume "Bang-a-dish" is a Wildean play on words for Bangladesh?'

Silence. Confusion.

The balding man glanced over Sawyer's shoulder to the door of the shop.

'Well,' continued Sawyer, 'this one is a geography issue. Sikhism isn't a major religion in Bangladesh, so I doubt there's any connection with...' He raised his eyebrows at the proprietor.

'Harmeet,' said the man.

The short one looked around, as if searching for hidden cameras. 'Is this a wind-up?'

The balding guy took a step towards Sawyer. 'Smart-arse, yeah?'

Sawyer smiled. 'Just a decent education. My mum was a teacher.'

The big man moved away from the counter. 'You need teaching some manners.'

'Nice,' said Sawyer, nodding. 'Nearly done, though. I'm reluctant to get into an economic debate about money being sent "back home", but I imagine for Harmeet, home is right here, which makes it hard for him to fuck off back there.' Sawyer pivoted, almost side-on to the group; he kept his eyes on the big one, whose hand was now in his pocket. 'And the other thing about that is that subcontinental immigrants have brought huge benefits to this country, particularly in the fields of science and medicine. Even if there was somewhere for his demographic to fuck off back to, then the likes of you three are hardly compensation for the resulting brain drain.' He moved to the left slightly, keeping the other two in sight while he concentrated on the big man. 'In fact, it would probably be best now if you all fucked off back to where *you* came from and left Harmeet alone to get on with his job.' Big smile. 'What do you reckon?'

The big man pulled out a serrated knife with a moulded steel handle and lunged forward, low. Sawyer sidestepped the stabbing motion, and drove his elbow down hard onto the man's forearm, forcing him to drop the knife. He moved in, grabbed the other arm and twisted it, forcing the man to face back towards the counter and holding him in a rigid armlock.

Sawyer edged backwards, into the aisle, dragging the man with him, causing his baseball cap to fall to the floor. The other two took a cautious step forward. Sawyer gripped the big man's thumb and tugged it to the side, away from the rest of the hand, dislocating it with a sharp crack. The man howled with pain, but Sawyer held him in the lock.

The other two froze.

Sawyer looked down at the knife. 'Looks like a Gerber. Tactical knife? Could be the most costly thirty quid you've ever spent. Judges really don't like them, and they regularly dish out four years for possession. And given what's just happened, local CID would probably push for attempted murder. So that's your life effectively over.'

'I'm calling the police.' Harmeet took out a phone and retreated into a back room, slamming the door behind him.

The big man groaned and writhed in Sawyer's grip. 'And you two would definitely go down for secondary liability. You probably know it as aiding and abetting.'

The two men stumbled over each other and ran down the left aisle, crashing out of the front door.

Sawyer released the big man, pushing him back down his aisle towards the door. He swept up the knife and slotted it into the zipped pocket of his hoodie.

The man faced Sawyer in the centre of the aisle, face red, eyes streaming, his injured hand tucked into his armpit. He crouched and picked up his cap. 'Fuck you!'

He backed away, towards the door.

'Get an ice pack on it,' said Sawyer. 'You can probably reset it yourself but it's really going to hurt. I would get yourself to A&E where they'll give you painkillers to get through it.'

The man opened the door.

Harmeet emerged from the back room. 'The police are on their way.'

Sawyer turned to the man. 'Before you go. Two last things. Tikka masala was probably conceived in this country, as a way to anglicise Indian chicken tikka. So, again. Geography. Secondly, if I ever see you in here again, I'll break your wrist. And then you're really in trouble, because you'll need to get a girlfriend to compensate.'

4

Terry Barker dropped four lumps of sugar into his mug and stirred, slow and ponderous, gazing into the swirling liquid.

'I don't think Sawyer is hiding in your tea.'

Barker caught himself, looked up at DCI Robin Farrell, leaning on the back of the green velvet sofa. 'Is this Earl Grey?'

'Yes. Why?'

'You drink Earl Grey as standard?'

'It's the Altrincham way.'

Barker took a slurp, lifting his little finger for comic effect. 'My old mum called it perfume tea.'

Farrell moved around and took a seat on the sofa, opposite Barker. He was a short, compact man with unnaturally thick black hair moulded into a waxy quiff. 'Let's skip the homespun insight.' Farrell's voice was flat and weary, with a permanent rattle of phlegm.

Barker sat back and drummed a rhythm on his cheeks with his fingertips. Farrell had led him, usher-style, to an unyielding armchair, and he shifted his obese frame around the seat, searching for a sweet spot.

Barker squinted through the vast bay window. Roofed

patio; golf bag propped up by the wall; table and chairs set into a purpose-built recess; a generous, well-tended garden with flat farm fields beyond. 'My old guvnor up in Leeds nick, back when I was a lowly old DC, he used to say, "follow the emotion".'

Farrell took a breath mint from a canister and flicked it into his mouth. 'And what does that mean?'

'Nobody wants to wake up somewhere that doesn't make them feel good, on some level. We can take a bit of hardship, but we're always trying to minimise it. If someone doesn't want to be found, it's a full-time job finding the balance between keeping yourself hidden and keeping yourself happy. And over time, the focus shifts towards the emotion, which leads to mistakes in the keeping yourself hidden part.'

'So we just have to wait a few more years, until he gives himself away by ordering a pizza?'

Barker rubbed at the bags under his eyes and looked down at the chess set on the glass-topped coffee table. 'Set up correctly.'

'You seem surprised.'

'Do you play, though? Or is it purely ornamental?'

Farrell sighed. 'I finished your book.' He took a paperback from the shelf under the coffee table. 'Ghostwritten, I assume?' The cover showed a much younger Barker: suited, hands clasped, gazing into the camera. *Three-Day Terry: My Life as the UK's Most Efficient Detective.*

'Yeah. I never paid a lot of attention in English.'

Farrell thumbed through the book. 'I enjoyed the chapter where you list all the cases you solved in three days or less.'

'Fewer. Even I know that one.'

Farrell squeezed out a smile. 'Like the case of the

Wakefield serial rapist, where you caught the culprit before the local paper even got to report on it.'

'Hence the subtitle.'

'Sawyer absconded five months ago, and you've been looking for him now for two months.'

Barker picked up the black rook, rolled it around his doughy fingers. 'You've been looking for five. I'm just one man.'

'Is it a question of resources, Terry? The funding isn't limitless, you do realise.'

'I appreciate that. Particularly when it's coming out of your own pocket. I assume I wouldn't pass the screening of your fine constabulary, given recent history?'

Farrell held the moment. 'Off the books can also be above board. Now. Progress?'

Barker leaned forward and took another sip of tea.

Farrell nodded to the reddened skin around his bald head. 'Nice weather in the Canaries?'

'Who told you Sawyer might be in Lanzarote?'

'Keating. He says he heard one of Sawyer's colleagues mention that he was a fan.'

'Well, he wasn't there.'

'And you've tried all his other happy places?'

'Yes. I even had a look round that fucking cave he likes. The steps nearly killed me.'

Farrell rolled the mint around his mouth. 'So, after all this time, the only thing we know for sure is that he stole a car from a side road near the hospital and ditched it in Calder Grove, close to the M1.'

'So he either went north or south.'

Farrell shook his head. 'You're earning your money.'

'He could be in Land's End, he could be in John o' Groats.'

'No connections in Calder Grove, Leeds, Bradford?'

'Not that I've shaken out. And I've done a lot of shaking. He ditched the car in plain sight, meaning he didn't care if we found it and connected it to him.'

'Meaning it's probably a decoy.'

'Or a double bluff. How clever is Sawyer, in your view?'

Farrell looked out to the garden. 'Very.'

'You're confident he's still in this country?'

'We've been doing regular all-ports checks, PND, NCA, the search compartmentalised by continent.'

'Just in case he found his way onto a container ship.'

Farrell shrugged. 'It happens. Nothing on social media. No likes or mentions. As you know, Sawyer transferred ownership of his house in Edale to his brother Michael a week before his disappearance. We only found out recently that he withdrew a lot of cash at that time.'

'Why only recently?'

'Admin error. I had an officer run over the figures again and he caught it.'

Barker smiled. 'It happens. So Sawyer had a go bag, which means it's unlikely that he's offed himself. You have spoken to his brother?'

'He's like a stone.'

'And how much cash did he take out? I assume you've frozen his account since?'

'Of course. A few thousand.'

'Can't be much of that left. Have you repeated the media release?'

'Yes. Couple of weeks ago. Nationals, a few regional hubs. Getting his face out there again. Offered a reward.'

Barker replaced the rook, picked up the knight, ran his fingers across the contours of the horse's head. 'From what I know about Sawyer, it's not surprising he's been difficult to apprehend.'

'And what do you know about Sawyer?'

'You've been trying to find him with directness, aggression. Chess masters know not to rely on a single idea. They develop many strategies as the game progresses, probing multiple areas for weakness, setting traps. The Norwegian grandmaster Magnus Carlsen defeated Indian grandmaster Viswanathan Anand in 2013 to become world champion. When Carlsen stuck to book moves, going toe to toe with a guy who had a big team analysing all the likely progressions, he couldn't overcome his opponent. So he accepted this weakness and drew Anand into his own style, forcing him to improvise, taking him out of his comfort zone. Sawyer can handle himself, he knows police processes, and he's got a lot to lose if he comes in. So he'll be resisting any risk-taking, or at least trying to. We need to improvise. Move off the edges of the map.'

'Or at least extend the boundaries.'

Barker caught Farrell's eye. 'Above board isn't cutting it.'

'If you're going to start hacking phones, I don't want to know. Plausible deniability.'

Barker tidied the line of pawns. 'I wonder if he's getting help, if someone might be hiding him, keeping him afloat. Someone who owes him.'

'It would be a big commitment, for five months.'

'Perhaps it's a big debt.'

5

'He had a dog.'

Linda Keller clasped her hands together, opened and closed her fingers. Flex, unflex.

'What breed?'

Maggie Spark rested a hand on Linda's wrist and tucked her rust-red hair behind one ear.

'A Yorkshire. Lovely little thing. It died last year and he didn't want to get another. I think he'd had it a long time.' She blew on her tea. 'It's cruel, isn't it? The way the things you love go away. The people you love.' She took a sip, replaced the cup onto the saucer. 'It feels like they're going to be around forever.'

Maggie withdrew her hand. 'Did you see anyone around Charles's house when you arrived? Anyone you didn't recognise?'

'No. I just let myself in. He had the telly on too loud. Never turned his hearing aid up properly. I put his groceries away, went into the sitting room and when I opened the curtains...' Linda screwed her eyes shut, opened them again. 'I can see his *face*, in my head. Then when I close my eyes, it's there again. At first, I thought there was a shadow over his eyes, but then I realised... There were just holes. And I thought he'd spilled his tea, but...' She got up from the sofa, walked over to the dining table, and took a tissue from the box brought by Maggie. She blew her nose. 'I've never seen so much blood. It was all down his front, all over the carpet.'

Linda hovered by the table; Maggie turned to face her. Linda's sitting room was small and overfurnished for a woman who lived alone. Too many chairs and side tables, too many family photographs crowded onto a wall shelf above the sofa, a display cabinet with enough crockery to serve a football team.

'My daughter wants a dog,' said Maggie.

Linda sniffed, dabbed her eyes with a fresh tissue. 'How old is she?'

'Thirteen.'

Linda smiled. 'Lovely age.'

'Not always. Linda...' Maggie leaned forward. 'It's important to seek counselling early. You've been through an awful experience. The after-effects can last for a long time, and they can rear up just when you think you're over it.'

Linda sat down again, on the sofa by Maggie. She stared ahead, unblinking. 'I've known him for ten years, been looking after him for five or six. I met him through a friend who does voluntary work. Charlie lost his wife, Penny, about ten years ago. He's never been the same, really.' She blinked, snapping out of the reverie, and turned to Maggie. 'Are you married, my love?'

'I used to be.'

'So did I. My husband seemed decent enough, but he just told me one day that he didn't love me anymore, and left soon after. He was shocked that I was so surprised. He said he thought it was obvious. It's funny how we seem to miss the things that are the most important. And I know

35

it's a cliché, but you don't appreciate the good things about people until they're gone. The more you're around someone, the more you notice the bad things.'

Maggie sighed, waited until she was sure Linda had finished. 'Was Charles a good person? Did he have any issues with anyone? Were you aware of anyone whose life he'd made difficult or who had any kind of grudge against him?'

'No, no.' Linda lifted her teacup. 'Charlie never hurt anyone. He didn't have any enemies, as far as I know. Or friends, either, really.' She clasped her hands again. Flex, unflex.

'Did you notice anything unusual about the house when you came in? Something out of place?'

Linda frowned. 'Not really. Didn't look like anything was missing. He didn't have much worth taking, though. He had a medal in a little case. His father's. Something from the war. They could have got a few quid for that, I suppose.'

'It's still there.'

Linda pointed at Maggie. 'Now I come to think of it, there was a funny smell. Sort of sickly sweet. I thought he'd bought a new aftershave. But I buy everything for him, including his food. He probably just used too much of some old cologne or something. He had a silly habit of dressing up sometimes, as if he was going out somewhere posh.' She dropped her voice to a whisper. 'He had these turns. Thinking Penny was still alive. He was definitely going a bit... You know.' She twirled a finger around her temple. 'But I'll tell you what. Charlie was strong for his age. I once saw him move one of his cabinets halfway across the room when he was looking for a lost glove. And he was still physically active.'

'But you did his shopping?'

'Yes. He got confused, as I say. In shops. Anything with numbers. Funny, as he used to be a maths teacher. He'd seemed a bit down on my last couple of visits, but not to the point where I'd be worried. I suppose at that age, in his situation, you have to try terribly hard to give yourself a reason to get out of bed, find the point of the day.'

A discreet knock at the door. A young detective—short, slim, suited—poked his head into the room.

'Coming, Matt.' Maggie squeezed Linda's hand. 'You must call the number I've given you, Linda. Talking Space. They're really nice, and they will be able to help. Don't make the mistake of thinking that you can just forget about something like this. It's like getting caught outside when it's about to rain. You can't stop what's coming, but you can take steps to make sure you don't get too wet.'

Linda squeezed Maggie's hand. 'So, this counselling. It's like an umbrella, is it?'

'Sort of.'

'Thank you, my love. You know what? Someone made a big mistake, letting you go.'

———

The mustard-yellow Range Rover settled into a tailback behind a behemothic farm vehicle. Maggie rested her head against the back seat and stared out at the empty flatlands of Sterndale Moor. She pressed the window button; nothing happened.

'Can you open this for me?'

DS Ed Shepherd turned in the driver's seat. 'Oh. Sorry. I use the central lock so the kids can't mess around.' He pressed a button in his door, and Maggie rolled down her window a few inches. Morning air whistled through the gap, warmed by the spring sunshine. The car filled with the sulphurous stink of farm waste. Maggie winced and closed the window.

'They're spreading late,' said Shepherd, glancing at Maggie in the rear-view mirror.

'That's human shit, you know.' In the passenger seat, DS Matt Walker loosened his royal-blue tie, keeping his eyes on his phone screen.

Shepherd shook his head. 'Bollocks.'

'He's right,' said Maggie. 'Sewage sludge. Something like three million tonnes of it. Reprocessed from water treatment works and resold to farmers as agricultural fertiliser.'

Walker grinned, looked back at Maggie. 'They call it biosolids.'

Maggie forced a smile, kept her gaze on the scrolling moors. 'Nitrates, phosphates. Nourishing the land.'

'Jesus,' said Shepherd with a shudder.

'Better than burning it,' said Maggie. She looked at Walker. 'Is that *Tetris*?'

'Yeah. Old-school.'

'I used to play that on the original Game Boy,' said Shepherd. 'Remember that?'

'No,' said Walker. 'I'm not old enough.'

Shepherd smiled. 'You had to sit under a light or you couldn't see the screen.'

'See, that doesn't sound like a finished product to me,' said Walker.

'Did either of you smell anything on scene?'

Walker paused the game. 'At Yates's place? No. You mean farm smells?'

'More like a cologne. Linda mentioned it. She said that Charles sometimes got dressed up, thought he was going out.'

'To the Old Boys' Social?' said Shepherd. 'Not quite the

full pack, then.' He caught Maggie's eyes in the mirror; she scowled at him.

'My nan used to call it "a bit simple",' said Maggie. 'Shorthand for everything from dementia to Down's syndrome.'

Walker got back to his game. 'Drummond says he thinks the killer used an ice pick. Or a screwdriver.'

'Either way,' said Shepherd, 'it wasn't deep enough to sever the carotid.'

Walker touched a hand to the scar around his Adam's apple. 'We're waiting for word from Sally's team. Doesn't look like there's much trace. Couple of shoeprints to eliminate.'

'We need to know more about him,' said Maggie. 'That's the terrible thing with the elderly. They're too easily dismissed as invalid, in the classic sense of the word. Irrelevant.'

'Invisible,' said Walker. 'I'm on it. Victimology.'

'Stabbing into the eyes,' said Maggie. 'That's about as personal as it could get.'

'I know,' said Shepherd. 'And not high on anyone's list of ways to go.'

'You probably think you're safe for a peaceful and easy death in your sleep,' said Maggie. 'Once you get to eighty-four.'

Walker glanced at Shepherd.

'Sounds like you're channelling our absent friend,' said Shepherd.

Maggie smiled, turned back to the window.

6

SEPTEMBER 2000

'I think I'll talk to you.'

The bright young woman raised her pint glass, and the sullen young man clinked it with his bottle of Grolsch.

He took a slug, studied her with his deep-green eyes. 'You've made a wise decision.'

'You in halls?'

'Got a shared flat on campus. Four teenage boys away from home for the first time. We drew up a strict cleaning rota on the first day.'

She frowned, swept her rust-red hair off her shoulders. 'Really? I'm impressed already, and we've only been talking for a few seconds.'

He smiled, activating a dimple in his right cheek. 'Of course not. We're keeping the Pot Noodle and Beanfeast people in business. There's an old Oasis poster on the wall in the bathroom. It's gradually disappearing, though. One wipe at a time.'

She grimaced. 'For God's sake. There is a thing called toilet paper, you know.'

He sipped from his bottle, nodding. 'I've got a personal stash. I'm not an animal.'

She tilted her head. 'Well. Looks like you're right. I did make a wise decision. Latching on to someone with good anal hygiene.'

He spluttered, laughing. 'Normally, I'd use the Oasis poster on general principle. But I prefer—'

'You know what? I think we should move the conversation away from...' She steadied herself, held her head high. 'Let's go old-school. Given names. I'm Maggie.'

He held out a hand; they shook. 'Jake.'

'Seriously? This formal? Now it looks like we're doing a drug deal or something.'

Jake smiled; the dimple returned. 'That would be a pretty bold move in a university lecture theatre, in full view of our future instructors.'

He looked over his shoulder; Maggie followed his eyeline. Thirty or so fellow students hovered near the attendant academics in front of the stage. Tables of finger food lined the back of the stage area, and a rack of documents had been propped at the front: reading lists, student society leaflets, lecture timetables, seminar groupings. A few students sat in isolated pockets of the tiered seating, eating and reading.

Maggie hunted through the pockets of her jeans. Jake held up a folded piece of paper.

She frowned. 'Did you steal that from my pocket?'

Jake ran a hand through his scruffy black hair. 'Yeah. One of my talents. Might be useful once I run out of money.'

'And is this a recently acquired skill?'

'I went through a shoplifting phase.'

'As an adult?'

Jake finished the Grolsch, clanked it down on the table behind, next to two empties. 'Technically, I haven't been an adult for long enough to go through a phase. It was when I was a kid. I stole some cigarettes from a shop. The owner chased me, demanded I turn out my pockets. The only place I could think to hide them where he wouldn't find them was on him. So I slipped them into his pocket. I just did the same to you.'

Maggie reached behind, pulled the folded paper out of her jeans back pocket. She eyed him. 'And what might your other talents be?'

'Sex. I'm really good at that.'

She gasped, mock shock. 'According to whom?'

'Joking.' He laughed, threw back his head. The overhead lighting caught his clammy forehead. 'I'm a decent goalkeeper. I do martial arts. I know a bit too much about films, particularly David Lynch.'

'I love him! I finally got round to *Twin Peaks* last year. So good. I like Hal Hartley. Have you heard of him?'

'Of course. *The Unbelievable Truth*, *Trust*. Romcoms with brains.'

'I suppose.'

'Lynch has better hair, though.'

Maggie opened the paper. 'I thought so. You're in my Environmental Criminology group. Have you bought all your books? I can't find the big one. The bible, apparently. *Media & Crime*.'

'I've got two copies of that. My dad used to be a policeman. He bought me one, didn't know I'd already got it. You can have the spare if you like.'

'That's kind of you. I suppose I should rescue it, before it finds its way into the bathroom.'

Jake laughed again, too loud. A lecturer—balding,

bearded—sent over a sharp look; Maggie returned a reassuring smile.

'Listen,' said Jake. He took Maggie's pint glass—half full—and set it down on the table next to his empties. 'Come over for a smoke, chill out a bit. Have something to eat. That's another talent. My scrambled eggs, with crème fraîche and chives.' He leaned in too close, unsteady, lowered his voice. 'You have to keep shifting them on and off the heat, so they don't overcook. And you don't put fucking milk in there.' He backed away, held out a hand.

Maggie smiled. 'It's okay, Jake. I can walk unaided.'

———

Maggie angled her head sideways and inspected the shelf at the far end of the bedroom. 'And here's another of your talents. Obsessively collecting true crime books.'

Jake sat on the edge of the bed, constructing a joint on a vinyl LP sleeve: *Morrison Hotel* by The Doors. The album played on an orange turntable on the floor, sandwiched between two tall Technics speakers. 'A lot of this course is stuff I already know.' He licked the gum, rolled the papers together.

Maggie squinted through the low lighting, mostly provided by a tall blue-and-orange lava lamp in the corner. *Whoever Fights Monsters, Killing For Company, Mindhunter, The Shrine of Jeffrey Dahmer*. She turned to him, smiled. 'All I know is that I know nothing.'

Jake lit the joint, spluttered on the first toke. 'Socrates. I read the classics as well as the lurid stuff.'

'My mum calls it "omnivorous". You must be omnivorous, she says. "You don't want to keep reinforcing the same old ideas. Get outside the conventional wisdom. That's where you discover new things."' She flopped into a dark-red beanbag by the window that overlooked the lamplit lawn at the heart of the campus. Jake passed her the joint; she took a cursory drag and handed it straight back.

Jake laughed and took a drink from his beer can. 'You not smoked before?'

'Not much.'

He nodded, smiling. 'Not ever. You should be omnivorous with experiences as well as reading. I like your eyes.'

'I was thinking the same about you. Green is much more interesting than blue.'

'Yours are hazel. My second favourite colour. After orange.' He tidied the dope paraphernalia into a metal tin embossed with the Jack Daniel's logo. 'Maggie's a cool name. Doesn't really suit you, though. It's a bit mumsy. Makes me think of another famous Maggie.'

'Thatcher?'

'Philbin.'

He got up and changed the record. The The. *Soul Mining*. 'What's your surname?'

'Spark.'

'Really? Did they call you Bright Spark at school?'

Maggie stood up again, and went back to the shelf. 'A few did.' A line of poetry books: Larkin, Hughes, Sexton, Plath. 'What's yours?'

He took another drag on the joint. 'Sawyer. Like Tom.' He inhaled, puffed out the smoke. 'I think I'll call you Mags. It makes you sound Nordic.'

'I don't look Nordic.'

Jake took another drag on the joint. 'No, you don't fit the cliché. Cold, aloof, abrupt.'

'This is a bit of a premature profile job.' She tilted a book out of the row. 'What's this one? *Whiz Mob*?'

'*A Correlation of the Technical Argot of Pickpockets with*

Their Behavior Pattern. David W Maurer. It's basically the manual for what I showed you before.'

'So, Mr Sawyer, are you interested in the prevention of crime or just crime itself? Why so fascinated with all this?'

Jake took a deep drink from his can, tossed the empty into a bedside bin. 'Know your enemy. I want to be a copper. Like my dad. There's a line in *Mindhunter*. "If you want to understand the artist, look at his work."'

Maggie leaned in to a framed photo at the end of the shelf. A young woman in an orange bathrobe, standing by a garden gate. Coils of black hair spilled out of the hood of the robe, down over her shoulders. The smile was indulgent, facing downward.

'Did you take this? Is it your sister?'

'My mum.'

Maggie turned. Jake had taken off his top and was pulling a grey Bruce Lee T-shirt from a drawer. His back was toned and muscular, with a fresh-looking tattoo written in neat, curlicued lettering between his shoulders: Κατά τον δαίμονα εαυτού.

He pulled on the T-shirt. 'It's Greek. It means "true to his own spirit". Jim Morrison's father chose it as the inscription for his gravestone. I've seen interpretations like "against the devil within him" or something.' Jake turned, grinned. 'But I'm on the side of the angels.'

Maggie laughed. 'Are you saying you were sent from heaven?'

He opened a new can. 'Not quite. Wardlow Mires. A village in the middle of the Peak District. Change the channel on the car radio while you're driving through and you'll miss it.'

'Ah! A proper country boy. I'm from Leek.'

'That's hardly the urban badlands.' He mouthed the

word, slurring. '*Leek*. It's not a good place name, is it? Like Staines.'

'Or Bognor.'

The song 'Giant' played. Electronic kick and snare, cycling bass riff. Matt Johnson sang of thinking of things he hoped to forget.

'You can't help where you're from,' said Maggie. She turned back to the shelf.

Jake got to his feet, stumbled onto the bed, laughing. 'No. It's all about where you're at.'

Maggie leaned in to the picture. 'Your mum is beautiful. What's her name?'

He lay flat on the bed, eyes on the ceiling. 'Jessica.' Another toke on the joint. 'She died.'

Maggie turned. 'What? When?'

'When I was young.'

Matt Johnson sang of turning his friends into enemies, of the past returning to haunt him.

She sat back in the beanbag. 'How young?'

'Five or six.'

'My God. I'm so sorry, Jake.'

'It wasn't your fault. People die.'

'No. Of course... I mean. I'm empathising.'

He sat upright, lunged for the record player, dragged the needle away, scratching the record.

Maggie winced. 'Jesus!'

'Sorry. Just...' Jake tried to tidy his hair, messing it up further. 'Let's change the subject. Dead mothers. Bit of a passion killer.'

She raised her eyebrows. 'Are you anticipating passion?'

Jake flopped back on the bed. 'We could give it a go. Or we could watch some films. Got loads of DVDs. Have you seen *Fight Club*? And if you're not into dope, we can try something stronger.'

Matt Johnson yelped and shrieked, and sang of not knowing himself.

Maggie frowned. 'What do you mean, something stronger? I had a bad time on ecstasy a couple of years ago.'

Jake lay flat on the bed, chest rising and falling, hand hanging over the side, joint between his fingers.

She stood up, walked over to him.

His eyes were closed, mouth open, head lolled over to the side.

She smiled, eased the joint from his hand, flipped it out on the ashtray, and crept out of the room.

———

On the way back to her accommodation block on the other side of the campus, Maggie diverted to the library building shown to the freshers earlier that day.

She swiped her card and sat down at an enclosed booth with a PC pushed to the back of a shallow desk. She accessed the university intranet and typed 'jessica sawyer' into the new Google search engine.

Maggie clicked on an image from the front page of the September 1988 edition of the Daily Mirror. It magnified, filling the screen with a headshot of the woman in Jake's bookshelf photo, beneath a screaming, double-stacked headline.

BEAUTY SLAIN BY A BEAST

Maggie leaned in to the screen, her eyes moving across the grainy typography.

Police are appealing for witnesses after a mother of two was brutally murdered in broad daylight on a country lane in rural Derbyshire.

Jessica Sawyer, 34, a teacher at Pioneer Primary School in Derbyshire, was walking her two sons home from school when the attacker struck.

She scrolled the page and studied the inset image: two young boys crouched beside an elaborate sandcastle.

TRAGIC KIDS: MICHAEL (8) AND JAKE (6)

7

PRESENT DAY

Curtis Mavers bowed his head and leaned forward on the sofa, resting his elbows on his knees. He inhaled, slow and steady, gazing down at the expensive-looking parquet flooring.

'Smells good in here, Jamel. A touch of oud?'

He raised his head, squinting through the eyeholes of the black balaclava.

A chunky thirtysomething man sat on a tall stool at the black marble breakfast bar. Ankles and wrists locked into cuffs; tailored white shirt, speckled red. He was mixed race, with cropped hair and a short beard, sculpted to taper into his sideburns. His nose was freshly broken, and he puffed a spray of blood into the air, holding his body upright, in defiance.

Mavers caught the eye of the tall man dressed head to toe in black standing at the far end of the breakfast bar. He stopped drumming his hands on the surface and tugged at his balaclava.

'You trying to look like a ninja?' The man in the white shirt tipped his head back in question.

Mavers nodded at the tall man who launched himself forward and drove a powerful punch into their captive's stomach, then hit him in the face with a right cross, which knocked him off the stool. He fell awkwardly, but just about managed to scramble up onto his knees.

He spat blood again, towards the feet of the tall man who had to step back to avoid it.

The young woman on the sofa next to Mavers wailed in alarm.

The captive man smiled through bloodied teeth and propped himself back up on the stool. 'Do you stupid bastards know who you're slapping around?'

Mavers sat back, glanced at the woman. Blonde, strapless black dress, heels. She held her hands over her face and rocked on the edge of her seat, keeping her body angled away from the action.

'You're Jamel Manley Perry,' said Mavers. 'You were born in Coldhurst, Oldham. You're thirty-three years old, but you probably knock a few years off for her benefit.' He nodded to the woman. 'For the last two years, you've been the head of an organised crime gang engaged in the trafficking of wholesale quantities of Class A drugs. Charlie, mainly. But also heroin, ecstasy. You made a lot of money, didn't you, Jamel? You spunked three hundred grand of it on a villa in Dubai, and another fat wad on a personalised numberplate for your BMW. *B055*. Oh, and your pig-ugly Rolex cost you thirty-five grand. I've got a copy of the receipt if you want to see it.'

'You a Scouser?' said Perry.

'Take off your clothes.'

Perry spat more blood, wiped his mouth on his shoulder. 'What?'

Mavers raised a Glock pistol, nodded at the tall man, who unlocked Perry's cuffs. 'Get 'em off. *Now*.' His voice hardened.

The woman groaned.

Perry flattened down his hair, wiped his nose. 'Fuck me. So you're a bin-dipper *and* a bender?'

'I'm going to ask nicely one more time. Then I'll start to get a bit more assertive.'

Perry hissed through his teeth. 'You're both in a world of shit, yeah? Me and Mel, we were going out tonight. It's her birthday.'

Mavers turned to the woman. 'Many happy returns, Mel.'

She gave a jerky nod, kept her eyes on the double-door fridge.

'So, let's say you fuck off now, let us carry on with our plans—'

'With a broken nose?' The tall man spoke: clipped, upper-class accent.

Perry smiled. 'Who's this? Your fucking brief? Yeah, with a broken nose.' He shrugged. 'I've done worse with worse.'

Mavers jiggled the gun around his hand. 'You were saying... We fuck off now. Then what?'

'Then when my boys catch up with you, I'll tell them to do you quick. If you keep this shit up, and ruin our evening, then I'll make sure they take their fucking time.'

Mavers dropped his head again, nodding. He got to his feet, sniffed. 'Actually, I think that's more sandalwood. Makes sense. You do strike me as more of a Body Shop type, Jamel.' He walked to the breakfast bar and stood over Perry, swaying a little. 'Take off your clothes. Or I'll have my acquaintance take off Mel's.'

Perry looked up, held Mavers's gaze. 'Fuck you.'

Mavers sighed. He raised the gun and brought the butt down hard on the side of Perry's head. Perry fell off the chair again. He howled in outrage and scrambled to his feet. The tall man walked over to Mel, grabbed her arm and yanked her upright. She cried out, but didn't struggle.

'Right! Okay.' Perry stripped off the shirt, unhooked his belt and stepped back, facing Mavers. He wore red-and-white Diesel briefs, and was in decent shape; a little tubby round the middle.

Mavers nodded. 'Carry on.'

Perry glanced at the tall man, holding Mel firm at the edge of the sofa. 'Yous are both dead men, y'know?' He pulled down the underwear, stepped to the side. 'You should start planning your funerals right now.'

The tall man pulled Mel in close. 'I might have a go on this fine lady, anyway. Teach this one a few manners. And show him how it's done.'

Mel sneered. 'You wouldn't know what to do with me.'

The tall man laughed: shrill and staccato, like a bleating goat. 'I *love* hard to get.' He leaned in to Mel and lowered his voice. 'Hard to get makes me hard.' He glanced at Mavers, who shook his head, then pushed Mel back down onto the sofa.

Mavers studied the manicured offering between Perry's legs. 'One thing is clear, Mel. You're with this fool for the money.' He held Perry's eye, then gave a sudden startle. 'Oh! Reminds me.' He turned, handed the gun to the tall man, and unzipped a backpack he'd placed by the side of the sofa.

The tall man waved the gun towards the breakfast bar. 'Up on there.'

'What?'

'Climb up on there and lie on your front,' said Mavers. 'Do it in the next five seconds or I'll have my ninja shoot you in the elbow.'

Perry clambered up onto a stool and lay face down on the breakfast bar.

'Now we're getting somewhere,' said Mavers.

The tall man reattached the cuffs to Perry's ankles and wrists, forcing him to stretch both arms out in front, hanging over the edge of the bar.

Mavers took a small steam iron out of the backpack and plugged it into a socket by the fridge.

'Jesus Christ,' said Mel. *'Please.'*

Mavers turned to Perry and spoke to the back of his head. 'Where is it?'

Perry twisted himself round, trying to see what Mavers had plugged in. 'Where's what?'

Mavers held up the iron to show Perry; steam rose from the base. 'Where is it?'

The tall man pocketed the gun and stepped to the side of Perry. 'Ah, look. He's trembling.'

'Fucking cold in here,' said Perry.

The tall man gripped Perry's ankles and held them firm, as Mavers swiped the hot iron over his skin, from the small of his back up to his shoulder blades. The scorched flesh sizzled under the heat.

Perry bellowed in pain and fury, as a dense plume of steam rose from his skin, engulfing Mavers. Mel twisted away, whimpering. She buried her face in the sofa, covering her ears.

Mavers held the iron between Perry's shoulder blades, and applied a moment of extra pressure, drawing another scream. He lifted it away and held it at his side. Strips of skin bubbled on the surface, dripping down onto the parquet floor.

Perry moaned and writhed, biting on his bicep. The tall man moved around and crouched down close to his face. He looked up to Mavers and grinned. 'His eyes are watering, but he's not crying.'

Mavers gripped Perry's chin and jerked his head up. 'Where is it?'

'*Where's what*?'

Mavers reached between Perry's legs and yanked his testicles up through the gap between his thighs, squeezing them into a tight ball. He held the iron close to them, letting Perry feel the heat.

'*There's nothing here, man*! No drugs. Money's in the basement safe, if that's what you mean.'

Mavers pulled the iron away. 'Got there in the end.'

Perry squirmed, trying to twist and face Mavers. 'Listen, though. It's all I've got, man. And I owe people, yeah?'

The tall man leaned in close to Perry's face again. He nodded, delighted. 'Crying now.'

'There's nothing else. Honestly. Please don't take it all. I... I won't come back at you. I swear on my kids' lives, man. If you take it all, I'm fucked. *Please.* You'll fuck me. You'll put me out of business.'

Mavers unplugged the iron. 'That's the idea.'

8

Sawyer pushed the copy of the *Derbyshire Times* across the wooden table and tapped a number into one of Ainsworth's Nokia 105s. He lingered for a moment, then pressed the call button.

'News desk.' Gruff estuary accent.

Sawyer took a breath. 'Numbers.'

A crackle on the line. Jostling sounds as the recipient moved somewhere. A door slammed.

'Well,' said the voice. 'Look what the cat dragged in.'

'Numbers, Logan. Let's save the passive-aggressive pleasantries for better times.'

'Where are you, Sawyer?'

'Wouldn't you like to know?'

A wheezy cough. 'Me and most of the senior coppers on this fair isle.'

'Get me a couple of numbers, and I'll give you the full story.'

'Of how you caught Bowman?'

'You asked for it, I said yes. Sorry for the delay. I've been busy.'

Dean Logan laughed, coughed again, caught his breath.

'You old dog. I knew you'd turn up eventually. You're like Lord fucking Lucan.'

'Showing your age, Logan.'

'They had officers rooting around everywhere. Even your dad's old place. Phone numbers?'

'Yeah. Civilian.'

'Why me? You can't have been doing this alone, Sawyer.'

Sawyer reached across the table and toyed with the Gerber knife he'd taken from the shop thugs. 'I am now.'

'How about a bit extra on the past few months? How you went AWOL on a murder charge.'

'They hadn't charged me when I went AWOL.'

'No, but you knew it was coming. Otherwise you wouldn't have legged it. Isn't this aiding and abetting?'

'We don't say that anymore. And it depends what happens to me. It's in your interest to help. Big scoop for you, too.'

'*We* don't say scoop anymore. I don't know the full details of your case, Sawyer. For all I know, I might be assisting a cold-blooded murderer.'

Sawyer ran his hand along the moulded handle of the knife. 'Are you seriously telling me you've found your moral compass after all these years?'

'I've always had a strong moral code, believe it or not.'

'Is that why you ended up at the *Derbyshire Times* instead of *The Sunday Times*?'

'I thought we were staying away from passive-aggression. Yeah, alright. And I suppose we didn't have this conversation?'

'Of course not. Where are you with the Yates murder?'

Logan sighed. 'Vicious bastard, whoever did that. For sure. Stabbed the poor guy through his fucking eyes.'

'Same blood, wherever it leaks from.'

'Good point, if a tad dispassionate. They also cut his throat. Talk about overkill.'

'And he wasn't robbed?'

'Doesn't look like it, no. Few drawers in his bedroom turned out. Probably not the best target for smackheads looking for iPads.'

Sawyer twisted the point of the knife blade into a notch on the table. 'Have you looked into Yates?'

'Course we have. Wasn't an ex-Nazi or anything. Upstanding bloke. Churchgoer, military background, ex-teacher.'

Sawyer got up and walked down the hall to the front door. 'They might need to think laterally. His kids or family have probably pissed someone off.' He opened the door and looked out through the trees, to the lake, sparkling in the moonlight.

'No kids,' said Logan. 'Or family. Where are you, anyway? You can't blame me for being intrigued. I'll keep the information confidential, naturally. Source protection and all that.'

Sawyer closed his eyes, savouring the evening breeze whipping through his hair. 'We'll get to that. First, numbers.'

9

'Come!'

Terry Barker stepped around the door, smiling. 'You're being ironic, right?'

DCI Robin Farrell leaned over the desk at the back side of the room and moved something around his computer screen. 'About what?'

'You'll be saying "Enter!" or "Approach!" next.'

Farrell took his seat: a padded office chair. Beige. Too big for him. The desk was the main feature of a first-floor home office that overlooked the back garden. Farrell had kitted the place out with cold functionality: computer in the desk centre, printer perched on an undersized side table, grey filing cabinet in the corner. Barker smiled at the room's only evidence of humanity: a framed photo on the cabinet featuring Farrell standing next to the British entrepreneur, Richard Branson. In the photo, Farrell grinned in triumph, head tilted back; Branson's smile was more watchful, almost pained.

'Nice little man cave,' said Barker, taking a seat.

Farrell eyed him. 'A little austere, I know. But it's for business, not pleasure.'

'Your missus calls it your study.'

'Well...' Farrell opened his canister of breath mints and flicked one into his mouth off the end of his bent thumb. 'Rose is just thankful it gives me the chance to be home more, even if I do have to work. I used to live in the office. You know what it's like.'

'I do.' Barker kneaded his ample cheeks with both hands. 'You're a strange one, Farrell. A lot of coppers have that irritating sense of keeping an eye on everything, even when they're not working. You know the type. Never really off duty, but there's still the real person up top and the copper never too far from the surface. With you, it's like you were always a copper. Like you were born that way. You came out of the fucking womb with your cap on.'

Farrell rolled the mint around his mouth. 'You've been off the force for too long, Barker. There's such a thing as the modern policeman. The best ones *were* born for the role. They see themselves as the arbiters in an amoral world. To them, it's a calling. Not just a nine-to-five thing that interrupts their time in the pub. Someone has to maintain high standards.'

Barker spluttered a laugh. 'You've done me there. I was never a great beacon of morality. Nobody drinks these days, though, do they? Not properly. Most of the younger officers I know are non-smokers, non-drinkers, non-anythingers. A small glass of craft beer with Friday dinner.' His eyes wandered to Farrell's screen. 'Robin and Rose. That's sweet. So what's up?'

Farrell turned the computer towards Barker. 'CCTV from a convenience store in Coniston.'

'Lake District?'

Farrell sighed. 'Yes. No sound. But it's a hell of a silent movie. I'll send you the full version, but here's my favourite bit.'

Barker leaned in as Farrell played a video file. A tall man in a hooded sweatshirt was attacked by another customer wielding a small knife. The hooded man disarmed the attacker with swift efficiency, pulled him into an armlock and pulled on his hand with a sharp sideways motion.

'Dislocated thumb,' said Farrell. Barker winced.

On-screen, another two men standing near the counter ran away down a separate aisle, out of sight. The hooded man released his captive, who followed them. After a brief conversation with someone off-screen, he also stepped out of the camera's range and the footage ended.

'Shopkeeper Harmeet Agarwal called it in,' said Farrell. 'The guy's hard to distinguish facially in the video, but Agarwal says he had green eyes and generally fitted Sawyer's description, although he was heavily bearded.'

'So you want me to have a mooch around the Lakes, keep an eye out for bearded men who look like they can handle themselves.'

Farrell rolled his tongue from cheek to cheek. 'Perhaps a little more strategic than that. If this is Sawyer, then he could be living in the area, he could have been passing through. No way to tell.'

'What did he buy?'

Farrell looked down at his notepad, raised his eyes to Barker. 'Monster Munch.'

Barker laughed. 'That's him alright.'

'What about you? Progress?'

Barker screwed up his eyes. 'I had a sniff around one of Sawyer's exes in London. Sheena Harley.' He shook his head. 'Took another pass at his ex-marksman pal Tony Cross. He told me to fuck off, but I'm not convinced he knew anything, anyway.'

Farrell steepled his hands in front of his face, rested his

elbows on the desk. 'I imagine you get told to fuck off quite a lot.'

A shrug. 'It can save time. Sometimes it's a red flag and gets me even more interested. You have to learn not to take fuck off for an answer.'

'What about Dale Strickland? You said there might be someone helping Sawyer who feels like he owes him. Sawyer saved Strickland's son from a kidnapping a couple of years ago.'

Barker made a face. 'Politics. From what I heard, Sawyer is on Strickland's shitlist. And even if he wasn't, I can't see him doing any favours as the new Deputy Mayor of Greater Manchester.'

Farrell bristled. 'He's not the Deputy Mayor. Well, not technically. It's nominal.'

Barker raised his eyebrows. 'He's technically your boss, though.'

Farrell stood up. 'If there's nothing else... Get up to Coniston, ask around, stake out the store, interview the owner. Assume Sawyer is there and try to get into his head. Where would he hide? Where would he live?'

Barker didn't get up. 'I think I already know that.'

Farrell lowered himself back into the seat. 'Do you?'

'Have you heard of a chap called Donald Ainsworth? Professor of Psychology at Strathclyde University. Sawyer saved his reputation a few years back when he exposed some charlatan clairvoyant who was exploiting Ainsworth's desperation to get in touch with his teenage daughter. She died in 2008. Anorexia. I went back to look at Sawyer's press cuttings. This is all in the *Hero Cop* story from the *Derbyshire Times*.'

'Most of which is ludicrous hagiography. Yes, but doesn't Ainsworth still live in Glasgow? Long way from the Lake District.'

Barker rubbed at the bags under his eyes. He took out his phone, navigated to an image, then turned the device around to show Farrell. 'Ainsworth bought this place with his ex-wife back in the late nineties. He's been renting it out for a few years, initially through Airbnb. But he pulled it from the site near the end of last year and switched to a private website. But that's not currently online.'

Farrell inhaled, held the breath, let it out. 'And where is it?'

'Just outside Coniston. About two and a half miles from Harmeet's shop. If I were you, I'd send the cavalry up there.'

Farrell shook his head. 'I can't trust anyone legitimate not to be in contact with Sawyer.'

'Well, it's good to know that you see me in such a positive light.'

'I mean official. Her Majesty's current civil servants. If Sawyer is there, I can't risk him being tipped off. This needs to stay quiet, off the books.' He stared past Barker's shoulder for a few seconds, then tapped out a short drumbeat on the edge of the desk. 'Do take a look, though. Keep a low profile. Sawyer has evaded me before by being forewarned. We need to be one hundred per cent sure he's actually there before we make a move.'

10

DSI Ivan Keating settled into his seat at the head of the Buxton MIT conference table. He removed his cap and scratched the white stubble on his scalp. His eyes betrayed a moment's distance, before flashing into character.

'Good morning, all. Full house today. Couple of outsiders but we're all friends, so share and share alike.' He nodded to DS Ed Shepherd, who swiped at his video monitor, sharing the content with the other touchscreens fixed into the table in front of the attendees. The image synced to a headshot of an elderly man, scowling into camera.

'Charles Yates,' said Shepherd. 'Eighty-four. Ex-teacher. Retired in 1999. Discovered at his home near Sheldon last Sunday afternoon by his carer Linda Keller.'

A few of the detectives tapped the gallery at the bottom of their screens and swiped through a series of crime scene photos.

'Charles was stabbed in each eye with a sharp, pointed object, and he had his throat cut, possibly with the same object.'

'I call ice pick,' came a deep voice from the far corner.

Its owner sat back in a separate chair, away from the main table. He was vast and rounded; shiny bald with a grey beard and semi-rimless spectacles. 'Maybe screwdriver.' He folded his arms. 'Or at least a thin-bladed knife, given the lack of impact on the surrounding eye sockets. Probably swiped it from the kitchen, took it with him.'

'Thank you, Frazer,' said Shepherd. 'The full pathology report is on HOLMES, and I urge you all to familiarise yourself with the details.'

Frazer Drummond unfolded his arms. 'One more thing, DS Shepherd. The carotid artery wasn't severed. It looks to me like the killer maybe slashed at the throat, changed his mind, then went for the eyes.'

Shepherd caught DS Walker's eye across the table; he looked away. 'Now, despite Charles's advanced years, we understand he was still physically strong and active, although we believe he was showing early signs of dementia. Undiagnosed, but his doctor concurs with our suspicions. The bedroom drawers had been pulled out, but, according to Linda, nothing obvious had been stolen, including an original bronze George VI World War II medal.'

'They're not worth much, anyway,' said a skinny detective in a light grey suit. 'But you'd probably assume it was and take it anyway.'

'DC Moran's brother is an antique dealer,' said Keating.

Moran shook his head. 'Yeah. He sells crusty old rubbish to people with too much money.'

'You're not an antediluvian aficionado, are you, Ross?' said Drummond, pale blue eyes twinkling.

Moran shot Drummond an indulgent smile.

'Trace evidence is nominal,' continued Shepherd. 'Sally O'Callaghan's report is also available on HOLMES.'

'And she's currently available for live consultation, DS

Shepherd,' said the fiftysomething woman with cropped, bottle-blonde hair, sitting beside Walker. 'No prints, no physical or tool marks. Nothing foreign at the scene. Plenty of shoe prints around the back of the flat, but only one static print with traces of blood.'

'Charles's blood?' said a hefty detective with tall, slicked-back hair, gazing down at the generic headshot on his screen.

'Yes, DC Myers. Size 7.' Shepherd swiped his screen and a photo of the shoe print appeared. 'Nothing unique about the heel pattern. Obviously, we need a suspect for a match. The back door was unlocked, unforced. Looks like Charles wasn't too hot on security.'

'The killer left that way,' said Walker.

'It's clear why you were promoted, DS Walker,' said Moran.

Walker ignored him. 'Also, Frazer said "him".'

'Sorry?' said Shepherd.

'The killer. We're assuming it's a he.'

Drummond's chair creaked as he shifted position, folding his arms. 'Well, we assume nothing, DS Walker. As you know. But from what I've seen of the body, and I have intimate knowledge, Charles Yates was robust for his vintage. There were two single penetration marks in the back of his armchair. So, two strikes.' He raised his arm and demonstrated. 'One, two. So the killer must have been powerful enough to subdue him and hold him in place for those two accurate stabs.'

'Or maybe the killer cut his throat first, which incapacitated him, then stabbed him in the eyes after. And he bled out.'

Moran smirked. 'I would say that DS Walker overrules you for experience in throat cutting, Frazer.'

Walker nodded, still not engaging with Moran. 'Strange that he didn't take the medal, at least.'

'I don't want to appear too unwoke,' said Drummond. 'But I submit that a woman with size 7 shoes, who would be around five foot seven in height, wouldn't be able to deliver such definitive injuries when faced with the sort of resistance that Charles would be capable of.'

'We're getting bogged down,' said Keating. 'Maggie, what was your impression of his carer, Linda Keller?'

Maggie tucked her hair behind her ear, sat upright. 'There's nothing to suggest she might have been involved in any way. I got the sense that she was in deep shock, and I advised her to take up the offer of long-term counselling. Linda said that Charles's wife died ten years ago, and he sometimes smartened up in the anticipation that they were going out together. So, there's clearly some dementia involved. It often starts with forgetfulness but then moves on to delusions, and sometimes hallucinations, or the inability to distinguish between the past and present, or even fact and fiction. My ex-husband's father would often say he could see children playing in the room, when there were no children present. Hallucinations, like trauma, are very real to the sufferer and can be distressing for their carers.'

'You said she thought there was a funny smell?' said Walker.

'Yes. Some kind of sweet cologne she didn't recognise. But then that could have been part of his getting ready to go out ritual, digging out something he used to wear when his wife was alive.'

'Okay,' said Shepherd. 'We'll do some cross-ref on the shoeprint, try to narrow things down. DS Walker is continuing with victimology, looking into Charles's history to see if there are any potential connections, anyone he's pissed off. Tomorrow, DS Walker and I will visit Esther Murphy, a friend of his wife's, to help with that. I'll then speak to Sally and assign Exhibits. DC Myers, Officer in the Case. DC Moran, Disclosure. Next briefing tomorrow morning at nine.'

'Before we go,' said Keating. 'I hope that nobody here feels that Charles Yates is any less of a victim because he was in his eighties. This is a horrendous crime, and I would like the maniac who committed it in custody as soon as possible. We have to assume he might do it again.'

Shepherd powered down the screens and they got up to leave.

'Sir,' said Moran. 'Is there any word on the other killer we have still on the loose?'

Keating glared at him. 'If you're referring to the DI Sawyer enquiry, DC Moran, no. There isn't.'

Moran winced out a smile. 'I was starting to think that all the violent crime round here had been jinxed by Sawyer's presence. Maybe this proves otherwise.'

'DI Sawyer isn't a killer,' said Maggie.

Moran tilted his head. 'I know you were at college together, Maggie. But you sound like a serial killer's mother or something.'

'Moran...' warned Keating.

'Oh, my boy would never do something like that,' Moran continued, in a mocking voice. 'Sawyer is a killer, Maggie. And we had evidence—'

'Testimony,' said Shepherd.

'We had evidence that Bowman's killing was a long way from self-defence. And we were about to question him on that, when he was tipped off by a colleague. Repayment for saving that colleague's neck.'

'I was visiting him,' said Walker. 'There was no tip-off.'

'*Enough.*'

Keating's voice silenced the room. The detectives froze. Drummond smiled, sat back in his chair and propped his arms behind his head.

Keating struggled to keep his voice low and steady. 'DI Sawyer conducted an operation of questionable legitimacy in which a suspect died at his own hand. According to DI Sawyer, the suspect attacked him and he was forced to defend himself. A witness testimony came to light during his suspension and we were keen to clarify this, but he absconded. The enquiry is being managed by DCI Farrell at Greater Manchester Police. Unfortunately, DI Sawyer has still not made himself available for further questioning, and we've heard nothing from him for over five months.'

'So,' said DC Moran. 'He's a fugitive, on suspicion of murder. A killer. And your past relationship with him can't change that, Maggie.'

Maggie scowled at him. '*Relationship*?'

'Whatever we all think about Sawyer's guilt or innocence,' said Keating, 'it all comes down to one question. Why would an innocent man, or a man convinced he'll be found innocent, run and hide from the police?'

11

Jordan Burns set down two pints of lager on the wooden picnic table and switched his phone to silent.

'Is this breakfast?' His companion hitched his Barbour jacket over the back of the chair.

'Close enough to midday to call it a lunchtime pint.'

The man—fifties, woolly sweater, wiry grey hair—sipped his drink, glanced back at the reservoir. 'Come here often?'

'Not lately.' Burns hunched his shoulders and buttoned up his cheap suit. A flash of wind swooped in off the surface of Ladybower, drawing a shudder. 'Used to walk a lot up here with Steph. Bamford Edge. Hope Valley.'

'How is she?'

Burns's phone vibrated with a call. He sent it to voicemail and took a slug of his drink. 'Things improved a bit last month, but now she seems worse than ever. She's still in pain from... what happened. Can't really walk far without...' He drank again. 'She went back to work a couple of weeks ago, but I think she took one look at the books and it set her back.'

'Your rental business?'

'Quality Cottages, yes. She's always ran the admin. I've tried to take it on, Lance, but... Spreadsheets, ROI, projections. It's not me.'

'I do sympathise.' Lance took out his phone, smiled, tapped out a reply to someone. Burns waited in silence, head down. 'Sorry about that. Well, we renovate rentals, prepare for sale. There are parallels, but—'

'Yes, I'm not great with the figures, close up, but I know the business.'

'My management roles are all occupied, Jordan. And anyway, for as long as I've known you, I wouldn't in good conscience think of you as a manager.'

Burns's phone vibrated. Again, he screened the call to voicemail. 'How about taking on QC?'

'Buy you out?'

'We have plenty of clients still on the books. All high-end places. Party-sized. No cosy granny cottages fit for two. The high rates reflect the quality and customer base.'

Lance looked away. 'Jordan, due diligence informs me that you've offloaded quite a few clients in recent months. Not through choice, I'd imagine.'

'Airbnb eating our lunch.'

'The internet has mostly just exposed inefficiency in offline practices. You need to be agile, adaptable, willing to take on risks. Innovate. Still, I'm not sure that your business is a level of risk I'm willing to take.'

Phone again.

'Sorry,' said Burns. 'Can I just... It might be important.'

Lance showed his palm; a grudging compliance.

Burns shifted his thickset frame to an empty table at the top of a verge overlooking the Snake Pass. He took the call.

'Jordan?'

'Yes. Who's this?'

'We're at a fork in the road.'

Burns sat down. 'Sawyer? Where are you?'

'Wouldn't you like to know?'

'Yeah, me and most people in Derbyshire and the surrounding region. Why are you... What—'

'Seems to me there are two choices of route from here.'

Burns took a drink. 'I could call this in, you know. There's a reward out for you.'

'You could, but what could you call in exactly? You don't know where I am and you don't know where I'm calling from. Could be Bamford, could be Budapest. The reward claim procedure is complicated, you know. They don't just hand over a bag of money over an alleged contact.'

'So what are the choices?'

A pause. 'One. I talk to Stephanie about your attempted blackmail. It won't be too hard to make her complicit. The two of you aren't exactly rock solid. It won't be good for your relationship status, or your not-being-in-prison status.'

'Or yours.'

'Precisely. Everybody loses. Me, you, Stephanie.'

'The way things are going right now, prison doesn't sound too bad.'

'I know. I've seen the accounts.'

Burns sighed, waited for a lorry to pass. 'And what's the second option?'

'Stephanie doesn't need to find out about your blackmail attempt. I will voluntarily help you financially, to re-establish your business. I have money, inherited from my dad.'

'And where do I tell Steph I got it from?'

'You can say that you legitimately convinced me to... provide the funds, given that I was involved in an aspect of her trauma. Stephanie gets the treatment she needs, and you get the kudos from her for being the big man who brought it home.'

Burns looked over at Lance, who was striding around near the table, engaged in a phone conversation of his own. 'So what do you want in return?'

'Stephanie just has to retract her version of events, that Bowman's death was self-defence, not cold blood. This way, only she, you and I need know we've had this conversation. It removes credibility for any legal action against me, stops me pursuing you for attempted blackmail, helps your business get moving again, gets Stephanie physical and psychological help.' Sawyer took a breath. 'It might also improve your personal situation. Remember, the reason Bowman took her in the first place was her use of the *Secret Encounters* website.'

Burns lifted the glass to his mouth, let the beer slop against his lips. 'If you'd just accepted my offer...'

'It was hardly an offer.'

'And this is?'

'You put me in this position. And, yes, it's an offer. Not a coercion. Here's a newsflash, Jordan, and I advise you not to share it. I'm coming home, one way or another. I'm just giving you the option of making that palatable to you and Stephanie. If you don't take this offer, then you're still in a bad way financially, and I can pursue charges for the blackmail. I might go to prison for Bowman, but you and Stephanie also stand a good chance of being indicted.'

'We go down with your ship, eh?'

'Think of it as a collaboration. If we don't all work together, then the future looks bleak for all of us.'

Burns took his time over a sip of his drink; Sawyer kept silent. 'And the police? How are they going to buy Stephanie's U-turn?'

'I'll fix that. You just have to keep this conversation

quiet for now. Don't tell Stephanie yet, and obviously keep it away from our friend, Mr Farrell.'

'There's a reward,' Burns repeated, draining his glass.

Sawyer laughed. 'Well, yes. But then we're back at the ugly old blackmail thing. And you run the risk of being convicted and it will just mean you get to buy a better class of bedding for your cell bunkbed. Listen. Jordan. You don't strike me as a blackmailer, or an extortionist. I assume the plan wasn't all your own work, and I have an idea who might have pushed you in that direction.'

'I had a conversation with DCI Farrell, yes. Mainly about convincing Stephanie to tell the truth.'

A pause on the line. 'Like I say, I'll fix it. That won't affect you or Stephanie.'

'Stephanie already suspects about the blackmail. She says she overheard me talking to Farrell.'

'Jordan. This works. We let the blackmail go. You were desperate. You were coerced. You were trying to help Stephanie. Look. I've found it in my heart to forgive you. Just see this as me accepting my role in the trauma suffered by Stephanie on seeing my killing of Bowman. Call it unofficial compensation.'

Burns looked over at Lance, now back at the original table, holding his palms out to Burns, shrugging. Smug and lordly. 'Okay. But now we have to get Stephanie behind the idea.'

'Just set up the time and date. I'll do the talking.'

12

The white Mercedes pulled in to the side of a lane at the edge of an upscale estate close to Bakewell town centre. Dale Strickland looked out of the back window, squinting at the largest semi in the block. 'Get me DCI Farrell, would you, Martin?'

The stocky man at the wheel connected the call and relayed it to the car's soundproof back seat.

'Robin Farrell.'

'Dale Strickland. Just checking in, DCI Farrell. I trust the effect of my narcotics initiative is meeting approval with Greater Manchester Police.'

'Nice to hear from you, Dale. The word I'd use would be "controversial". A few see the policy as the first steps towards decriminalisation.'

'The mayor agrees that drug abuse is a social problem, Robin. And we're not in the business of criminalising social problems. We're trying to reduce drug-related deaths. Changing the equation. The idea is to make your life easier, not cram more people into overcrowded prisons.'

Farrell made a non-committal noise. 'I can't quite work you out, Dale. Are you radical left or soft right?'

A tall woman in tracksuit trousers and a yellow hoodie emerged from the house. She heaved a loaded rubbish bag into the wheelie bin, swishing her long black hair off her shoulders.

'I'm neither, Robin. I'm more of a pragmatist. We're living through the post-ideological age. Those who cling to the old definitions, the old loyalties, will realise that soon enough.' He watched the woman as she re-entered the house. 'I was speaking to Russell, sorry, the mayor, about a loose end. Something he sees as an embarrassing civic matter. Embarrassing for you personally.'

Farrell scoffed. 'We're confident that Jake Sawyer will be apprehended soon.'

'The mayor doesn't share your confidence. And he'll be making a representation to the Greater Manchester Chief of Police next week. As the detective tasked with both the enquiry into the death of David Bowman in Sawyer's custody, and with bringing Sawyer to justice, I feel that your name may well enter the conversation.'

'What do you want, Dale?'

'I have an idea. Something that could help you to flush him out. Do you know where he is?'

A pause. 'I'd rather not say.'

'I'd rather you did.'

'With respect, you're not my line manager.'

Strickland laughed. 'You see, Robin? Line managers, corporate hierarchy, established processes. Things that are worth getting done, they don't get done that way, not anymore.'

Farrell cleared his throat. 'I'd be happy to hear your ideas on Sawyer. If you bear with me for a few more days, then I'll be able to give you more detail.'

Strickland's tone darkened. 'You should learn to take yes for an answer, DCI Farrell.'

He nodded at Martin, who disconnected the call, as Strickland stepped out of the car.

———

The tall woman opened the front door of the large semi, and stepped into the frame, blocking Strickland's passage.

'You need to warn me if you're coming.'

Strickland tried on a smile. 'You make me sound like a threat, sweetheart.'

She shook her head. 'It's Eva to you.'

'Is the little man in?'

Eva folded her arms. 'He's at school. And his name is Luka.'

Strickland nodded. 'Luka Strickland, not Gregory.'

Eva peered over Strickland's shoulder. 'Nice car. Not yours, though.'

'Technically, no. Not like this one.' He nodded to the silver Mazda parked in the drive. 'I bought this for you. Twenty-eighth birthday, I recall.'

'It's generally accepted that gift ownership is transferred to the recipient, Dale. Although I know you don't operate by everyone else's rules.'

Strickland plunged his hands into his suit trouser pockets, ran his eyes up and down the contours of her long body. 'Do you know something, Eva? You're one of those women who would look good wearing a potato sack.'

'You always were the one for compliments.'

'I'd like to see Luka, for his birthday. His twelfth.'

Eva reeled in mock shock. 'Well remembered. If it helps with your latest act of over-compensation, he's into twenty-year-old guitar bands at the moment, and he plays an online game thing called *Team Fortress* something or other, talks to his mates over a headset. And he's lost the red glasses now.' She touched her own dark brown Tom Fords. 'I think he's finally starting to accept some influence from his mother.'

'The little man no more.' Strickland leaned to the side, looked into the hall and spotted the large portrait photo of Luka: small, skinny, scruffy blond hair. He took off his glasses, cleaned the lenses with his shirt cuff. 'Remember when that photo was taken? Things were good, sweetheart. We were planning a playmate for him.'

Eva drew the door closed behind her, blocking Strickland's view of the house. 'Well, I was planning. You were busy, with your so-called business.'

'We drove to Mablethorpe with Luka that weekend, stayed with my parents. He lost his spade on the beach. Again.'

Eva smiled. 'If losing your spade was an Olympic sport...'

Strickland replaced his glasses. 'What say we go round again, Eva? We've... strayed off the track, but we can get back on it.' He took a step closer, onto the porch. 'Fast-forward a year. Teenage Luka, helping us with his baby brother or sister. A bigger house, nearer the city. Better school for Luka. My career and salary would mean you could choose your own work, focus more on your photography.' He reached out and took her hand. 'I could be a father to Luka again. It's not too late. Look at me. I'm a success story. I used to be wanted by the police, but now I practically run the police. There are some who would call me a bit of a catch.'

Eva lifted Strickland's hand away. 'It's a tempting prospect. But I've moved on, Dale. I'm seeing someone.'

Strickland closed his eyes. When he opened them again, the light had dimmed, and his stare drilled into her. 'I take it you haven't seen too much of him lately, though.

Nobody has, have they? Understandable, given what he's accused of.'

Eva eased herself back into the hall, preparing to close the door. 'If you're asking whether I know where he is, then no, I don't. I'm sure that whatever he's doing, wherever he is, he has his reasons.'

'Are you seriously telling me that you have more faith in a bent copper than the Deputy Mayor of Manchester?'

'Whatever Jake turns out to be, I do have faith in him. And however nicely you ask me where he is, I can't tell you. Because I don't know. So you'll have to try another way to find him.'

13

Sawyer sat cross-legged in front of the TV, jinking his on-screen spaceship through the blizzard of projectiles. He blasted the insectoid attack craft sequentially, based on colour and type, maximising his score, smiting his infinite digital enemies.

He pressed Start on the PS4 controller, pausing the game, replacing the synthetic zaps and booms with the drowsy trilling of the birds in the woodland outside his window. He tipped back his head, slowed his breathing. In the hour since he'd first fired up *Bullet Symphony*, the room's natural light had retreated and the wood burner flames had dwindled to flickers.

The clock on his CD player read 17:40. Around an hour to dusk.

He sprang to his feet and swiped his iPod Mini and headphones from the table. Then, the usual rituals: windows locked; all blinds down and flattened to the panes by clothing or towels; an outside check of the view in from the windows to make sure there was nothing obvious on display.

He locked the front door, pulled on a beanie and took

his standard route: into the shelter of the trees, up to Grizedale. With no need to head into the village, he could run for an uninterrupted hour, which gave plenty of time for a full listen to his favourite album: *Loveless* by My Bloody Valentine. As he climbed the trail for his warm-up walk, he cued the music: vague, sighing female vocals; an amniotic squall of guitar.

The forest had cleared of tourist walkers and he had the trails to himself, holding a steady pace for the initial incline, then pushing harder as the ground flattened and the trees thinned, opening up the views down to Coniston Water.

At the halfway mark, Sawyer felt a twinge from his hamstring and slowed to a brisk walk, turning back towards the house. He would have to defer the 10k to another time.

He ducked into a thicket at the top of an overgrown trail, and sat down on a fallen trunk. A bracing wind, restless for nightfall, swirled around his collar. He palpated the back of his thigh, wincing, closing his eyes against the pain.

'You've overdone it, my darling.'

He kept his eyes closed. 'No. I just rushed the warm-up.'

A gentle laugh. *'Dad would always rush to pick you up when you fell. I thought you should be able to do it yourself. As long as it didn't look too serious, of course.'*

Sawyer eased his eyes open. A woman stood leaning against an ash tree, almost obscured in the shade from its overhanging branches.

He peered through the shadows, but his mother's features remained vague. Usually, she was vivid, undeniable; but today she was defined only by her familiar mannerisms.

'I remember,' said Sawyer. 'I came off my bike. Pushbike. Stabilisers. I still have the scar on my hip. Dad was fussing and you were there. Almost overseeing.'

'It's not that I didn't care, you know that. At first I wanted Dad to be softer with you. He could be old-school. He would always storm out if you ever started to cry or have a tantrum over anything.' Jessica's Bible-black hair danced in the wind. 'But I also wanted you to learn about looking after yourself. For the time when you would have to.'

Sawyer tugged on the rim of his beanie. 'I'd love to hear you talk more about memories, about what life was like for you, before me. Before Michael, even. To find out more about who you were. It would help—'

'To let go?'

He shook his head. 'No. It's more complicated than that.'

A vibration in his pocket. He took out a plastic oblong, about the size of a cigarette lighter. The LED light, usually green, flashed red.

Sawyer hurried back along the track, limping a little. As he neared the house, he crouched down and crept along a rough path parallel to the woodland around the back of the house, giving him sight of the dirt track that connected to the main road and the tree where he'd set up the motion sensor and camera brought by Ainsworth.

A blue VW Golf was parked halfway down the track, and a man—rotund, in a saggy suit—stood at the front window of the cottage, pushing his head close to the glass. He trudged around the side, and swore as he stumbled in a patch of mud.

Sawyer moved off along the parallel path, staying low. He emerged, with caution, near to the car, making sure it was empty. He crouch-walked to its side and looked in the passenger side window.

Large, empty packet of Doritos in the passenger footwell; reusable coffee cup in the holder; cigarettes in a tray beneath the dashboard; duffel bag on the back seat.

He tried the door: locked.

A distant cough from near the cottage. Sawyer memorised the registration and scurried back into cover, as the man waddled back along the track.

He lurked behind a thick tree, at a distance safe enough not to be spotted but too far to pick out the man's features as he heaved himself into the car, lingered for a few minutes, then drove away.

14

'Oh, Charles is as dull as they come.'

Esther Murphy balanced two mugs of tea on wicker coasters in front of Walker and Shepherd. They leaned forward in unison, shuffling to get comfortable on the low sofa.

Esther caught herself. 'Sorry. Was.' She fumbled her way to her armchair, steadying herself along the edge of the coffee table. Walker raised himself to help, but she made it to the chair at surprising speed, and slumped down, smiling at each detective in turn. She was slight and angular, well into her eighties, with a shameless blue rinse bouffant to match her cobalt cardigan, fully buttoned up.

Walker reached for his tea. 'You were close to Charles's wife, Penny?'

'Yes, I'd known her all my life. Both of us, Bakewell born and bred. She was a bit wayward in her youth. Then Charles came along, settled her down a bit.'

'Were they a happy couple?' said Shepherd.

An unkempt Bichon Frise fussed around Esther's feet; she scratched it under the chin as she spoke. 'Content, I'd say.' She chuckled. 'You get to a certain age, and that's the best you can hope for, really. You become each other's carer. As long as you do actually care about the other person, then it can be fine. That's what they seemed like to me. Fine. But you can never tell for sure, can you?'

'You say Charles was dull,' said Walker. 'In what way?'

She smiled, waved a hand. 'Oh, I'm not going to speak ill of the dead.'

'They can't hear you,' said Shepherd. Walker eyed him.

Esther raised her eyebrows. 'No, I suppose not.' She picked up the dog, planted it on her knee. 'He was just... Not really one thing or another. He used to be a teacher. Pioneer Primary in Wardlow. I was a governor for a while, when my two were there.'

'Good place?' said Shepherd.

'As far as I know, yes. Charles was always helpful to me. Seemed like a good teacher, a good man. He used to be an excellent cook. He would make these wonderful pies. I think he was the custodian of the kitchen, even when Penny was still alive. After she died, I don't think he kept it up. Charles was a runner for a time, then he took to walking. Kinder Scout, Castleton. The kind of routes you wouldn't expect for a man of his years. He was fit and active. Physically strong.'

'Was he one for cologne, Esther?' said Walker. 'Aftershave?'

She laughed, shook her head. 'I wouldn't know about that. I doubt it.' She toyed with the cameo brooch at the top of the cardigan. 'I suppose he could be a little old-fashioned.'

Shepherd nodded. 'Unreconstructed?'

She frowned. 'He had his ways.'

'When was the last time you saw him?' said Walker.

Esther pondered. 'A couple of weeks ago. A guided walk near Longnor. I was with a group but he was alone. We crossed paths briefly. I'm still not sure that he knew who I was. He seemed quite vague.'

Shepherd shuffled his bulk to the edge of the sofa. 'Can you think of anyone who might want to hurt Charles, Esther?'

'Goodness me, no. I never heard a bad word against him.' She rubbed at her eye. 'Poor, poor Charles. Was it all over money? Did they steal from him? I don't think he had very much.'

'We don't think anything significant was taken, no,' said Shepherd.

Esther set the dog down on the floor, and gazed off into space. 'What sort of a person would do this to an elderly man, living out his final days? Do you think you'll catch them?'

'We have lines of enquiry,' said Shepherd. 'We'll do our very best.'

'Maybe I could get a few of my friends in on the case? If we put our heads together we might be able to help.'

Walker glanced at Shepherd. 'I think it's probably better if you concentrate on keeping yourself safe. Make sure your house is secure, and don't answer the door unless you're sure who's there.'

'Oh, I'm always careful with things like that.' The dog fussed around Walker. 'And Betsy might not look like much, but she's a good guard dog.'

―――――

Rain rattled against the bonnet of the old Range Rover, as Shepherd threaded through the steep side roads, away from Bakewell.

Walker fiddled with his phone, trying to connect to the car's sound system. 'Good job scaring the old lady to death.'

'Better than saying there's nothing to worry about, which we both know isn't true.'

Shepherd didn't slow for a dip in the road, and the car thumped through a deep puddle, showering the windscreen.

Walker shot him a look.

'Sorry... I'll talk to Sally about trace, try to get a clearer forensic view. You look into the school. There must be something interesting about Yates. So far, all we know is that he was an old fella who was losing his marbles, and in decent nick for his age.'

Walker gave up with the music. 'Maybe we're after someone who gets his jollies from the old folks.'

'Which is why I was warning Esther to stay alert.' Shepherd slowed for the junction that turned into the road back to Buxton.

'Gerontophilia is rare. Gerontophile killers rarer.'

Shepherd nodded. 'Ken Erskine. The Stockwell Strangler.'

'Erskine sodomised his victims. No sexual abuse of Yates's body.'

'And I assume gerontophile homosexual killers are—'

As Shepherd emerged onto the Buxton road, he was forced to brake hard, as a car heading towards the town swerved to avoid him. The driver gave an angry blast on his horn and waved a hand out of his window.

'Fuck!' Walker lurched forward, locked in by his seatbelt.

Shepherd drove on for a few seconds, then pulled the Range Rover into a lay-by and switched off the engine.

Walker gathered himself, looked at Shepherd. 'Didn't you see him?'

Shepherd sat upright, eyes closed. He shook his head.

'Jesus Christ, Ed. Are you okay? That was close.'

Shepherd's breathing quickened; he kept his eyes closed.

'Take it easy. Hold the inhales for a bit longer. Slow it down.' Walker unscrewed the cap from his water bottle and offered it to Shepherd, who took a few thirsty gulps and handed it back.

Shepherd widened his eyes, wiped his brow. 'I'm fine. Just a shock.'

'Your breathing is still pretty fast.'

'It'll pass.' His hands gripped the wheel, trembling.

Walker studied him. 'Take your time. I can drive if you like.'

'No. I'm fine. Just give me a minute.'

Walker turned to look out of his window. The rain spattered into the leaves of a high hedgerow at the side of the lay-by. For a few moments, he kept his eyes away from Shepherd, listening to his slowing breaths: in through nostrils, out through mouth.

'Slow breaths,' said Walker. 'Take your time.'

'Sorry, Matt. I'm okay. Just... Didn't see him.' Shepherd started the ignition and pulled out onto the road.

Walker glanced over. Shepherd's forehead glistened with sweat. He scrubbed at his goatee, shook his head, forcing himself back into focus.

They drove on.

'So I'll look into the school,' said Walker. 'Maybe ex-colleagues of Charles. See if anyone can think of a reason why he might have been targeted, if it was personal.'

'Maybe nothing was taken because the killer was disturbed by Linda's arrival.' Shepherd's voice wavered. He checked his rear-view mirror, then wing mirror, rear-view mirror again.

Walker turned back to the window. 'I was just thinking—'

'There's your first mistake.'

'You'll hate this.'

Shepherd glanced over. 'Go on...'

'What would Sawyer do?'

Shepherd laughed, uneasy. 'I don't think that's a healthy thought experiment.'

'Do you think Maggie knows?'

'About what?'

'Where he is. They've known each other for a long time.'

Shepherd slowed again for traffic. He rolled his head around, crunching the neck muscles. 'I spoke to her about it a couple of weeks ago. I don't think she's holding out much hope.'

15

NOVEMBER 2000

'Put your valuables in there!'

The man threw a large, open sports holdall into the middle of the sitting room floor.

'And turn the fucking music off.'

A pallid male student in a black-and-red top with *KEELE RUGBY* on the back pointed to a stacked sound system near to the intruder, who wheeled around and twisted the volume dial, silencing Eminem.

The intruder stepped towards the student and raised his sawn-off shotgun to his face. He was small, stocky. Wild eyes. Petrified but empowered.

'This your place, eh?'

The rugby man nodded. 'I live here, yeah.'

'Right. Well, your guests need to fill that fucking bag, or you'll be the first who gets this.' He raised the gun in the air, pointed it at the group of young men and women who had backed into a cluster by the bay window.

A few began to edge forward and throw wallets and watches into the bag.

The man in the rugby top reached into his back pocket and the intruder swung the shotgun towards him again.

'He's just getting his wallet,' said Maggie Spark, moving into view at the side of the group.

The intruder pointed the gun at her, then back at the man. 'Hurry up! But do it slow.'

Someone sniggered.

An adjoining door opened and Jake Sawyer emerged, carrying a full-to-the-brim glass of red wine and a plate of cheese and crackers. 'What happened to the music?' He froze, surveyed the scene, then walked towards the man with the shotgun. 'Try this cheese. Seriously. It's Roquefort. French. They make it from sheep's milk. It's so good.' He held the plate up to the man, who scowled and raised the shotgun, pushing the barrel into Jake's head.

'Get over there with the others.'

Jake glanced at the man and shot him a dimpled smile. 'The story is, there was a farm boy or something...' He was flushed, speech slurred. 'And he was eating a standard chunk of cheese, but he saw this gorgeous girl and went to speak to her. When he came back to the spot, weeks later, the cheese had moulded, and, y'know...' He took a slug of wine. 'The rest is history. Cheese history.'

'Put your wallet in the bag and get over there.'

'And this,' Jake held up the wine, 'this is Barolo. Jesus, it's the drink of the gods. You can only find the grapes in a certain part of Italy. It's special because of the soil or something. Makes the wine age quicker. I don't know.' He took another slurp. 'I'm not an expert. Seriously.' Jake held up the plate. 'If you're not a drinker, just try the cheese.'

The man lowered his gaze, but kept the shotgun pointed at Jake's head.

Jake nodded at the gun. 'Is that a Weatherby? My dad's got one.'

The intruder reached out to the plate and took a chunk of the cheese. He glanced up at Jake, who nodded, smiling.

He popped the cheese into his mouth, chewed, raised his eyebrows.

'How good is that? Now try this.' Jake raised the wine glass to the man. 'Hey. No tricks. Look.' He took a drink himself.

The shotgun drooped as the man snatched up the wine and took a sip, then another. He tilted back his head and drained the glass.

The man held eye contact with Jake for a few seconds, the toughness melting from his features. He looked around the room, confused, surprised. 'I don't...' He set down the gun on the floor. 'Sorry. I'm in the wrong place.'

He turned and walked to the door, then pivoted, came back to Jake and retrieved the gun and bag, and walked out, down the hall, through the front door.

The room held its stunned silence, as the students huddled around the window, watching him move off down the street.

'Call the police!' a woman shouted, breaking the spell. 'He's got my fucking purse.'

The rugby man took out his phone and tapped in a number.

Jake slumped into a chair at the side of the room. He gathered up the remaining crackers, brushed the cheese off them, and posted the plate underneath the chair.

Maggie walked over and crouched beside him. 'How much have you had to drink? He could have blown your head off.'

Jake looked over to her, his green eyes swimmy and distant. 'Could he?'

'Yes, you idiot. He could.'

'With an unloaded gun?'

'How do you know it was unloaded?'

He munched on a cracker. 'There's a little button by the trigger. The shell elevator. It wasn't released. And you could see the bolt was still open.'

Maggie stood upright, folded her arms. 'This is the first I've heard about you being a cheese and wine aficionado.'

'I'm not. Just got it all from the kitchen. The wine is alright, but the cheese is hideous. It's got *mould* on it, for fuck's sake.' He looked around, reached for an abandoned glass of white wine. 'I need a drink.'

Maggie got there first, and held the glass out of his reach. 'I disagree, Jake. Time to quit while you're ahead.'

———

Jake fumbled beneath the bed and pulled out the metal Jack Daniel's tin.

'Oh. The Aloof. I love this album.'

Maggie flicked through a stack of vinyl records pushed up against the wall, her face illuminated by the glow from the lava lamp.

'Yeah. They're a London version of Massive Attack. Never get the respect they deserve.' He pulled a red study folder from his bedside cabinet and shook out a mound of white powder onto the plastic surface.

'Do you have any music recorded after 1996?'

'Yeah, I didn't bring everything. Lots still back at home.'

'In Wardlow.' She tidied the pile. 'You brought the nineties stuff, though. That's your comfort era.'

He glanced up, smiled. His eyes had fuzzed over and he swayed in place. 'You're quite the analyst.'

Maggie put the album on. Clattering, processed percussion. A deep, pulsing kick drum. Intoned, reggae-ish vocals. She stood, looked along the bookshelf. 'Yeah. I'm erring more towards prevention, rather than policing. Helping people not to become criminals in the first place, giving them the tools to live better lives, regardless of their backgrounds.'

Jake rolled a five-pound note into a straw-like tube. 'So you're on the nurture side of the debate.' He sniffed up a line.

Maggie glanced over her shoulder, frowned, turned back to the books. 'Your background, past experiences, are important. But there's a process of rebuilding, reinvention. Not everybody with a difficult background goes on to be a serial killer.'

'No...' He rubbed at his nose. 'But it's usually a factor.'

She studied the photograph of Jessica Sawyer. 'Between the stimulus and the response, there's a space—'

'—and there lies the opportunity for growth and freedom.'

Maggie turned, eyebrows raised. 'I think that's Viktor Frankl.'

He chopped out another line. 'Not sure. It fits his ideas, though. He believed we're all on a permanent quest, a "will to meaning". To find a point to our existence, no matter how miserable.'

'Yes, he had quite a Stoic attitude. He said that when we can't change a situation, we should seek to change ourselves.'

'And of course, the main situation we can't change is what has already happened to us.'

She stepped towards him. 'The past.'

He nodded, re-rolled the five-pound note. 'Do you want some coke?'

Maggie grimaced. 'No, thanks. I hate that horrible taste you get at the back of your mouth.' She lowered her head, jiggled to the music. 'The singer sounds like Horace Andy.'

'Plenty did back then. I suppose Massive Attack were the aspirational artists.'

'I know about your mother, Jake.' He didn't flinch. 'She was a teacher, wasn't she? I read about what happened. Have you ever spoken to anyone about it?'

He leaned in, snorted the line hard. 'Aren't we doing that now?'

'I mean professionally.'

He shrugged.

'That's what might be driving this.'

'What?'

She waved a hand towards the powder. 'And risky behaviour, disregard for consequences.'

'Shall we move down to the sitting room so I can lie on the couch?'

Maggie sat on the bed next to him. 'The future doesn't just happen. We shape it with our choices in the present. I'm just saying that it doesn't feel like you're making good choices.'

'In the space between stimulus and response.'

'You suffered a terrible trauma.'

'Not as terrible as my mum's.'

She reached over, lifted the powdery study folder off his knee and placed it on the floor by her feet. 'I just don't think you can find your will to meaning with short-term chemical changes. You have to expand your view. Find something bigger than yourself and dedicate your life to it.'

He lay back on the bed. 'I remember the week before... she died. We'd been looking after this bird. We'd found it on the back door step, just standing there, making no attempt to get away. It was like it had given up. It must have injured its wing or something. I looked after it, kept it in a shoebox. She said it was probably in shock and if we gave it some time, it might recover and fly away. It died, of course. And we buried it. I remember the *finality* of it. How one second, there's this marvellous little creature, full of potential, and the next... But my mum said that the dead body wasn't really him. It was only a vessel, and the part that was really him had gone to a place where he didn't need it anymore. But I couldn't get over that feeling of not being able to help it, despite our best intentions. I couldn't change its course. I remember crying and saying it wasn't fair.' Jake raised his head, looked at Maggie. 'But that's just what kids say, isn't it? Imposing this higher sense of justice on everything. In fact, it's all random, and there's nobody in control. I don't think that we have control. It's a comforting illusion. There's no point dedicating your life to something bigger, whatever that is. It's all... stuff that happens and you have to react on the fly.'

Maggie smiled. 'Please don't tell me you're a fatalist.'

'No. I'm not saying we can't influence things. But I think we over-estimate our ability to control the present and build the future. We have this arrogance, and we think that if we can do good then we'll get karmic payback. But no sooner have we set something in motion, allowed ourselves to feel attached to something, it spirals away, on its own path.' He sat up. 'You could say that the moment we feel connected to something is the moment we have to get used to the idea of one day letting it go. We're helpless products of our past. And we don't get what we deserve. We get what we get.'

She sighed, took his hand. 'Jake. You are really going to have to work at your seduction technique.'

16

PRESENT DAY

Dale Strickland sat on the edge of his desk and faced the floor-to-ceiling window. Streaks of water raced each other to the bottom of the pane.

'Does it rain this much in Liverpool?'

Curtis Mavers angled his head, glanced at the tall man at his side. 'Yeah. You don't notice as much, though. The drops get stolen before they hit the ground.'

Strickland didn't indulge him with a laugh. He turned. 'Drink?'

Mavers shook his head. The man at his side—tall, dressed in fitted black jeans and a tight black polo-neck—took a step forward. 'What's on offer?' He ran his fingers through long greasy blond-streaked hair.

Strickland smiled, in surprise. 'Well, you certainly don't sound local.'

The tall man held out a hand. 'Levi.'

'Like the jeans,' said Strickland, shaking.

'That's Levi's.'

'This is Levi Wilmot,' said Mavers. 'An old cellmate at Manchester. He's sound. Helped me out in a few scrapes there.'

Wilmot smiled. 'Indeed. And I've been looking forward to working with Curtis.' He held Strickland's gaze.

'A pleasure,' said Strickland, sitting. Mavers did the same.

'Love the suit,' said Wilmot. 'Gucci?'

'Brioni. I'm not normally so fashion-conscious, but I need to be in character, in my other life. Now. Curtis. Housekeeping.'

Mavers spoke while Wilmot remained standing. 'This fella, Marian. Nothing. I've tapped up all my finest bottom feeder buddies. If they don't know what's happened to him, it can't have been good.'

Strickland took off his glasses, cleaned them on his shirt cuff. 'Let's defer that one. And the other thing?'

'Austin Fletcher,' said Wilmot, beaming. 'He's quite a specimen.'

'No sign of him, though,' said Mavers. 'A few rumours, but nothing solid. Trickier than fucking Dynamo.'

'An upstanding purveyor of violence.' Wilmot finally sat down. 'I'd love to meet him.'

'Join the queue,' said Strickland. 'I'm sure they'll surface eventually. For now, we have a new game. Our Oldham friend was a big success. You've stirred up plenty of paranoia among the gangs. Rusholme, Fallowfield, Moss Side. Hopefully, it'll kick off a turf war. Knock a few of the main pieces off the board.'

'We left a lot of blood on his floor,' said Wilmot. 'I had to exercise extreme restraint with his woman. I really don't see why I shouldn't indulge in a little leisure—'

'They'll want revenge,' said Mavers.

'I take it you didn't use each other's names.' Strickland glanced at Wilmot. 'Particularly since one is so distinctive.'

'Of course not,' said Mavers. 'He clocked my accent, though. They might join things up. Recent releases with histories of violence. Beefs with drugs.'

Strickland shrugged. 'They're thugs.'

'They don't have the perspicacity,' said Wilmot.

'No,' said Strickland. 'I suppose they don't. And how heavy was your burden on the way out?'

Mavers scowled. 'Not heavy enough. Five figures. It's in safekeeping, needs washing.'

Strickland waved a hand. 'I'll arrange that.'

'Got a few replicas, cloned plates. Thing is...' He sat forward. 'Cunts like that are mid-tier. We've pruned a bit off the middle of the tree. But we need to go for the roots if we really want to disrupt things.'

'And the Deputy Mayor gets a big tick on his performance review,' said Wilmot.

Strickland shot him a glare. 'I can work some indirect contacts and come up with bigger names. But it'll take time.'

'Can't you call in some insider help? There must be loads of rotten filth at GMP.'

'I'm working on that. But the pace is too relaxed.' He picked up a fountain pen, tapped it on the desk. 'You know, we could join a few dots here. Make some progress on the other problem we talked about.'

Mavers nodded. 'Mr Sawyer.'

17

Sally O'Callaghan swiped at her touchscreen, revealing a gallery of six images with different angles and details on various shoeprints.

'Nothing new on the size 7. The visible print with Charles's blood matches these others taken from around the back of the flat. Looks like the killer entered through the back door, walked through to the sitting room, walked back out again. The back alley on that side leads to Sheldon village. We found the same pattern on the bedroom carpet.'

Sitting beside Keating, Maggie paused from her note-taking, tucked her hair behind her ear. 'I spoke to Linda again, Charles's carer. Apparently, a lot of people use the back way almost like an alternative front because it's the most direct route up from the village.'

'Any prints at the front of the house?' said Myers.

'There's nothing to suggest any movement into any other parts of the house. Nothing at the front door or hallway. We used electrostatic lifting to get them off the lino, then made the cast you can see bottom-right.'

'Is there any way to link the print with a brand?' said Walker, looking up from his screen.

'The files are with a specialist shoeprint and tyre track analyst. I hope to have the findings back in a day or two.'

'Can't you just do a reverse image search or something?' said Moran. 'Algorithms can work wonders, these days.'

Sally smiled. 'DC Moran. The International Association for Identification recommends over five hundred hours of training before it will recognise an analyst as competent. Some things are still beyond the reach of the Silicon Valley venture capitalists, and we have to rely on pesky human expertise.'

'Also,' said Shepherd, 'it's more about detecting blemishes and damage, to link the print to a specific shoe. Just matching to a style of outsole would be too broad.'

'And we still need a suspect to match,' said Keating. He sat back in his seat, stared up at the conference room ceiling.

Shepherd took it as a cue. 'Do some house to house. Sightings of anyone around the back of Yates's place around time of death. The description will have to be vague as there's no clear correlation between shoe size and height, correct?'

Sally shook her head.

'CCTV?' said Keating.

Myers cleared his throat. 'Nothing from any of the pubs or businesses around Sheldon. ANPR records not much use without a potential suspect vehicle. We have an officer working with Rhodes on doorbell cams.'

'Since it sounds like the killer would probably have come to the house from the village, talk to the people in the shops around Sheldon. Anyone unusual, strange behaviour.'

'We also spoke with one of Charles's old colleagues,' said Walker. 'An ex-governor of the school where he used to teach. Pioneer Primary. The only thing we really learned was that he made a mean pie.'

Shepherd shut down the shared screen system. 'Keep us informed about forensics, Sally. DC Myers, DC Moran, keep HOLMES up to date. Drummond says his toxicology will be ready tomorrow morning, so I'll add anything new once he reports.'

Maggie raised her head. 'Pioneer?'

'Yes,' said Walker. 'I have an appointment later to see another teacher who worked there. A colleague of Charles's.'

She nodded. 'That's the school where Sawyer's mother taught.'

Moran gave a theatrical sigh. 'And this is relevant how?'

'I want to see deeper work on victimology,' said Keating. 'Any family connections, old grudges. Most vics know their killer. Could he be someone local? Go deep on the house to house. Get Rhodes to go broader on the passive data. Mobile masts, all the off-high street CCTV bases covered. Go back further than the few days before the murder in case the killer was staking things out. Look for repeat appearances.'

'And finances,' said Shepherd. 'Doesn't look like the old boy had a lot stashed away, but is there anyone who might gain financially from him not being around anymore?'

Walker eyed Keating. 'It still seems strange that nothing was taken. And why do it in broad daylight? Why not just wait until dark? Much safer. Maybe it says something about the killer's arrogance. Sawyer once told me that you should pay attention to anything—'

Keating slammed both palms on the table and pushed himself to his feet. 'DI Sawyer is not a part of this investigation, DS Walker.' His voice was raised, borderline shouting, and all the detectives lowered their heads. Maggie kept her gaze on him, and he directed his final remark in her direction. 'We are all capable of functioning without DI

Sawyer. It's time we got used to the idea that he is part of this unit's past, and has no role in its future.'

18

'No sign.'

Terry Barker crashed into the chair opposite DCI Farrell, who reached for his canister of breath mints, realised it was empty, and flicked it aside in irritation. 'And how hard did you look?'

'I waited for a while, made sure all was quiet, then I had a good snoop around the building. Nothing. Blinds all down, blacked out.'

'And what if Sawyer had emerged while you were pressed up against one of his windows?'

Barker shrugged. 'Lost fisherman.'

'Any cars outside?'

'No. In my typically humble opinion, it didn't look like the place had been lived in for a while. Sorry to burst your bubble, but if I was a betting man—'

'And are you?' Farrell picked his nose, wiped something on his knee.

'No. But if I was, I'd say that Sawyer knows we're onto him somehow, and he's moved somewhere else.'

'You think he's realised that the fight in the shop might have exposed him?'

Barker took out a bottle of water. 'It was hardly a fight.' He took a drink. 'Maybe. He might also have seen me arrive and kept his head down. We can't be sure unless we set up an extended surveillance. Probably using a CROP crew.'

Farrell rummaged in his drawer. 'He'd know.'

'Fucking hell, Farrell. He's not Jesus.'

'No, but we have to be lateral. Stay off the books, particularly with your good self involved. The moment we start getting official is the moment Keating will get wind of it all and his cronies will muscle in.'

Barker smiled. 'You know what? This logic in bypassing the regulation channels is sounding suspiciously similar to Sawyer's justification of his raid on Bowman's place. It's almost like you're trying to settle a score.'

'Or play him at his own game.'

Barker stood up and walked to the window. He looked out at the neat back garden. 'Who's got the green fingers?'

'Not me.'

'I don't have the patience for gardening. I like the idea of an allotment, though.'

Farrell scoffed. He unwrapped a new canister of mints and popped one into his mouth. 'Go back up there. Rent somewhere nearby. Put a regular watch on the place. Get some night goggles or something.'

Barker turned. 'Like in *Silence of the Lambs*. I've always wanted a pair of those. And I'll see if I can source a stingray. A cell site simulator which can catch nearby calls.'

'An IMSI catcher,' said Farrell.

'The very same. Although there may be civil liberty issues.'

Farrell rolled the mint around his mouth. 'Just make sure they don't become issues for me personally. We need to hold steady, be one hundred per cent that Sawyer is there. If we squeeze too tight now, he'll slip away. Remember, there's a lot at stake for him. He'll be taking precautions. We have to keep everything watertight, purely between you and me. Nothing leaves this room. Our little secret.'

Barker approached the desk, leaned on the back of the chair. 'Yeah. On that...'

'What?'

He took out his phone. 'A key thing about surveillance. Make sure you're not being surveilled, too.'

'You mean Sawyer is watching us?'

'No. But someone is.' He turned the phone screen around to reveal a photograph, taken from distance. 'Two fellas in a black Audi TTS, parked quite a way down the street, but with an excellent view of your front door.'

19

Sawyer stood, topless, before the half-length mirror at the foot of his bed. He closed his eyes, slowed his breathing, and eased into the first Wing Chun Kung Fu form, *Sil Lum Tao* ('Little Idea'). His arms chopped at the air, rehearsing the blocking and parrying techniques, reinforcing the core principles, working around an imaginary vertical centreline for absolute efficiency, unwavering economy.

He warmed down, dressed, poured himself a glass of water. He placed Ainsworth's laptop on the sitting room table, and took two fresh Nokia 105s from the box under the bed. He started one up and connected a call.

'News desk.'

'Car reg.'

'Top of the morning to you, too, Sawyer.' Again, the sound of Dean Logan moving into a private room. 'You're using another new phone. I love this. You're quite the gamekeeper turned poacher.'

'Let's be nice. And quick. I'm picturing your desk surrounded by NCA spooks with sophisticated tracking equipment.'

Logan spluttered. 'I wish. Spare hot desk office.

Nothing here but a chair and a company computer. The previous bloke has left a fucking apple core in the wastebin. I'm surrounded by savages, Sawyer.'

'Car reg. LD71 BXY. Whatever you can dig up about the owner would be most appreciated.'

'Anything else? Can I order you a pizza or something? Let me know your address and topping.'

Sawyer opened the laptop and started it up. 'Almost had me there, Logan. You haven't lost your wily ways.'

He hung up, took out and snapped the SIM card, then connected the 4G cellular dongle to the laptop and opened the video conference software. The signal was weak but serviceable, and he dialled in. After a few seconds, the software window showed a man and a woman sitting side by side, with Sawyer's face in the top-right corner.

The room at the other end was dark, and as Jordan Burns loomed into the image, too close to the camera, his shapeless black T-shirt gave the impression that his head was disembodied. He was at least ten pounds heavier than the last time Sawyer had seen him, over five months earlier, and had grown a thick salt-and-pepper beard, mostly salt.

Stephanie Burns stared into the camera, distant but with an air of defiance. Her blonde hair had been cut short and her features had filled out slightly, the dark circles under her eyes pitted in the harsh glow from the computer screen.

Sawyer sipped his water. 'Can you hear me okay?'

They both nodded.

'Can I say something first?' said Stephanie. She spoke in a hoarse waver, almost a whisper; it was the voice of a woman twenty years older.

'How are you, Stephanie?' said Sawyer.

She squeezed out a smile. 'I'm surviving, thank you. I wanted to apologise for all the trouble I've caused you.

Jordan has told me about your offer, and I... understand. We were badly advised, and I hope you can appreciate how awful things were last year.'

'I just want everyone to get their lives back. This way works for us all, I think. You say you were badly advised. By whom?'

Jordan looked at Stephanie, who continued. 'The detective. Farrell. I overheard him speaking to Jordan in the corridor when he came to see us, investigating what happened at the...' She lowered her head; Jordan put an arm round her shoulders, but she didn't lean in to accept the comfort. 'I've tried to exercise, get myself back into some kind of shape. But I still suffer so badly from pain, where I was restrained. And the nightmares go away for a while, then come back worse.'

'She needs proper physical and mental therapy,' said Jordan. 'NHS options aren't doing it.'

'And there's also the guilt about not being able to maintain our business.'

Jordan pulled her close. 'That's not your fault, babe.'

She turned to him and snapped, 'I know.'

The image froze for a moment, then resumed. Sawyer glanced at the signal icon; the second bar of three flickered. 'What did you hear in the corridor, Stephanie?'

She paused, looked at Jordan. He dropped his head. 'I heard Farrell talking to Jordan, pushing him into getting me to change my story, to say you weren't acting in self-defence. I was desperate, so I...' She held her head in her hands. 'I'm so sorry, Mr Sawyer. Jordan said that Farrell told him we'd be—'

'Generously compensated,' said Jordan.

Stephanie held up her hands, pleading to the camera. 'Isn't that a form of blackmail?'

Jordan kept his head down.

'It's over-promising, maybe,' said Sawyer. 'But not blackmail. I'm making this offer because I want to help, and... I understand the nightmares, Stephanie. The trauma. I've suffered similar for my whole adult life, and most of my childhood.'

She nodded. 'Goodness, your poor mother.'

He took a deep drink of water. 'I used to feel that everyone was redeemable. But there are some people who forfeit the right to share the earth with everyone else. You were unfortunate to meet one of them. And so was I.' He leaned in. 'I'm just trying to pay something forward. My father was also a victim of what happened to my mother, and he channelled his pain into his art. And when he died, I benefited.'

'Financially,' said Stephanie.

'Yes. I was fortunate. And I want to use that good fortune to help you to restart your business and get your health back. It will help us all, but I see it as my way of taking the horror faced by my parents, and turning it into something good.'

Stephanie's cheeks ran with tears. 'A "fuck you" to the people who tried to ruin our lives.'

'It helps me to see it that way, yes. I hope it's the same for you.'

Jordan pulled Stephanie in for a hug; this time, she submitted. He passed her a tissue and she mopped at her eyes and nose.

'What do you need from me?'

20

'What can I get you to eat? There's not a lot in.'

'I'm fine. Thank you.' Walker hung back by the front door, giving Dorothy Butcher plenty of time to hobble down the hall towards the kitchen.

She looked over her shoulder. 'I'm asking what you want to eat, love. Not do you want something.'

'Really, Mrs Butcher—'

'I've just made Graham some tongue sandwiches. I always make too many.'

He followed her into the kitchen. 'Thank you, but I've already had lunch.'

'You wouldn't know you ate at all, looking at you. And you can call me Dot. Because you're a policeman.'

Walker smiled. 'Special privilege.'

Dot peeled the clingfilm off a plate of triangular sandwiches. Walker looked past her, through an adjoining door that led out to a conservatory overlooking a modest garden. An elderly man sat in the centre of a sun trap, in a high-backed wicker chair, angled towards the lawn.

'We've got a bit of apple juice.' Dot bent forward to open the fridge: circa 1975, no freezer compartment. It contained several glass bottles of milk and a large slab of cheese, also wrapped in clingfilm. 'We hardly use this thing. I keep all my food in the pantry. Keeps it nice and cool. I don't like food too cold, do you?'

'Depends, really. You don't want warm ice-cream.'

Dot made a face. 'Never liked ice-cream. We have a nice jam sponge cake for our treat.' She extracted a sandwich from the pile and transferred it to a smaller plate. 'During the war, I was evacuated to a place in Devon. I had sponge cake there for the first time, and I've never lost the taste. Butter cream will do for me.' She handed the plate to Walker.

'Thank you, Dot. Did you mention to Graham that I wanted a quick word?'

'Yes. Come through. He's had his snooze.' She lowered her voice. 'He can be a bit sharp, so don't mind him. He used to be so polite. Couldn't do enough for you. These days, though, I'm not sure he's all there. He drives me up the wall sometimes, asking me the same thing over and over.'

Walker stepped into the conservatory. 'Mr Butcher?'

The man squinted up at him. He was a gnomish seventysomething with wispy white eyebrows and an undersized head that squatted low, between his oddly broad shoulders. A large salmon-pink birthmark sat at the top of his forehead.

He hitched himself up on the chair and put on a pair of silver-rimmed glasses. 'Are you the police? What do you want?' His voice was feeble and wavering, with a bass note of derision.

'Detective Sergeant Matthew Walker, sir. Pleased to meet you.'

Walker put his plate—and sandwich—on the glass-topped table at Butcher's side. He waved it away. 'If that's for me, you can shift it. I've had enough. She keeps making 'em even though I hate the bloody things.'

Dot laughed. She raised her voice and adopted a condescending tone, clearly well practised. 'I keep making 'em because you keep eating 'em, young man.'

Butcher groaned in disagreement and shuffled in his chair, trying to get comfortable.

'I'd like to ask you a few questions, Mr Butcher. It won't take long. It's about a chap you used to work with. Charles Yates.'

He tossed his head. 'That fucking ponce.'

'Graham!' Dot leaned down in front of Butcher, forcing herself into his field of view. 'Watch your language.'

'Well. I always thought he was one of them. And I'm too old to mince my words.' He took a good look at Walker. 'You look like that cricketer. What's his name?'

Walker smiled. 'I don't follow cricket.'

Butcher threw up his hands. 'Oh, for fuck's sake. You're not a ponce, as well, are you?'

'Graham!'

'It's okay, Mrs Butcher.' Walker held a hand up in submission. Dot got the message and left the conservatory. 'Mr Butcher, you worked with Charles at Pioneer Primary School in Wardlow.'

'Yes, I bloody well did. He did the numbers. Maths. I could never stand numbers. I was more about words. I taught those kids how to speak and write properly. You wouldn't fucking know it to hear them talk nowadays, though. Some of them can barely spell their own names. What's going on with Charles, anyway? What's he been sniffing around?'

Walker took out his notepad. 'What do you mean?'

The hand wave again. 'Could never keep it in his

trousers, so I heard. Not that there was much down there to write home about.'

'He was murdered last Sunday.'

Butcher screwed up his face in confusion. He peered through the glass, out to the garden. 'Who would bother killing that silly old bastard?'

'That's what we'd like to find out.'

He scoffed. 'They need a firmer hand.'

'Who does?'

'Kids. That's the trouble. You can't lay a finger on them, these days. They need to feel a bit of fear. It keeps 'em in line. He was always soft with them. And always sucking up to Welch.'

Walker checked his notes. 'Norman Welch. Head teacher.'

Butcher nodded. 'Bighead, we called him. Not to his face. He had a temper on him. Loved his cane. He made sure he was the only one in that school allowed to cane the kids. Everyone else had to use slippers and rulers.'

'Had to?'

Butcher glared at Walker. 'Yes. You're not listening, are you? I've just told you. They need a firm hand. Let them get away with too much and they think they're in charge.'

'Corporal punishment was banned in British state schools in 1986.'

Butcher laughed, shook his head. 'You *are* a fucking ponce, aren't you? Are you married?'

'Can you think of anyone who might want to harm Charles? Anything recent?'

Another hand wave, more violent this time. 'How should I know? I haven't seen the bugger in twenty years.'

'Do you remember anything else about the school? Any other teachers?'

He shrugged. 'A few. It's funny. I can barely remember

the last time I had a piss, but a lot of that stuff is like yesterday.'

'How about a woman named Jessica? Jessica Sawyer?'

A leering smile formed on Butcher's crumpled features. 'Oh, I do remember her. Yes. A decent little teacher. Bit of a do-gooder, though. She snuffed it a while back, didn't she?'

'She was murdered, yes. It was an appalling—'

'I know, I know!' Butcher raised his voice, just about managed to hold back a coughing fit. 'She was a little slag, though. Putting it about, I heard.' He shook his head, tutting. 'Married, as well.'

'That's a bit crass, if you don't mind my saying.'

Butcher jerked his chair forward and leaned in towards Walker, scrutinising him. 'You're a sensitive young lad, aren't you? It's touching, it really is. I bet you were one of the good boys at school. Snitching on the smokers. One of these prefect types. *Please, sir. Thank you, sir.*' He sat back, smirking. 'Let me tell you, lad. There was a lot of that about then. Women not knowing their place. She got her comeuppance, if you ask me. She made a promise to one man, then had it away with another. She got what she deserved. She got taught a lesson.'

Walker's face reddened. 'And what kind of "lesson" was that?'

Butcher slapped his fist into his palm. 'That all actions have consequences, lad. The wages of sin. We all have to pay up in the end.'

21

Farrell powered down his office computer and turned his chair to the window. Daylight was fading and, after a busy day, he found it soothing to gaze down from his perch on the top floor of the GMP building and watch the East Manchester street lighting flicker into life.

He dug an index finger into each nostril, one after the other, repeating a circular rooting motion.

A double-tap on the door. His PA poked her head into the room. 'Visitor, sir.'

Farrell turned his chair, stood up. 'I was about to leave, Alice. I wasn't aware I had any more meetings scheduled.'

Dale Strickland pushed the door wide and strolled in. 'Robin. Sorry about the lack of appointment. I was in the area on mayoral business. Just a quick one.'

Mavers and Wilmot followed him into the room.

'These your new aides?'

Wilmot walked over to the window, past Farrell. 'Nice view, officer.'

'Detective Chief Inspector.'

'Forgive the gaucheness,' said Strickland. 'This is Levi, and this—'

'I know who he is.' Farrell sat down. 'Curtis Mavers. What is this, Dale? Some kind of day release scheme?'

Mavers grinned. 'I'm a free man, Detective Chief Inspector. I made my mistakes, ate my porridge.'

Strickland took a seat. 'Curtis and Levi are helping me with a couple of projects.'

Farrell switched on his notary desk lamp; the light cast the room in a mild green hue. He drummed on the desk, gazing at Mavers. 'Theft and handling. Assault with injury. Offensive weapons.' He took out a breath mint. 'Bit of burglary, as I recall. Dealing.'

'That wasn't me,' said Mavers. 'No drugs.'

Farrell flicked the mint into his mouth. 'Of course it wasn't.'

'Where's Jake Sawyer, Robin?' Strickland tidied his tie, crossed his legs. 'The last time we spoke, you promised me more detail.'

'I don't want to jeopardise things by sharing information too soon. But I will, of course.'

Strickland nodded, no smile. 'Of course. And your operation to uncover Sawyer is, I take it, all official?'

Farrell looked at Wilmot, then Mavers. 'Sawyer is an embarrassment to the police force. We're moving heaven and Earth to apprehend him.'

Strickland reached into his inside pocket and pulled out a paperback. He read aloud from the cover. '*Three-Day Terry: My Life as the UK's Most Efficient Detective*. Have you read this?'

Farrell sighed. 'Yes.'

'Terry Barker,' said Wilmot. 'I've heard of him. Quite a force in his day.'

'Shame he had to ruin things with...' Strickland raised his hand to his mouth, made a drinking motion. 'In the book, he describes how the pressure eventually got to him. He had what they used to call a breakdown. These days, it's all mental health issues and stress-related illness.'

Wilmot walked around to the front of Farrell's desk. 'Three-Day Terry was dismissed after being caught with a prostitute. Underage.'

'Sex worker,' said Farrell, crunching into the mint. 'And he wasn't aware of her age.'

'Ignorance isn't an excuse, is it, Robin?' said Strickland. 'And clearly you're not ignorant about the ignominious end to Mr Barker's career. As a civic official, I'm concerned about why you would feel that one disgraced detective is an embarrassment to the force, while another you seem to view as a friend. Not a work colleague, though, I assume? I can't imagine he's visited you on official territory.'

Farrell shrugged. 'I knew him briefly back in Leeds. His instincts are good. It's purely advisory. I'm not breaking any regs.'

'I do understand the softly-softly approach, Robin. I really do. But the optics are unpleasant, wouldn't you agree? A high-ranking detective using the... unofficial services of one disgraced detective to find another disgraced detective, who evaded his custody in the first place. It almost looks desperate. Now.' He leaned forward. 'Jake Sawyer. Where is he?'

Farrell held his gaze. 'We think we know. Barker has a bead on him.'

'From what I've heard about Sawyer,' said Mavers, 'if you've got close, then he'll already know. And if we don't get a move on, he'll slip away.'

'"The wise warrior avoids the battle",' said Strickland.

'Is that Confucius?' said Wilmot.

Strickland shook his head. 'Sun Tzu. "Through the

promise of gain, an opponent is moved about, while the team lies in wait."' He sat back. 'I can flush Sawyer out, Robin, and you can take a share of the spoils.' He tossed the paperback onto the desk. 'Or you can leave it to this idiot and get nothing.'

22

Sawyer scrambled down the shallow, lower slope of the Old Man, and joined the perimeter road on the village outskirts. He tapped the volume increase button on his iPod Mini, and The Avalanches' 'Oh The Sunn!' soundtracked his run alongside the western shore of Coniston Water.

As the song's choral refrain drove him on—exhortations about passing tests and never turning back—he pushed through a drag of fatigue, and dropped into a sprint for the final three minutes. Exhausted, he turned into the boating centre and walked out to the edge of the launch jetty, where he stopped to refill his lungs and soak up the view: the lake surface rippling in the early evening breeze; the sun submitting to the surrounding ridges, painting the clouds with smears of sandstone.

He closed his eyes, tuned in to the lapping water, the chug of the pleasure boats on the south shore.

'I keep thinking you're going to jump in.'

Sawyer turned. A white-bearded man in a crimson sailing jacket squatted at the base of the jetty, winding an armful of rope around a lakeside post. 'No. Just admiring the view.'

The man nodded, kept his eyes down on his work. 'Seen you a few times over the past few weeks. I keep wondering, "What's he looking at?" But then you don't see it when you're used to it, if you know what I mean.'

Sawyer hitched down his hood and walked back to the shore. 'Lived here a while, then.'

He laughed. 'Oh, yes. No plans to live anywhere else. I was born up by Wastwater but moved down soon after. I was here when Campbell went for the speed record in '67. Saw it all happen. They didn't bother to recover the boat and body for thirty-two years. I run a diving club here, so I assisted with the operation.'

'Do you still dive?'

'Not these days. I help out with the steam gondola. Tourist stuff.' The man peered through the dusk light at Sawyer. 'Are you here alone, then?'

'Writing a book. I rented a place so I could get away from it all and concentrate.'

The man nodded, doubtful. 'So, what is it?'

'The book?'

'The thing you're looking at.'

Sawyer gave him a quizzical look. 'Nothing, really. Just... running things through my mind.'

The man secured his rope with a sturdy knot. He stood up and brushed down his jacket. 'When I look out there, I think of what's underneath the surface. Nature puts on this beautiful show, doesn't it? But it's really hidden depths, underwater currents, probably a few bodies.' He wheezed out a laugh. 'I've dived around the country, wrote up plenty of wrecks in my logbook. The M2 submarine in Dorset, the Lucy liner on the Skomer Reserve. I used to be fascinated by all of that. Couldn't wait to get down there. But it's all in your head, you know. When you're a young man, you get caught up in the... silly stuff.'

'The romance?'

'Yeah. The romance of it all. But then you grow old and you start to see things for what they really are. Your experience catches up with your imagination. There's no treasure to be found down there. Just rotting steel and silt. Household appliances.'

'People dump things like that in here?'

'Oh, yeah. I've seen bikes, cars. Bones.' He winked. 'Mostly animal. The history, the life that the vessels had when they were above water, it's all gone for good. You can't recapture it or make sense of it with a canister of Nitrox and a pair of flippers, and you're an idiot if you think you can.'

———

Back at the cottage, Sawyer stripped and stood before the half-length mirror. He raised the clippers to his face and traced the contour of his chin, taking small strokes at first, but soon building to long swipes. He played Nick Cave's *Ghosteen* album as he worked, the music's hymnal reverence chiming with the ritualised reveal of his features as he stripped away the layers.

Half an hour later, the floorboards around his bare feet were thick with black beard hair.

He wet-shaved the rest, showered and dressed.

At the sitting room table, he took a Nokia from the box and made a call. The reception crackled, then sounded a ringtone. After half a minute or so, he was about to disconnect, when Dean Logan's voice broke through.

'Mr Sawyer, I presume?'

'Are you alone?'

More crackling on the line. 'You're never alone with a Sasha Grey video, Sawyer.'

'Nice.'

'I think this might be her finest performance.'

'Let's move swiftly on to the car reg. Anything?'

A slurp as Logan took a drink of something.

'Back on the meths?' said Sawyer.

'Nice pint of Caffrey's. Just polishing off a pizza, too.'

'You're watching porn while eating pizza?'

'Doesn't everybody?'

The motion sensor in Sawyer's pocket vibrated. He took it out; the LED flashed red. 'I haven't got long, Logan. The line is terrible, and I hate to keep you from your entertainment.'

'It's a Golf. Owned by a Mr Terence Barker, AKA Three-Day Terry. Ex-copper from Leeds, also worked in Greater Manchester in the nineties. Bit of a celebrity in his day. I'm guessing he's been sniffing round you?'

'Probably for a lot longer than three days.'

'He's an old colleague of your soulmate, DCI Robin Farrell. This doesn't sound like good news to me, Sawyer.'

Sawyer walked to the blind and peeked out. Headlights, full beam, cutting through the total darkness on the dirt track. 'Didn't he get kicked out for some corruption scandal?'

Logan laughed. 'Better than that. Got done for drink driving, then his missus left him after it came out he was seeing prozzies.'

The lights swung past the window. Engine cut-off.

Sawyer walked back to the table, faced the front door. 'He must have been doing something right, though.'

Another slurp. 'He wrote a book and it was panned for being too... hold on... *solipsistic*. I'm a man of letters, but even I had to look that one up. I thought it was a fucking indigestion cure or something.'

Car door thunk.

'But he did notch up plenty of collars.'

'No doubt. So maybe he's not a man to underestimate. But if I were you, I'd hire a couple of go-go dancer bodyguards. That should keep him busy.'

Footsteps on the path.

'Thanks for the tip.'

'Sawyer. Look. Before you hang up and put your foot through the phone. How long do I have to play Google for you until I get my exclusive?'

'I'll be in touch.' Sawyer hung up, dealt with the SIM card.

The footsteps came to a halt on the porch.

He opened the door.

Ainsworth stood in the glow from his phone light. 'I hope you haven't groomed yourself on my account, Jake. Nice to see what you look like, though. I'd almost forgotten.'

Sawyer sucked in a deep, deep breath through his nose, held it, exhaled. 'Let's go.'

23

Shepherd jabbed the button for the basement level. The ageing lift grumbled into life and began to sink through the shaft at Sheffield's Northern General Teaching Hospital.

'Well, this is life-affirming,' said Walker.

'Tell me about Butcher.'

Walker laughed. 'A lovely fella. Where do we start? Homophobe, misogynist, an advocate of corporal punishment for children.'

Shepherd whistled. 'Jesus Christ. Generational, I suppose. Was he close to Yates?'

'That's probably a stretch. Said he was a "ponce" who "couldn't keep it in his trousers". Didn't show much compassion when I told him about the murder.' Shepherd gave him a look. 'He didn't do it. I'm not sure he could even walk. Long-suffering wife keeping him in disgusting sandwiches.'

'Disgusting in what way?'

'Tongue.'

Shepherd grinned at him. 'My great auntie used to swear by that. It's a post-war thing. During rationing, that was their idea of luxury. I suppose they carried it over and never kicked the habit. Did you partake?'

'The smell was making me gag. Told her I'd already eaten. She wrapped one up for me and made me take it when I left.'

'Bless her.'

The lift car ground against the walls as they descended. Shepherd looked up at the flickering light. 'No hint of animosity between Butcher and Yates?'

Walker grimaced, shook his head. 'Not that I could see. I also looked into Yates's finances. Nothing to suggest he was in debt or he might have been murdered for money.'

They were silent for a moment.

'Oh,' said Walker. 'He knew Sawyer's mother. She taught at the same school. Well, she started as a teaching assistant and then taught full time for a while.'

Shepherd stared down at the lift floor. 'Shame we can't talk to her about Yates. Sawyer's dad worked with Keating at Buxton, you know. In the 1980s.'

'I know. Do you think Keating knew Sawyer's mother?'

Shepherd shrugged. 'You can ask Sawyer yourself, when he turns up.'

'Have you heard from him at all?'

Shepherd hit him with a hard stare. 'No. I haven't.'

The lift gave a loud clunk and froze in place, buffeting Shepherd and Walker into the walls. Walker gave Shepherd a quizzical look as the mechanism strained and whined.

The overhead light went out.

'*Fuck*,' said Shepherd.

'Probably a temporary power thing.'

Shepherd took out his phone and turned on the light. 'Just my luck to get stuck in a lift with another bloke.'

Walker's face loomed out of the dark, elongated and

warped in the phone light. 'I got stuck in one when I was in training. My girlfriend lived in a high-rise. We were on our way out. Took two hours for them to get it moving. I know what you're thinking, and yes. We did.'

Shepherd's phone dropped to the lift floor, falling on its front and dampening the light to a thin glow at foot level.

Walker took out his own phone and lit up the car.

Shepherd squatted in the corner, head down, breathing hard and fast.

Walked crouched down, put a hand on Shepherd's shoulder. 'You okay?'

Shepherd wiped his brow, nodded. 'I'm fine. I get this sometimes.'

'You claustrophobic?'

The lift light flashed a few times then stayed constant. The engine whirred and they continued their descent as if nothing had happened.

Shepherd brushed Walker's hand away and got to his feet, steadying his breathing. 'I'm fine. Really.'

————

'I'm going to rule out suicide.'

Frazer Drummond led Shepherd and Walker down the main corridor of the pathology suite and through a pale green door into a converted storage room. Couple of low-grade chairs, cheap beechwood table.

Shepherd closed the door behind them. 'Is that something you'd been considering?'

Drummond turned and scrubbed at his shiny scalp. 'Oh, I always consider it. I like to cross it off as soon as I can.'

'His carer said he'd been a bit down lately,' said Walker.

Drummond lowered his head and looked over the top

of his glasses, training his icy blue eyes on Walker. 'Haven't we all?' He crashed down in one of the chairs. 'Suicide isn't always the end point of depression, you know. Herbert Hendin also defined it as a form of self-punishment, for individuals who have a high and rigid sense of self-esteem and can't cope with a perceived mistake or failure, because that would be too far from their high opinion of themselves. And people do cut their own throats, you know. It's one of the rarer forms of suicide, particularly in the western world, but it does happen. The thing with auto-throat slashers, though, is you normally get several hesitation marks.' He tapped at the front of his neck. 'They feel their way, taking little nicks with the knife as they pluck up the courage for a *coup de grâce*. So you usually see little tell-tale pre-cuts to the osteocartilaginous tissues around the neck and throat. There's only one attempt at a throat cut, though. Decisive. Any sign of the weapon?'

'We didn't find anything at scene,' said Shepherd.

'Right. Then he must have taken it with him.'

'He or she,' said Walker.

Drummond grinned. 'Point taken. Getting stabby isn't that common for female killers, though.' He rolled up his shirt sleeves and consulted a folder of notes. 'Blood was pooled at the base of the body, around the floor. Not a lot of spatter or splashback. I'd say the killer kept him steady, possibly gripping him by the jaw and holding him still, took this slash at his throat, but then changed tack, and went for the eyes.'

Shepherd had a go at sitting on the other chair but changed his mind and remained standing. 'Why do you say that?'

Drummond turned his eyes to Walker again. 'Sorry to raise this, but it's the same thing that happened to you, Matt. Trachea severed, hence the blood. But the carotid was only nicked, otherwise we'd have seen blood on the facing wall, and the telly. I've seen carotid jets so powerful they've broken windows.'

Walker winced and bowed his head.

'Sorry.'

'Toxicology?' said Shepherd.

'Nothing unusual. It's all about the wounds, gentlemen. I put TOD only an hour or two before his carer found him. Lividity, rigor, rectal temp. I call exsanguination.'

Walker sat in the second chair. He looked pale. 'Why would you inflict such violence on an elderly man, and not take anything for your trouble?'

'Maybe he had a hidden stash of cash,' said Drummond, 'and they took it without you knowing.'

Shepherd caught Walker's eye. 'Feels like a reach.'

Drummond laughed. 'Maybe they lost their nerve after the stabbing. Maybe they were disturbed and didn't have time to take anything. This is your gig, fellas. I'm just a humble body person. I'll tell you what, though.' He ruffled his beard. 'Throat cut, stabs to the eyes... But no defensive wounds. No sign of struggle. This guy was knocking on a bit, but I'd expect a bit of resistance.'

'He was relatively active for his age, apparently,' said Walker.

'Nothing under his fingernails, either. You often find a bit of skin or hair. Those stabs to the eyes are both so bloody definitive. *One! Two!*' Drummond demonstrated with two sharp movements. 'They're accurate. No attempts that landed to the cheeks or middle of the face. There's a bit of bruised tissue around the old boy's neck, which indicates that the killer held on to him, but still... Even with an eighty-four-year-old, you'd have to be seriously strong to keep him still enough to land those stab wounds so accurately.' He heaved himself upright and let out a cavernous sigh. 'Congratulations, detectives. You've found yourself one scary individual here. It's just a shame that our resident expert in scary individuals is living in a hole somewhere.'

24

Wilmot drummed an intricate pattern on his knees. 'What's the logic behind the kid thing?'

Mavers shrugged. 'It's what he wants.'

They sat in Mavers's Audi at the junction end of a cul-de-sac. Tidy bungalows, lawns like golf greens, not a wheelie bin out of place.

Wilmot sighed. 'Enlighten me again as to this charming locale.'

'Marple. Some village near where your man lives.'

'Dylan Hall,' said Wilmot, pressing his nose against the passenger side window.

'You what?'

'My first fight. I was twelve, he was thirteen.' He glanced at Mavers. 'And a big thirteen.'

'Fisticuffs over the cucumber sandwiches?'

Wilmot turned to him. 'Inverted snobbery. My parents had money, Curtis. But they weren't royalty. People assume that correct enunciation means you're easy pickings for the bullies. With me, they only made that mistake once.'

An olive-green Mercedes turned in to the road and parked in the first drive on their left.

'Oi-oi,' said Mavers. 'Time to get into character.'

'He tried to force me to kiss his arse. Fucking brute. Sat on my chest, facing away.'

Mavers frowned. 'Like reverse cowgirl?'

'On my chest, Curtis. Not my penis.'

A fortysomething man in a black Fred Perry hoodie got out of the Mercedes. He opened the back door and two children got out, one after the other. Teenage girl, younger boy.

'And did you?' said Mavers.

'Did I what?'

'Did you kiss Dylan Hall's arse?'

'No, I did not. I reached across the pavement and grabbed a chunk of stone, smashed it into the side of his head. They had to take him to hospital. Fractured eye socket.'

Outside, the man walked up the path and opened the door. The children dawdled by the car. The girl was tall with bright blonde hair and wore a close-fit padded jacket with a fur hood. She tapped at her AirPods and peered into her phone.

Mavers and Wilmot each pulled on a black balaclava.

Wilmot grinned. 'I don't kiss anyone's arse unless they're wearing Coco de Mer lingerie.'

The children wandered up the path and stepped past the man into the house. He followed and closed the door.

They got out of the car. Mavers walked faster, ahead of Wilmot. He rang the doorbell.

The girl re-opened the door. Mavers pushed his hand over her mouth and stepped inside. She wriggled, but he held her firm from behind and hustled her away from the door into a narrow hallway.

Wilmot followed and closed the door.

The boy—short and skinny, also blond—appeared

131

from the sitting room on the right. He startled at the sight of the men and let out a cry.

'Freddy?'

The man burst into the hall; Freddy cowered behind him.

'Jesus! Who the—'

'You Justin?' said Mavers.

The man's eyes darted between Wilmot, Mavers. The girl implored him with wide eyes.

'Yes. Look—'

Wilmot sprang forward and delivered a powerful punch to Justin's nose, knocking him sideways into the sitting room. He grabbed Freddy and produced a cut-throat razor, which he flicked open, holding the blade to his face.

Freddy whimpered as Justin scrambled to his feet, clutching his face.

Wilmot stepped around into the sitting room, followed by Mavers, dragging the girl.

'What we do next,' said Wilmot, 'is we kneel. Just over there by the delightful granite-coloured sofa. Also, we keep quiet.'

Justin backed away towards the sofa. Blood seeped out of his nose, staining the front of his hoodie. He stood on the Moroccan-style rug, holding his hands out, palms up. 'Look. I... *Please*. Don't—'

'He said kneel,' said Mavers.

Justin caught the girl's eye. She scowled and shook her head. As Mavers moved her around into the centre of the room, she jerked to the side and almost forced herself out of his grip. Mavers secured her, but she twisted her head and freed her mouth from his hand.

'Dad! *Don't*. Tell him to f—'

Mavers clamped his hand over her mouth again.

Wilmot gripped Freddy's forehead, forcing his eyes

wide. He held the blade close to an eyeball. 'Get down onto your knees now. Or I will slice this boy's eye in two.'

'Okay!' Justin lowered himself to the rug.

Wilmot moved in close and held Freddy firm by the back of his neck.

Mavers smiled. 'Listen to me, Freddy. Your dad is about to have a really bad morning. He'll be okay. Nothing a decent doctor can't fix with a few... hundred stitches. But it's going to hurt. How old are you, Freddy?'

Freddy's eyes raised to Mavers. Reddened with tears, flaming with fear and hatred. 'I'm nine.'

'Make a fist,' said Wilmot.

The girl writhed in his grip, but he held her solid.

'I'm going to do a deal with you, Freddy,' said Wilmot, 'if you can show me a good, clean punch. A *man's* punch. Then I promise we won't hurt your dad too much.'

'I know you're not a big lad, Freddy,' said Mavers. 'But you look like you've got a good punch on you.'

Wilmot crouched down beside Freddy. He softened his voice. 'I know you love your dad. But think of all the times he's upset you, disappointed you, let you down. That's got to be worth at least one punch, yes?'

Freddy sniffed. 'No way. I'm not hitting my dad.'

'If you hit him now,' said Mavers, 'then it'll save him later. Trust me. You have the power, Freddy.'

Freddy turned to the girl, tearful. 'Mia!'

Mia wriggled her mouth free of Mavers again. 'Leave him alone. He's nine years old.'

Mavers took a reel of duct tape out of his jacket pocket.

'My mum works with the police,' said Mia. 'You're in a load of trouble.'

He tore off a strip and pressed it over Mia's mouth.

Justin held his head high. 'Do it, Fred. It's just a game. It'll be okay. Really.'

Freddy looked up to Mavers, then back to Wilmot. He screwed his eyes shut and shook his head. 'I'm not doing that.'

Mavers screamed in pain as Mia drove her heel down on the front of his foot. He dragged her to a sturdy radiator pipe at the bottom of the far wall and produced a pair of handcuffs. He forced Mia's arms behind her back and locked one clasp over both wrists, then attached the second clasp to the pipe. Mia slumped against the wall, glaring up at him.

'Fuck this,' said Mavers. 'We'll just tell him it happened.' He beckoned to Wilmot, who hustled Freddy over to a separate radiator pipe, out of Mia's reach. Mavers pressed a strip of tape to his mouth and secured him with another set of cuffs.

Wilmot smiled at Mia and crouched beside her. He ran his fingers over her hair; she jerked her head away. 'How old are you, Mia?' He dropped his voice, close to a whisper and turned the hair over on the blade of his razor. 'Are you a woman yet?'

Justin turned to face them. 'Don't you touch her.'

Wilmot kept his eyes on Mia. 'Why? Are you going to sue me, Mr Barrister?'

Mavers hauled Wilmot to his feet. 'Let's get this done.'

Wilmot turned to face Justin. 'Here's what we do next. We walk to the black Audi as if it's the most normal thing in the world. As if we're just three friends off for a round of golf.'

'I'm not leaving the children here,' said Justin.

Wilmot nodded. 'Yes, you are. They'll be okay, until you return. But if we make any kind of scene on the way to the car, then I'll toss a coin. Heads, I take off one of Mia's ears. Tails, same for Freddy.'

Freddy sobbed harder; Mia glared up at Wilmot.

'What is this about?' said Justin. 'Something to do with a case? I don't do criminal trials anymore.'

'We'll be gone less than an hour,' said Mavers.

Justin got to his feet. 'Where are we going?'

Wilmot grinned. 'To take some pictures.'

———

Wilmot grabbed a fistful of Justin's hair and held his head in place, while he drove punch after punch into the centre of his face before throwing him to the ground.

Justin bent over, spitting blood. His shirt was torn, with a dark stain across the collar and most of the chest. He groaned and crawled away from Wilmot, feeling his way across the grimy stonework of the aqueduct arch, towards the cover of a dense thicket of trees.

Wilmot ran at him and drop-kicked him in the stomach, almost lifting him off the ground.

Justin dropped to the floor, retching.

Mavers stood by the Audi, arms folded, keeping watch. It was early, Saturday, in a spot with no clear footpath. They were undisturbed, and it was likely to stay that way for some time.

Wilmot grabbed Justin by his shoe and dragged him back to the centre of the wall. He propped him up and began to work on him again. Right hook, sit him back upright, a few jabs to the mouth followed by another right hook.

'Sit up straight, man!'

Justin leaned to the side and spat: blood and bile.

He vomited, and Wilmot clocked him with a hammer right to his cheek as he raised a hand for mercy.

'You not got a left?' said Mavers. He walked over and

hitched Justin upright by the lapels. 'Here. Get hold of him.'

Wilmot held Justin firm while Mavers worked on his stomach: alternating lefts and rights. He drilled the punches deep each time, and Justin cried out with each blow. When Mavers took a rest, Wilmot stepped in, aiming at Justin's bruised eyes and cheeks, now swollen and cracked, streaming with blood.

Mavers struck him with a left cross punch. Justin's nose gave a wet crack, and showered Wilmot with blood.

'Oh, nice shot!' He swiped himself clean with a forearm.

Justin keeled over and curled into a ball, howling and sobbing. He seemed to be babbling a single syllable through his bloated lips, over and over. Wilmot leaned in close, staring into his eyes, half-closed inside the inflamed tissue.

'What's he saying?' said Mavers.

Wilmot looked up at Mavers. 'He's calling for his mum.' He laughed, cruel and hissing. 'I don't know about that, Justin. But you can have a look at your daddy.' Wilmot tugged off his balaclava and leered into Justin's face.

Mavers leapt across and pushed it back over his head. 'Get that back on, you silly cunt. Let's get these pictures and knock off.'

Wilmot stepped back and took several phone shots of Justin, slumped over. Defiled, debased.

Mavers spread a layer of towels over the back seat of the car, and they bundled Justin inside. Wilmot closed the back door. Mavers gripped his arm and pulled him away from the car, to the edge of the trees. They both panted from the effort of the beating.

Mavers slapped Wilmot on the cheek. 'The fuck was that about? With this?' He pulled at the balaclava material.

Wilmot shot him a dangerous glare. 'The mask? He can

barely see, anyway. And he's practically unconscious.' He leaned forward, getting in Mavers's face. 'I know what I'm doing, okay? I once beat a man so badly he had to have both testicles removed.' He turned away, stared up to the top of the aqueduct. 'I have a question.'

'What?'

A sordid smile. 'The girl.'

Mavers turned away. 'No. Don't even—'

Wilmot scurried around Mavers, back into his line of vision. He held his hands together in a parody of prayer. 'Fifteen minutes. *Ten*. Oh, Curtis. She smells so good. So... unpolluted.'

Mavers leaned in, eye to eye. '*No*. Job done. No extras. Let's get him home before the car-cleaning bill costs more than we've earned.'

————

Mia kept her eyes on Freddy, across the room.

When he made eye contact from time to time, she nodded, as if to reassure him.

The men had taken their phones, but the wall clock told her they'd been there for almost an hour.

A car outside, reversing onto the drive.

Mia raised herself upright.

Doors clunking.

Wilmot pushed his way in through the side door, with Justin over his shoulder. She gasped at her dad's bruised and battered face, but didn't turn away.

Wilmot dropped Justin onto the floor and stood at the door, leering at her.

Mavers pushed past him and tore the tape off their mouths.

Mia thrashed around. *'Dad!'*

Mavers held a finger to his lips, shook his head. 'He's okay.' He unlocked her handcuffs, gave her the key. 'You did good. Now keep it up.' He set down their phones on the floor. 'Give it ten minutes before you call anyone. Do it any quicker and you'll be seeing us again.'

'I hope we didn't scare you too much,' said Wilmot.

Mia raised her head to him. 'You don't scare me.'

Freddy groaned. 'Mia, leave it.'

She got to her feet, leaned in close to Mavers. 'Do I look scared?'

Mavers smiled. 'No, love. You don't. I'll give you that.'

'Yeah,' said Mia. 'I'm not the one who has to hide behind a mask.'

Wilmot laughed. 'Oh! We have, I think the phrase goes, got a live one.'

'Ten minutes,' said Mavers.

They walked outside and drove away.

Mia unlocked Freddy's cuffs and went to her dad, cradling his head in her lap.

He was barely conscious. She fetched a flannel and wiped the crusted blood from his face; he winced as she touched the livid skin, stained with angry red bruising.

He managed a clear word. 'Drink...'

Freddy rushed to the kitchen and brought him a glass of water.

They stepped back as he sipped, face crumpled in pain.

Mia hugged Freddy tight, and he sobbed into her shoulder.

'We need to get Dad an ambulance,' he said. 'And call Mum.'

Mia reached for her phone.

Freddy pulled away and wiped his arm across his nose. 'And Uncle Jake. We should call Uncle Jake. Where is he?'

'Nobody knows,' said Mia.

25

Felix Parks hauled himself upright and embarked on his slow, steady expedition across the communal lounge. Only two of the other residents—Kenneth and Malcolm—were still up. Malcolm had nodded off, with his head tilted onto his shoulder; Kenneth was still relatively alert, and the night's film—Hitchcock's *Frenzy*—flashed over the thick lenses of his glasses.

A partially eaten birthday cake sat on the coffee table in the TV corner. As he passed, Parks helped himself to a slice. The cake's topping had been iced with a wobbly number fifty-five, and was all that remained of the day's party for the head housekeeper, Kim.

Parks hobbled across the fawn carpet, past the beige high-backed chairs, and the tightly packed dining tables set for tomorrow's breakfast. He carried a heavy load—COPD, left-sided sciatica, hypertension—and he was down to two living relatives: a bed-bound sister, and a son who ran a leisure park in Wales and who hurried through a shortening phone call every birthday and Christmas.

In his room, Parks closed the door and set down the cake on his bedside table.

'Fifty bloody five,' he said out loud. 'In twenty-five years, she'll be me. Poor sod.'

He changed into his pyjamas and shuffled into the en suite shower room. He extracted his dentures and dropped them into the cheap plastic bath on the cabinet shelf, then filled the bath with warm water before closing the lid.

He ran a flannel under the tap and mopped his face, forever appalled at the folds and gutters, how they flapped and wilted as he dragged the fabric over the skin.

He stared into the mirror; as ever, the years stared back. A topography of erosion. Stains, blemishes, liver spots, yellowed eyes, furrowed forehead with an aura of ghost-white fluff.

Had he ever been young? Unruined? These days, his fading memory spared him the worst of the nostalgia pangs, but the faces and moments still reared up in his dreams: a buckled pedal bike; a scrappy rugby try; a gashed knee; his late wife perched on a rock in Capri, leggy and sun-baked, revelling in the moment.

Parks settled onto his lumpy mattress and reached for his Ludlum novel. But his eyelids lolled, and he flicked off the light instead, alone with the dark, and the rise and fall of his addled lungs. He would wake early, as ever, and savour the cake for pre-breakfast, to the chatter of *Farming Today*.

He turned a few times, slipped into sleep, but then stirred, strangely alert.

A firm grip on his arm. His pyjama top pulled to the side.

A pinch in the centre of his shoulder.

The curtain over his full-length window flapped, admitting light from the veranda outside.

A smell. Sweet, chemical.

A shadow loomed.

He startled, tried to cry out, but something clamped over his mouth, forcing his head deep into the pillow.

He thrashed an arm out, swiping the cake slice off the plate and onto the floor.

A hot rush, surging through his veins.

He slumped, stopped flailing, went limp. His breathing grew shallow.

A smothering from within: fiery and absolute, seeping through his core.

His legs spasmed, and he turned his head, searching for his assailant in the blackness.

Another pinch in his shoulder. A second dose.

Warm breath at his ear. A rasping whisper.

'Burn in hell, you evil bastard.'

26

'Have a seat, DCI Farrell.'

Keating looked up from his computer. 'You know Callum and Simon.' He gestured to the two men sitting around the circular table in the corner of his office: one slim and bearded with rimless glasses; the other older and balder, in a saggy suit.

IOPC Lead Investigator Callum Whitehead nodded to Farrell; Federation rep Simon Gail raised his hand in greeting. Gail, the younger man, gazed into an open laptop while Whitehead rolled a ballpoint around in his fingers. Both avoided Farrell's eyes.

Keating turned to a separate laptop on his desk and opened it. 'I appreciate you driving over on a Saturday, DCI Farrell. But I'm eager for progress. And I have a conference next week.'

Farrell sat opposite Keating. 'Not a problem, sir. Actually, there's been some development with the DI Sawyer investigation.'

Keating nodded, kept his eyes on the laptop as he typed. 'Do enlighten us.'

Farrell glanced at the other two. 'I've received some interesting information about Sawyer's potential whereabouts. But I need a little more time to clarify its veracity.'

'What's your source for this information, DCI Farrell?' said Gail.

Farrell smiled. 'I'd rather not reveal that at the moment. But I hope to have more the next time—'

'I've also been privy to some development.' Keating turned the laptop to face Farrell. The screen showed a video window. 'Again, hence the urgency. I would like to clear this up before my conference. We received this yesterday on a USB stick. I've followed it up and can confirm its authenticity.' He pressed Play.

The image faded up to show Stephanie and Jordan Burns, sitting beside each other on their living room sofa. The lighting was dim; Jordan leaned forward and turned on a lamp.

He looked over at Stephanie, smiling, and placed his hand on hers.

'My name is Stephanie Burns.' Her eyes found the camera. 'In September last year, I was kidnapped and... brutalised by a man called David Bowman. He took me to a location near to Dovestone Reservoir in Greater Manchester, and it's my belief that he was planning to murder me. He had already murdered several other women, and another man, Julius Newton, who was...' She bowed her head. Jordan put an arm around her shoulders. 'Julius Newton, who was killed in the same room when I was unconscious.'

She took a few breaths and continued.

'A police detective, Jake Sawyer, tracked me down and confronted Bowman. Sawyer was incapacitated by

Bowman, but managed to recover and defend himself. I watched this happen. Bowman attacked Sawyer with an axe, which Sawyer managed to wrestle away from him. In the struggle, Sawyer struck Bowman in the neck with the axe, and... he died.'

Farrell sat forward. 'This is nonsense. She's on record as saying that Sawyer killed Bowman in cold blood.'

Keating held up a hand as Stephanie continued.

'I recently claimed that Sawyer did not act in self-defence, but I wish to officially retract that version of events, which was delivered while I was under a great deal of mental strain and confusion. I have suffered deeply at the hands of a brutal killer, and if it had not been for Detective Sawyer's actions, I firmly believe that I would not be here today. I owe him my life, and I apologise for any harm I may have caused him with my inaccurate account. I will not say any more on this matter and I now wish to focus on my physical and mental rehabilitation, and on rebuilding my life and business.'

Keating tapped the space bar, pausing the video.

Farrell looked at Gail and Whitehead, then back to Keating. 'This is absurd. Sawyer himself must be behind it, coercing them in some way. Stephanie was clear in her previous statement—'

'I spoke to Mr and Mrs Burns yesterday.' Whitehead turned toward Farrell. 'The IOPC has laboured on this case for many months now, DCI Farrell, at great expense. And it's my view that there are no grounds for sanction or conviction on DI Sawyer's part.'

Farrell turned his head away, then back again. 'So, that's it? All the police time, all those resources, just written off?'

Keating closed the laptop. 'I thank you for your efforts, DCI Farrell. And I can imagine this must be frustrating for you. But in my view, we have no reason to continue to pursue DI Sawyer on a serious charge. The CPS has lost interest. There's no credible external case to build against him.'

Gail piped up. 'And, as I understand it, the IOPC are satisfied that there's no grounds for any further internal investigation into Sawyer's conduct.'

Farrell exhaled, shaking his head.

Keating sat back. 'But that's not the case with your own conduct.'

'How do you mean, sir?'

'Stephanie and Jordan have registered an official complaint against you, over the way you tried to influence them into changing their story to incriminate DI Sawyer.'

Farrell's eyes widened. 'You can't seriously—'

'Stephanie says she overheard you attempting to influence Jordan by implying that it wasn't fair for DI Sawyer to avoid sanction over his actions while they had to suffer. She says you claimed that he was "financially secure".' Keating leaned forward. 'That sounds perilously close to an incitement to blackmail.'

'DCI Keating,' said Gail. 'We still need to carefully consider—'

'And, if you're looking for a cherry on top,' said Keating, 'we've also received information about the nature of your investigation into DI Sawyer's whereabouts. An ill-advised association with one Terence Barker.'

'Who,' said Whitehead, 'apart from being a private individual with no official capacity—'

'Is also a convicted sex offender,' said Keating. 'A man who enjoyed a brief period of success in the service, but who was dismissed for gross misconduct.' He frowned. 'No wonder you're not keen to reveal details of your development, DCI Farrell.'

Farrell shifted in his seat. 'Barker is an ex-colleague, sir. I was merely consulting with him, as he does have an excellent record of solving difficult cases. And this is all hearsay. And it's all Sawyer. Can't you see? He must have got to Stephanie and Jordan. And he must have spotted Barker and linked him with me. I assume you received that information anonymously?'

Gail cleared his throat. 'DCI Farrell, in one of our recent meetings, I recall you holding quite the moral high ground over not being above the law. And now we learn that you've been consorting with a man whose career ended because he felt the rules didn't apply to him, and who went on to commit a serious offence and was additionally banned for driving under the influence of drugs and alcohol.'

'The IOPC will speak to Stephanie and Jordan Burns,' said Whitehead.

Farrell shook his head. 'About me?'

'About you, yes. About your conduct. I'm also keen to learn more about your activities with Mr Barker, and I'll be scheduling a private meeting on that matter, at GMP.'

Farrell slumped in his chair. 'So, that's that? Sawyer just gets away with murder?'

'*No,*' said Keating, raising his voice. 'He doesn't. Because he didn't commit murder, DCI Farrell. I've reinstated DI Sawyer's status and access, effective earlier today. He was lucky to escape the confrontation with his life, as was Stephanie. Bowman's death is regrettable, and Sawyer will receive an official reprimand for acting outside of his jurisdiction. But I believe he acted in good faith, as he had reason to believe that Stephanie's life was in immediate danger.'

Farrell rubbed at his eyes. 'Section 17.'

'Yes,' said Keating. 'Section 17.' He glanced at Whitehead. 'Life, limb or property.'

'It's all down there in the PACE manual, DCI Farrell,' said Gail.

Keating softened his tone. 'Robin, we all have our victories and defeats. I accept that you pursued this case with high moral intentions, because you considered the reputation of the service to be at stake. But it's time to let it go. My team here is investigating the brutal murder of an elderly man in his own home, and I need all of my best detectives—' He stopped, distracted, then frowned and shook his head.

The gesture was aimed over Farrell's shoulder, through the window, at the MIT office outside.

Farrell turned.

Three taps on the office door.

Sawyer entered. Blue suit, white shirt, orange tie.

He nodded at Gail and Whitehead. 'Gentlemen.'

Keating got to his feet. 'DI Sawyer—'

Sawyer nodded at Farrell. 'Sir.'

'We're busy,' said Keating. 'Can't this wait?'

'No,' said Sawyer. 'Sir, I've been reviewing the HOLMES detail on the Charles Yates murder. The pathologist reports.' He caught his breath. 'The precision of the wounds. The lack of struggle. The blood behaviour.'

Keating sighed. 'Yes. We can recap in a briefing before I leave later.'

Sawyer pushed on. 'I don't think it was a murder, sir.'

Keating frowned at him. 'Drummond isn't considering suicide.'

Sawyer stepped forward, closed the door. 'No. You've... *we've* been looking for a big, strong attacker. Someone who could subdue Yates powerfully enough to deliver the injuries.' He gripped the edge of Keating's desk and leaned forward. 'We need to change approach. We need to get Drummond to revisit.'

'So what do you mean, you don't think it was a murder?'

'Technically, no. I don't think Yates was murdered, sir. I think he was already dead when the killer arrived.'

PART TWO

SONG OF LIFE

27

OCTOBER 1975

'All things bright and beautiful. All creatures great and small. All things wise and wonderful. The lord God made them all...'

The assembled children trailed off at the close of the hymn and lowered themselves to the hard wooden floor.

A short man with thinning brown hair Brylcreemed across his scalp turned away from the piano keyboard and faced the other teachers, lined up across the back of the stage. The hall remained silent until another man rose from a separate seat off to the side and began to pound his chunky palms together. He walked to the front of the stage, prompting applause from the teachers and children.

He indulged the commotion for a few seconds before buttoning up his olive-green suit and tilting his head back, keeping his eyes down on the children: a signal that their contribution was complete.

As the applause died down, he pivoted to the piano man. 'Thank you, Mr Parks. A fine rendition.' He turned to the crowd. 'Good morning, children.'

They sing-songed in chorus. *'Good morning, Mr Welch.'*

'Thank you all for being in such excellent voice. I hope you've had a constructive week. Friday is the day when we look forward to spending time with our families and friends, but it is also when we look back and reflect on our performance, and behaviour, in the week that has passed. Most of you have worked hard, and we've had a good start to the new term here at Pioneer Primary. But, as is the sad tradition, I'm now called upon to address the actions of a few individuals who haven't quite measured up.' He darkened, and ran a hand across his short, tightly curled hair. *Bartley, Warburton, Frain.'*

Three boys rose from the ranks and trudged their way up the steps to face Welch.

Parks stood, and slid a crooked wooden cane from the top of the piano. 'Headmaster.' He handed the cane over with ceremonious portent, nodding and retreating back to his piano stool.

Welch ushered the first boy forward.

Bartley took a deep breath, tucked in his shirt and held out his hand, palm up.

Welch addressed the throng. *'Stand.'*

The children all got to their feet. Welch rested the cane shaft on Bartley's palm, getting his bearing, then raised and, with a swish, whipped it down, striking the hand with a terrible ferocity, sending a loud crack around the assembly hall.

A few children gasped, and shuffled in place.

Bartley scuttled off stage and rejoined the crowd, wincing and clutching his hand.

Welch punished the other two with equal force and efficiency, then handed the cane back to Parks. He turned to the children. 'As ever, let that be a lesson to you. I will not tolerate misbehaviour in my school. If any of these boys face me next Friday, they will receive two lashes, and so it will continue. Now. Work hard today, and, if you're lucky, the next time you'll see me will be at assembly on Monday morning.'

A loud thunk came from the back of the hall. One of the second-year girls had tumbled to the ground; two other girls held her up by the armpits.

One looked to a young woman with long dark hair standing at the side; a teaching assistant. 'She's fainted, Miss.'

The woman sprang forward and crouched by the girl, who had opened her eyes. 'Are you okay, my love?'

'Did she hit her head?' said Welch, louder than necessary.

The woman looked up to the stage. 'No, headmaster.' She guided the girl out to the side and sat her down in her own chair.

'Feel a bit sick, Miss Sawyer.'

She smiled and rubbed the back of the girl's hand. 'Take your time, Rachel. Deep breaths. You'll be okay.'

The children dispersed and headed into their form rooms.

Welch marched away, through a door at the side of the stage.

'My lot! Hurry up and sit yourselves down.' A teacher in a brown suit with a birthmark on his forehead hurried a group of children into a form room at the far end of the hall. 'Come on. *Come on.*'

Inside, he closed the door and dumped a pile of purple textbooks—*Mainline English*—on his desk.

'Latham, Hawkins. Hand those out.'

A blond boy stepped forward. He took half the books

from the pile and walked around, tossing one onto each wooden flip-top desk.

'*Place* them, Latham,' said the teacher. 'Show the books a bit of respect.'

Latham complied. 'Sorry, sir.'

A girl—blonde, slender—stood up from a desk in the front corner, set away from the others, and gathered up the rest of the books. She wore a florid skirt and a two-tone anorak: royal-blue with a white stripe around at chest height. Her left leg was covered by the standard knee-length white sock, but her right had been swaddled in a thicker, bandage-like material, which unbalanced her as she walked.

'Gazzer!' called a lad from the back. 'Let's have one of yours.'

Latham smiled. 'Ah, I've ran out, Halesy. Soz. You'll have to get the Hawko germs.'

'*Latham,*' warned the teacher.

He finished distributing the books and took his seat.

'How's the hand, Frain?'

At the back, Steven Frain sat with his caned hand tucked into his armpit. 'Hurting, sir.'

The girl placed each of her books over the pencil grooves at the top of the desks. One of the boys snatched up his book and immediately wiped it down with his blazer sleeve. He pulled the sleeve over his hand and reached back to the boy behind, who recoiled.

'Gerroff, y'dirty—'

'*Right!*' The teacher walked to the blackboard and squeaked out a word in the centre.

ADJECTIVES

'Page fourteen. I'm going to write out a sentence, and someone will read out the description of an adjective and someone else will pick out the adjectives in the sentence. Are we clear?'

He spoke each word as he chalked it up.

THE QUICK BROWN FOX JUMPS

With the teacher's attention on the blackboard, Latham took a deep breath and used both lips to blow a loud raspberry over the back of his hand.

Titters.

The teacher paused, then carried on with the sentence.

OVER THE LAZY DOG

He turned, smiled. 'And who did that?'

Latham kept his head down, but couldn't suppress his giggles.

'I think we have to move you again, Gary.'

'Oh, no. Please, Mr Butcher.'

Butcher smiled. 'Go.'

He sighed, and stood up. 'But she stinks, sir.'

Laughter from most of the class.

The girl finished handing out her books and took her seat at the separated desk in the corner. 'I don't want him next to me, sir. Please.'

Butcher waved a hand. 'Michelle. Think of it as your way of helping me control the class.'

Latham walked out to the front, paused in front of Butcher's desk. Michelle folded her arms.

'Now, Michelle. Unless you want a few strokes of the ruler.'

Michelle lurched out of her seat in fury and dragged a spare desk beside her own. She sat back down, and turned toward the window.

Latham sat in the desk next to her, making a show of pulling his chair over to the right-hand side and turning towards the blackboard, holding his nose.

A knock at the door. A tall, athletic-looking male teacher entered.

'Mr Yates?' said Butcher.

'Sorry to interrupt, Graham. Headmaster wants to see Hawkins.'

Michelle gave a shout of protest. 'What have I done?'

'You'll have to go and see, won't you?' said Yates.

She sprang up and stormed out of the room, across the assembly hall.

Miss Sawyer was still attending to the girl who had fainted. She looked across as Yates caught up with Michelle and roughly ushered her towards a door at the side of the stage. 'Everything okay, Michelle?'

She didn't make eye contact. 'Yes, Miss.'

'Everything is fine, Miss Sawyer,' said Yates. 'You concentrate on playing Florence Nightingale and leave the discipline to us.'

Yates and Michelle disappeared through the door and began to climb the steps. Miss Sawyer looked up to Welch's office, above the stage.

The headmaster stood at the window.

He looked out, caught her eye, smiled.

———

'Sit yourself down, Michelle.'

Welch pushed a wheeled chair over and sat at his desk, which faced the window overlooking the assembly hall.

Michelle sat down, wary.

Yates walked to the side of the desk and turned his back on the window.

Welch shifted his chair to face Michelle. 'You can take off your coat, my dear.' He gestured to a portable heater. 'Nice and cosy in here.'

She took off the blue anorak and hung it over the back of her chair.

'Mr Welch. I didn't do nothing.'

'You mean you didn't do *anything*. An important distinction.'

Welch's office was compact but seemed larger due to the lack of clutter. His desk was immaculate, and the only other furniture, apart from the chairs, was a tall, well-stacked bookshelf topped with a row of sporting trophies.

He sniffed the air. 'I must say, Michelle, you seem much more fragrant at the moment.'

She tugged at her plaited ponytail. 'I've got tablets, sir. For my abscess. Steroids. It keeps coming back but not as much as before. And I've got a special cream that smells nice.'

Welch smiled. 'Well, in that case, I can get a little closer.'

He walked his chair across the floor, taking slow and steady steps, and stopped in front of her, smiling.

His desk phone rang and a green light flashed.

'Parks,' said Yates. Welch turned to him. 'I didn't say—'

'Let's leave him out this time.'

Yates nodded and pressed a button on the phone. The light went off.

'Michelle,' said Welch. 'Your form teacher Mr Butcher tells me that your behaviour can be a touch difficult. We call it *insubordination*.'

'Am I gonna get the cane, sir?' Michelle dropped her head, struggling to hold back tears.

'No, no,' said Welch.

He gave Yates a barely perceptible nod; Yates leaned

forward and closed the blind, then flicked on Welch's low-wattage desk light.

'I know things have been difficult, Michelle, with your condition. But I'm here to help you. I can make it better. I can make you feel better. Do you understand?'

She looked up into Yates's eyes, now bulbous, gazing down at her, as if entranced. 'Not really, sir.'

Welch wheeled a little closer. He reached out and took her hand. 'All I ask is that you do something for me, too.' He dropped his voice to a whisper. 'And you have to promise to stay *really* quiet. And you must never tell anyone, because then all the children will be asking me for the same treatment.'

'And we reserve it for the special girls,' said Yates, still staring.

Welch smiled. 'Absolutely. And you're certainly special, Michelle.' He moved round to her side, keeping hold of her hand.

Yates folded his arms and, for the next fifteen minutes, kept his gluttonous gaze fixed on Michelle.

Staring, scrutinising.

Feasting on her pain.

28

PRESENT DAY

Maggie reclined on her chocolate brown Heal's futon and opened her laptop. She streamed an album—*Let Love Rule* by Lenny Kravitz—to the Sonos, and reviewed the week's patient notes, cross-checking with her schedule for the coming month.

But her eyes kept sliding from the booking website to the window: the Staffordshire Roaches in spring afternoon widescreen, the moorland tones deepening under a golden sky. Sparkling greens, glimmering purples.

Thudding footsteps from upstairs. Mia, awake at last. Early for a Saturday.

Beside her, Sawyer's wiry black-and-white cat Bruce startled at the noise, and she petted him. The cat settled, and Maggie pushed the laptop aside and padded over to the cabinet. She was barefoot, in full gym wear, ready for an online yoga session in half an hour.

She opened a cabinet drawer, digging out a scented

candle: True Grace, 'Lemon Tree'. She peeled off the protective cover and held the candle to her nose. Citrus, a touch of lavender.

Bruce miaowed: one of his yelps for attention. A mini alert.

'I know, I know.' She smiled, glanced at the pretentious description on the candle's box. 'Tell me about it.'

The cat sloped off the futon and hurried away, towards the door.

'Hey. Big man.'

She froze, and turned.

Sawyer stood in the doorway, in suit and tie. Bruce curled around his legs, purring.

He crouched, scratched the cat under the chin.

Maggie stared at him.

He offered her a dimpled smile. 'Mags.'

Hand shaking, she set down the candle, keeping her eyes on him. 'And where have you been?'

'Lake District. Professor Ainsworth owns a cottage. Remote.'

She guided herself to her armchair. 'How did you...'

He held up the front door key. 'Still had it, from when you gave it to me at the hospital.'

'You could have—'

'No, I couldn't.' He walked towards her. 'You know that.'

'What about the suspension? Bowman?'

He sat on the futon. 'That's gone. We worked it out, like good soldiers.'

She nodded, studied him. 'You're bigger. Not... in that way. Bulkier up top.'

'Been working on myself. Not many other options. Winter wasn't fun.'

'So, you've basically been hibernating.'

'Reading, had to sort out a few things. Ainsworth kept me supplied. Had to stay dark, of course.'

Maggie dropped her gaze. 'Justin was attacked.'

'Attacked?'

'He was badly beaten. Broken nose, minor concussion, cracked ribs, a few stitches. They jumped him at his place. Dragged him to Marple Aqueduct, spent an hour… dropped him back home.' She looked up, anger blazing in her eyes. 'Mia and Freddy were there. They cuffed them to the radiators, Jake.'

He winced. 'Jesus, Mags. Any ID? Did Justin recognise them?'

She shook her head, her gaze fixed on him. 'They were wearing balaclavas.'

'How is he? How are Mia and Freddy?' Sawyer started to reach out to her, then drew his hand back.

'How do you think?'

Bruce hopped up onto the futon and settled next to his owner. Sawyer dropped his gaze. 'Thanks for looking after him. Did Michael not—'

'Was it you?'

'Mags…' He looked up again.

'They attacked me to get to you, didn't they? Did they do the same to Justin? Is that what made you come back? Is there still something you need to "sort out"?'

'I'll look into it. Justin is a barrister. He might have pissed off the wrong person in court. I'll cross-check his recent cases.'

Maggie took a breath, dragged both hands through her hair. 'So. You've parachuted back in, then. All forgiven with Keating?'

'Haven't seen him to discuss that. But, yes. I'm a civil servant again. Stephanie Burns retracted her account.'

'Of her own volition?'

He paused, petted Bruce again. 'As far as I know.'

'They wanted to station a guard here, and one at Justin's. But I said no.'

Sawyer stayed quiet, focused on the cat. 'You don't exactly seem ecstatic to see me.'

'I'm happy to see you, happy that you're safe. But I've been thinking. You're dangerous, Jake. Dangerous to know. Dangerous by association. And no, not in an exciting way.'

He shifted position, reclined along the length of the futon. 'This is assuming a lot. You don't know why Justin was attacked.'

'Intuition is real. Remember *The Gift of Fear?*'

'You should take the official protection until we work out what happened. I'll oversee it.'

'What?'

'Your safety.'

'Ah. You'll stick around now, will you? Keep me safe?' Maggie sat back in the armchair. 'One of my clients told me this African saying. "Be careful when a naked person offers you a shirt."'

Sawyer gave a grim smile. 'Like I said, I'm working on myself. I've had a lot of thinking time.'

She tucked her hair behind her ear. 'Alex is back from her travels.'

'Is she working again?'

'She's just doing Skype and Zoom consultations for now. Maybe ease your way back in.'

He stood up, stretched. 'I've seen the reports on the Yates case. You spoke to the carer, Linda Keller. Interesting details. Lack of struggle. The strange smell.'

'Are we talking shop now? Has the friends part finished?'

Sawyer rose to his feet, and walked over to Maggie.

She got up, faced him. 'Before you say it, so did I.'

'Before I say what?'

'Some line about how you thought we were more than friends.'

Sawyer laughed. Maggie tilted forward, and he took his cue, embracing her, squeezing.

Maggie's eyes shone with tears, and she pushed her forehead into his shoulder. 'I really thought that was that. You'd become part of the past.'

'*Uncle Jake?*'

They pulled away. Mia stood in the doorway.

She ran to Sawyer; they hugged.

Bruce leapt from the sofa and scurried away.

Sawyer held Mia out in front of him. 'This is a cliché, but you're growing at an alarming rate.'

She tutted. 'You make me sound like a weed. And why are you so surprised? People don't shrink, do they?' She threw herself onto the futon. 'Where've you been, then?'

Maggie caught Sawyer's eye. 'We'll get to that, honey.'

Mia tossed her hair over her shoulder. 'I'm worried about Freddy. He won't come out of his room.'

'That doesn't sound too unusual for a nine-year-old,' said Sawyer. His phone sounded an alert and he took it out of his pocket.

She chewed gum and watched Sawyer. 'No, but it's just different. He doesn't say much.'

Sawyer checked his phone.

Mia pointed. 'Mum tells me off for that. And what kind of phone is that, anyway? Looks well old.'

'On the contrary,' said Sawyer. 'It's a new model. Secret. Only police can get them.'

She snorted. 'So are you going to find the people who attacked my dad?'

'Among other things,' said Sawyer. 'I've only been back five minutes and my in-tray is filling up.'

Mia frowned. 'You mean inbox.' She shuffled forward onto the edge of the futon. 'Look. You've got to get them. They're sick bastards.'

'Mia...' said Maggie.

'Well, they are. They tried to get Freddy to hit Dad. To punch him. But he wouldn't do it. I was *so* proud of him. I mean, why would they do that?'

'And they wore masks?' said Sawyer.

'Yeah. Balaclavas. Like the guy who got me out of that house. I'm still messaging the boy who was there with me.'

'Joshua,' said Sawyer.

Mia raised her eyebrows. 'Yeah. He's like a friend now. Not, like, a boyfriend friend.'

'I'll see what I can do about the men who attacked you and your dad,' said Sawyer. 'Most importantly, though, are you okay?'

Mia tipped back her head and nodded, imperious. 'Dad didn't want to call the police. I think they told him not to. Hey...' She sprang up. 'Give me your number, Uncle Jake.'

Sawyer eyed Maggie. 'Okay. Then you can call me if you're worried about anything.'

She smiled, shook her head. 'I can let you know if one of my friends is selling their phone.'

'I'm getting something new soon. Your mum can send you my number.'

'Okay. Do you want a drink? Cup of tea? We don't have cake, sorry.'

Sawyer laughed. 'Unbelievable.'

'Milky coffee? You like that, right?'

'Sold.'

She bounded out of the door. 'Won't be long.'

Maggie walked to the futon and tidied the laptop.

'There's a briefing tomorrow,' said Sawyer. 'Sunday, because Keating's away next week.'

'It'll be a shock to your system. Going to work after all that time doing press-ups and playing computer games.'

He smiled. 'Video games.'

Maggie stood there for a moment, gazing at him. 'Justin said that one of them took off his mask briefly.' She set up the candle on the cabinet shelf and lit it. 'So, what do you think? Is it about you?'

'It could be. Trying to get my attention.'

She angled her head. 'Urging a young boy to punch his own father. What's *that*?'

'Yeah,' said Sawyer. 'Interesting.'

29

The taxi turned off at the Hayfield crossroads and headed towards Edale, along the narrow, tree-lined road that cut through the lower slopes of Kinder Scout.

Sawyer lowered the back window an inch and inhaled the scent of home. Pure air, wildflowers, petrichor. A broad bank of gunmetal cloud lurked above the moorland plateau; the peak of the Peak. The Lake District was topiary in comparison; landscaped and manicured for the Instagrammers. Here, the fells seemed to swell and undulate at will, unhurried by the seasonal swarms.

Larkin came to mind again. *Here is unfenced existence: Facing the sun, untalkative, out of reach.*

He took out his phone and studied the image retrieved by the motion capture camera, sent via MMS. The blue VW Golf again. Terry Barker. Image dated late the previous evening.

Sawyer got out a few hundred yards from the cottage, and whirled on his jacket: both arms in at once, over the head and around. He shouldered on his backpack, hopped over a drystone wall and squelched along the edge of a field, around the back of the house.

A hefty man in a crimson jacket hauled a full rubbish bag over the driveway bridge, down to the roadside wheelie bin. Sawyer quickly crouched and dislodged the loose brick at the bottom of the wall. He took out the cellophane bag of brown powder and stuffed it into his pocket.

As the man lifted the bag into the wheelie bin, Sawyer walked over to the orange-and-black Mini Convertible, parked in the drive. He squinted in through the windows, cupping his hands around his eyes. Hoodie draped over the passenger seat, McDonald's milkshake cup, books and bags on the floor.

'About fucking time!'

The man hurried back over the driveway bridge and launched himself at Sawyer, holding him in a powerful bear hug. Sawyer held on for a few seconds then pushed him back.

Sawyer grinned, nodded to the car. 'Do you actually drive this thing or are you using it as a litter bin?'

Michael Sawyer gulped down a big breath and looked up at the sky. 'Hold on.' He looked back at his brother, rubbed his eyes. 'Yeah. You're definitely here. Come inside. Your timing's perfect.'

Sawyer followed him. 'Kettle on?'

'About to leave. I'll make a quick brew before I go, though. I'm only here weekends. Got a place in Sheffield.' He gestured to the Mini as they passed. 'And, yeah. You can gladly have that back. I feel like fucking Noddy in it.'

They ducked under the low beam and Sawyer closed the front door behind them.

Nothing had changed. L-shaped sitting room with galley kitchen and dining table. Bedroom and en suite bathroom at the back. Side door through to the patio and picnic bench.

'I love what you've done with the place,' said Sawyer.

Michael shrugged. 'I knew you'd be back. Your friend Maggie gave me her spare keys. I got your land registry details, but didn't complete it all. Place is still technically yours. Couldn't keep the cat, though. Sorry. Allergic. Maggie took him.'

'That's okay.'

'They want a dog, though. You might have to welcome him back.'

Sawyer eyed the gaming clutter by the TV. 'New controller?'

'Yeah, yours was a bit sticky. Been playing *Dark Souls III*. Brutal.'

'Not really a game, though, is it? More of an ordeal.'

Michael filled the kettle, set it to boil. He'd shorn down his grey hair, surrendering to the bald patch. His green eyes flitted over the surfaces, alert and alive. 'So is this an official visit? Did I actually see you?'

'Yes. I'm no longer a fugitive.'

Michael folded his arms. 'How come?'

Sawyer edged around the coffee table and fell onto the sofa. 'It's complicated. So what's in Sheffield?'

'Work. The flat is a shared place. Pretty decent. I'm working with a small developer. Taught myself a couple of coding languages.' He brought the tea over. 'Games, a few commercial gigs. I want to set up on my own, though.' He sat down, smiled. 'True to my own spirit.'

Michael took off his jacket. No new scars on his arms.

'You're looking good, Mike.'

Another shrug. 'Hasn't been easy. But like I told you at the hospital, I feel better. I decided to give it a go.'

'What?'

'Life.'

'That it will never come again, is what makes it so sweet.'

Michael slurped his tea. 'Dylan Thomas or something?'

'Emily Dickinson.'

Michael nodded. 'They asked me where you were. I told them nothing, Jake. I swear.' He beamed at his brother. 'Mainly because that's what I knew. Nothing.'

'I wanted to reassure you, make contact. But I couldn't. Mainly to protect you.'

'I know.' He stared into space for a few seconds. 'But you've been protecting me long enough.'

Sawyer took a sip of tea.

'Sorry about the lack of biscuits,' said Michael. 'Trying to lose a bit of this.' He grabbed a fistful of belly flab. 'Looks like you've been on the weights. Where did you go?'

'Lakes. Cashed in a favour. So what happened to Rosemary House?'

'Checked myself out. Said farewell to Mr Chris Hill. It's funny, Jake. It's like I had to hit the bottom before I could... get the purchase to find my way up again.'

Sawyer nodded. 'How are your memories?'

'Still fuzzy.'

'I've been having trouble in that department myself.'

Michael laughed. 'Bit early for early onset dementia.'

Sawyer set his mug down on the coffee table. 'I see Mum, Mike.'

'What do you mean, see?'

'Not really hallucinations. She feels real. She's right there, in front of my eyes. But even while we're talking, the rational part of me refuses to accept it.'

Michael squinted at him. 'Since... the thing...'

'Your suicide attempt. You can say it.'

He sighed. 'Since my suicide attempt, it's like... My memories have scrambled. The painful stuff, it's died down. I don't see it so clearly. It's more of an ache than...'

'An affliction?'

'Yeah. Do you still get flashes?'

'Sometimes. Not a lot lately.'

'I used to get them all the time. It was a full-time job keeping the distractions going. But now, they've gone. It's like my brain had reached its limit and switched off the dark side. It's given me access to things I didn't even know were still there. I do still get a few bits of the bad memories. Mum and Dad arguing, in whispers. The way we both used to stay up and listen through the wall, trying to work out what they were saying. Remember?'

'Of course.' Sawyer leaned forward. 'What do you remember about Mum?'

Michael smiled. 'I always had a terrible memory. Oh!' He sprang up. 'Got you something.'

He opened a kitchen cupboard and pulled out a carrier bag. 'The people who live at our old house had some work done, and they found this.' He pulled a battered-looking koala bear toy from the bag. 'They sent Dad a package and letter, forwarded to you.'

'And you opened it? Outrageous.'

'Checking it wasn't important.'

Sawyer took the bear. One of its button eyes had become dislodged, but it was in surprisingly good condition. He sniffed the fur. Sour, earthy.

'Your old comfort toy,' said Michael. 'I used to be jealous of it. I remember I once stole it and tried to hide it up that little fireplace in Mum's study, where she used to listen to her records. But it wouldn't fit.' He sat down again. 'But it triggered something else. I remembered there was a book up there, pushed into a little groove in the chimney. A hardback notebook.'

'Did you look at it?'

'No. I was terrified she'd come in and find me, so I just put it back.'

Sawyer picked at the bear's eye. 'Who lives there now?'

'Some couple. I've got their details in the letter. Listen. I need to go. Sorry about the car. I'll clear it out and order a cab.'

Sawyer moved to stand. 'That's mad. I'll drive you—'

'No, Jake. I'm good. I'm going to spend the rest of my life thanking you for keeping me going, for looking out for me. Let me just...'

'Give it a go.'

'Yeah. Like I said, I feel better.'

30

Keating took his seat at the head of the conference room. He smiled, looked around at his team. 'Morning all. I see Sunday eyes. Maybe a few sore heads behind them.'

'Can we start with the new guy, sir?' said Moran, scowling at Sawyer. 'What's the story?'

'The IOPC investigation into DI Sawyer has concluded and I'm pleased to say that he's back with us.'

Moran scoffed, shook his head.

Keating clasped his hands together on the table. 'Do you have an issue with that, DC Moran?'

Moran looked at Myers. 'He's like fucking Houdini.' Sawyer grinned; Moran turned to him. 'That's not a compliment.'

'Did anyone bring popcorn?' said a scrawny, moustachioed detective sitting next to Sally O'Callaghan.

Keating glared at him. 'Rhodes...'

'Pleasantries over,' said Sawyer. 'Shall we dig in? We're here because I don't believe we're dealing with a murder.'

'So Yates stabbed himself in the eyes and cut his own throat?' said Moran.

'From the HOLMES reports,' Sawyer continued,

'which you've also had access to, DC Moran, I suggest that the Yates scene tells us several things that we haven't yet fully investigated. No struggle, no violent blood spatter, precise wounds, and no apparent motive.'

'Drummond is looking into it all,' said Sally. 'Trying to get a more specific TOD, among other things.'

'We're not looking for a murderer. But we are looking for someone who arrived at Yates's house with the intent to murder him.'

Walker looked round at the confused faces. 'Are you saying he was already dead, but the... potential murderer slashed his throat and stabbed him in the eyes for kicks?'

'Pretty much. The killer must have walked in on Yates while his blood was still liquid and moving through his veins. So, recently dead. The throat slash feels standard, not interesting. But the stabbing in the eyes is too specific not to be significant.'

'Also,' said Shepherd, 'no struggle.'

Moran leaned forward. 'There could have been more than one killer. One holding him down, keeping him steady, while the other attacked.'

'There's no evidence of that,' said Sally.

Moran waved a hand. 'You haven't found any evidence of anything.'

'We've been looking really hard, DC Moran. Cross my heart.'

'We do have a shoe print,' said Keating. 'It's too generic to help by itself but once we have a suspect, we can cross-check.'

'Maybe it was supposed to be a robbery,' said Moran. 'Some kid. Drugs. Didn't find what he wanted, just a dead old man. Stabbed and slashed him in frustration, didn't see his medal or just thought it wouldn't be worth stealing.'

'That's a big maybe,' said Sawyer. 'I'd like to focus on

the certainties.' His phone buzzed in his pocket. 'We need to scrutinise Yates's connections, past links, any slights or feuds. This stuff doesn't shake out easily, so dig deeper.'

'Rhodes,' said Keating. 'Any passive? Anything on dashcams or doorbells? Any sightings around the back of Yates's place on the day?'

Rhodes shook his head. 'Not a sausage. Even if we did know who we were looking for, there's no coverage in that part of the village. This is sleepy Sheldon we're talking about. Doorbell cams are the work of Satan.'

'I'll check in with Drummond,' said Sawyer. 'Shepherd. Find me something worth knowing about Yates. Whoever delivered those wounds, I'm confident we'll be seeing them again.'

'You SIO now, then?' said Moran.

'Yes,' said Keating. 'He is. I'll be away for a few days, and when I return I want to see some progress, and everyone playing nice again.'

'You know, Moran,' said Sawyer, 'if you think I escaped some kind of justice or got away with something, and it's going to impact on your professionalism here, then I completely understand. I'd be happy to help with a potential transfer to Manchester, since you seemed to get on with our friend DCI Farrell so well.'

Sally laughed. 'A fine bromance.'

———

Shepherd followed Sawyer into his office.

'Sir.'

He shut the door behind him.

Sawyer pulled up the window, turned. 'You're going to say that you had to think of your family. That Farrell pressured you, forced you to choose.'

'There was no choice.'

'I know.' Sawyer's phone rang. 'Apparently, Farrell had a PI hunting for me in the Canary Islands.'

'I didn't tell him about that.'

Sawyer smiled. 'I know.' He waggled the phone; Shepherd exited and closed the door.

Sawyer took the call.

'How are you settling in?' Ainsworth's voice was a balm; one of the few comforts and certainties of the past five months.

'A warm welcome. What's up?'

'Did you see my message?'

'Been in a meeting.' Sawyer pulled out his desk chair and sat down, shuffling into his sweet spot inside the seat mould.

'My cleaning company went to the cottage. There was a package for you. I have it here.'

'Open it.'

Rustling at the other end. Sawyer closed his eyes.

The barking usually came first; then his mother's shattered face.

Sobbing and screaming.

But there was nothing.

He looked over to the corner table, half expecting her to be there, gazing out of the window.

'*Jesus Christ*.' Ainsworth coughed, caught his breath.

Sawyer sighed. 'It's photographs, isn't it? A man, beaten up. Location isn't clear but there's probably a wall behind him. Dark stone.'

31

Farrell rode a crowded lift to the top floor of Broadhurst House, the GMCA headquarters on Manchester's Oxford Street. He shouldered his way into the corridor and scurried through the open-plan offices to a generous reception area, furnished with kidney-shaped sofas in vivid greens and blues.

A youngish biracial man in a remote headset and immaculate formal dress leaned over a desk, typing into a raised laptop.

He smiled at Farrell. Salon hair, good teeth. 'Detective Chief Inspector Farrell?'

'Yes.'

'I'll let him know you're here.'

Farrell hovered by one of the sofas. 'He already knows.'

The man looked up, surprised. 'Yes, but I'll—'

'Robin!' Dale Strickland emerged from the left-hand door of a large partitioned office space. He held the door open and Farrell walked past.

Dale slapped a hand on the young man's shoulder. 'Thanks, Oliver.'

He closed the door.

The office smelt freshly cleaned; it was sparse and bright, with a glass desk, another curved sofa in silvery grey, and a ceiling-high window looking down on the Manchester rooftops.

'Don't your staff have chairs here?' said Farrell, dropping onto the sofa.

Dale took his seat behind the desk. 'Quite a few of Oliver's generation prefer standing desks. And when you factor in his... orientation, the figure is even higher.'

'Is he queer?' said Farrell.

Dale laughed. 'You see, your terms are now so unreconstructed they've come round to be acceptable again. And for a policeman, your gaydar is commendably evolved.'

'Sawyer's back,' said Farrell.

Dale frowned. 'At Buxton?'

'Yes. Got back yesterday. Working a case already. All is forgiven.'

Dale sipped from a mug. He held it up to Farrell, who shook his head.

'That's an impressive whitewash, even for him. Did they drop the charges?'

'The woman he got out switched her story.'

'Stephanie Burns.'

'Yes.'

Dale stared into the mug. 'Okay. Not good timing. But we'll have to defer for now.'

'Defer? They know about me and Barker. They don't know that I was paying him from budget allocated to official resource only.'

Dale nodded. 'Awkward. And I assume they don't know about the deeper history between you and Barker?'

Farrell swept back his hair. 'No. They don't. And I'd rather it stayed that way. If they start digging into Barker—'

'Some of the soil might fall on you.'

'A delightful analogy. And I'd rather they didn't link me with the fine gentlemen you employed to put pressure on Sawyer. How far along did that go?'

Dale looked out of the window. 'I assume Sawyer has seen the results by now.'

Farrell sighed. 'Terrific. So, if we'd waited, as I suggested, he was planning to come back of his own accord. I wasn't going to get any of the "spoils" you mentioned, anyway, and now we wouldn't have to clean up.'

'He'll get snared up in new cases. It'll fade.'

Farrell leaned forward, propped his elbows on his knees. 'It's messy.'

Dale shrugged. 'Talk to Barker. Hush money. He seems the type who wouldn't turn down a few weeks somewhere tropical. I'll bet my left bollock he's into ladyboys.'

'He's not an idiot. He'll see Sawyer's return and recognise he has one over on me. And if he starts to get chummy with Sawyer directly, then I'm fucked.' Farrell took out his canister of breath mints, found it empty. 'I take it the Jamel Perry attack was something to do with you? The one that's set the gangs actually collaborating to try and find out who it was.'

'It's a good thing. Let them fight it out. Disruption.'

'And how does your boss next door feel about these methods of isometric warfare?'

Dale turned his chair to face Farrell. 'You know what, Robin? This could work out.'

'How?'

'Symbiosis. Instead of you wafting over this soap bubble of a threat, I can help you and you can help me.' He stood up, walked over to the sofa, and took a seat next to Farrell. 'I need bigger names.' Dale kept his voice low. 'The front channel info isn't quite spicy enough. A few street gimps in Moss Side pulling out each other's fingernails. So what? I want to go up a few pay-grades. Bypass the generals and shoot for the field marshals. But these people keep their heads down. I don't have the names, and I can't get them by asking nicely.' He patted a hand on Farrell's knee. 'If only I had access to a friendly neighbourhood senior detective who could get me the names. Then we could have a conversation about sending the upstanding Mr Barker on a once-in-a-lifetime trip.'

Eva Gregory wrapped and unwrapped a curl of black hair around an index finger as she studied the menu.

The boy puffed his floppy blond hair up out of his eyes, focused on his iPhone game. 'Mum always does this.'

'Does what?' said Sawyer.

'She takes ages to decide what she wants and then changes her mind when the waiter asks.'

Sawyer smiled. 'Ah, but does she really have the free will to make the choice anyway, Luka?'

He frowned. 'What do you mean?'

'We like to think we have control, shaping our futures with careful decisions in the present, but where do those decisions really come from? Some people would say that we're just slaves to our impulses, and we comfort ourselves with the idea of free will.'

Eva sighed, set down the menu. 'I can safely say that nobody else in this burger joint is having a conversation about fatalism.'

'Determinism,' said Sawyer.

She pursed her lips. 'Are you really mansplaining philosophy concepts?'

Luka laughed. 'You've been by yourself for too long.' He eyed the waiter, in deep conversation with the diners at another table.

'Slow service,' said Sawyer.

Eva paged through the menu again. 'It's busy. Give them a chance.'

Luka sat back, petulant. 'We should tell them it's my birthday. It might speed things up.'

'They'll probably spit in your relish,' said Sawyer.

Luka leapt to his feet. 'I need a wee. Can you just order me a cheeseburger with fries. Vanilla Coke.' He hurried off towards the toilet at the far end of the restaurant.

Eva propped her elbows on the table, rested her chin on her clasped hands. 'Alone at last.'

The music switched: loping hip-hop with heavily Auto-Tuned vocal.

Sawyer tipped his head back and sighed.

Eva leaned forward. 'What's up?'

'The music. Making things note perfect. Modulating out the humanity, when that's the part that's the most interesting.'

She smiled. 'You sound old.'

'Just a more developed taste. We can't be that far from algorithmically developed music. Cut out the people altogether.'

Eva eyed him over the top of her Tom Fords. 'When we all live on the moon?'

'I feel like I have been living on the moon.'

She reached over, rested a hand on his. 'I'm still picturing you chopping logs and... wrestling bears.'

'In the Lake District? More like red squirrels.'

'Dale came over.'

'Of course he did.'

She sat back. 'And you're still convinced he's some kind

of gangster? In disguise as the Deputy Mayor of Manchester?'

'Pretty much.'

'Maybe it's all for me. Maybe he wants it all back.'

'Wants what back?'

She swept an arm over herself. 'This. Birthday dinners. Domestic bliss.'

'Dale is the type who gets his kicks by stopping people from having the things he can't have, even if he doesn't want them himself.'

'Are you saying he doesn't really want me?'

He held her eye, smiled.

Eva shook her head. 'I know you've been alone with your thoughts for a few months, Jake, but not everything is about you.'

'This is. You think he's worked his way up to some position of civic respectability so he can get back into your life. I think that would be more of an added extra. Narcissists, sociopaths. They're not good with empathy, with give and take. They like things to be the way they are because of their decisions. Anything else is an affront, an inconvenience. To be worked around, or removed.'

'Ah. So it is about you.'

'I'm just saying that Dale's beef with me is more existential. It's a power trip. Not just because I stole his woman or whatever.'

She nodded, took a sip of wine. 'He thinks you're a bent copper.'

'What do you think?'

Luka emerged from the toilet and started to make his way back to the table.

'Is that a serious question?'

'Yes. Am I really better for Luka than his father?'

She winced. 'Don't be ridiculous.'

Almost at the table, Luka bumped into the waiter, who managed to hold on to his tray of drinks. He apologised and took his seat. 'The toilets are mental. They're sort of gargoyle heads and you have to wee into their mouths.'

'Lovely,' said Eva.

Luka turned to the waiter, who had approached another table. 'Excuse me!' He waved a chunky ballpoint pen high above his head.

The waiter turned, frowned and walked over.

'Is that—'

'Yeah,' said Luka. 'You dropped it.' He handed the pen over. 'While you're here, I'll have a cheeseburger with fries and Vanilla Coke.' He pointed at Sawyer, who smiled.

'Same. Diet Coke.'

Eva shook back her hair. 'Chicken special, please. And a green salad. Tap water.'

The waiter gave a curt nod and scribbled down the order, leaving without another word.

Luka beamed at them both.

'Did you lift it?' said Sawyer.

He nodded.

Eva spoke to Luka but kept her eyes on Sawyer. 'Jesus Christ, Luka.'

Sawyer's phone buzzed with a call. He checked the ID. Shepherd.

'What?' said Luka. 'It worked, didn't it?'

'You're twelve years old. I'd rather you didn't pick people's pockets.'

Sawyer got up. 'Sorry. Need to take this.'

He moved out to the entrance lobby and took the call.

'Okay to talk?' said Shepherd.

'Something new on Yates's background?'

'No, but... and I have so missed using these three little words, sir.'

'Go on.'

Shepherd sighed. 'You were right. Drummond's put up the bat signal.'

33

Frazer Drummond closed the pale green door behind him and settled his vast frame into one of the frail-looking chairs around the beechwood table.

'I'd love to say that's it's a pleasure to see you again, Sawyer.'

Sawyer leaned back against the wall, shoulder to shoulder with Shepherd. He gave Drummond the dimple smile. 'But you can't, right?'

'No.' He slurped at a plastic cup. 'Because it isn't. Because you're already causing trouble.'

'How do you mean?' said Shepherd.

'I had the Yates thing nice and clear, but now I'm not so sure. Accurate time of death is notoriously tricky, particularly for anything above ten hours since the last breath. Get to twenty and you're basically guessing. This one, though...' He took out a case folder, slipped on his glasses. 'Gentlemen. We all have three deaths, you know. Physiological, legal, estimated. I'd say Yates's carer found the body at 3:15pm, not much more than two hours after his physiological death. The attendant doctor officially, legally, pronounced him dead at 3:45pm. And then I gave my estimated TOD as sometime around one.'

'Cause of death, exsanguination from the throat wound.'

Drummond nodded. 'I'd say so. Tox is negative, no external wounds, organs and bloodstain analysis confirm. So, we have the killer entering, holding Yates down, slashing the throat, then holding him still and going for the eyes. The adrenaline would keep him going but he'd lose consciousness quickly and death from exsanguination could occur in as little as five minutes.'

Sawyer pulled up a chair and sat opposite Drummond. 'But is it possible the killer discovered Yates already dead?'

Drummond sighed. 'Yes, it is. But I'd like to hear your logic, before I give you my view.'

'No defensive wounds. No sign of struggle. Two clean, accurate stabs into a tricky area. And there's a dissonance.'

Drummond closed his folder. 'In what way?'

'There's not enough violence. This isn't a robbery with violence. That's just presentation, misdirection. Yates's medal is sitting there in plain sight. It's the first thing a robber would swipe.'

'As opposed to rifling through his undies drawer,' said Shepherd.

'Yes. This isn't incidental violence. It's directional, specific. There's a lot of anger.'

'Personal,' said Drummond.

'More than that. I think the killer did know Yates. They had planned to kill him, and I think they'd been planning it for a long time. There's more than anger here. There's frustration. I think Charles Yates sat down in front of the television and expired right there, a lonely old man.'

Drummond grinned. 'And very soon after, our killer enters, finds the body—'

'And is denied the opportunity to kill. They grab a weapon from the kitchen and in frustration, deliver the stabs to the eyes.'

Shepherd stepped forward. 'But why not stab the chest, or the neck, or anywhere?'

'Exactly,' said Sawyer. 'That's too unusual to ignore. And it introduces some interesting questions. Why? What's the motive? Who? How did they know Yates? What's their problem with him? Or, more specifically, what's their problem with his eyes?'

'And is this a one-off,' said Drummond, 'or does our killer have a checklist? Are we going to get more?'

Sawyer gazed at a cup stain on the table. 'Or have there already been more, and we just don't know yet?' He stood up. 'We have to double down on Yates. His connections, the connections of his connections.

'We have eighty-four years to dredge up,' said Shepherd. 'There will be something, someone, who sticks out.'

Sawyer kept his eyes on the stain. 'Start with the school. Pioneer. That's where he spent the main part of his working life. Check on the health of all the teachers, anyone he might have fucked over, ex-teachers.'

'What about your mother?' said Drummond.

Sawyer looked at him. 'What about her?'

'She taught there, right? Maybe she knew Yates?'

'Unfortunately,' said Sawyer slowly, 'we can't interview her. But we can cross-check with anyone with connections to the school or with Yates's activities since leaving, and anyone who has a subsequent record, or who has been linked with similar offences. Particularly if their shoe size tallies with the print found at scene.'

'It's like a messed-up version of *Cinderella*,' said Shepherd.

Drummond spluttered on his coffee. 'In that case, we're

all fucked.' He nodded to Sawyer. 'You're going to have to play Prince Charming.'

34

Sawyer parked the Mini at the end of a rough farm track and followed the signs for Adlington village. He stayed close to the grass verge, guided by the full moon that squatted on the horizon, beyond the ploughed fields. An evening chill slipped down his collar, and he hitched up his shoulders and sank deeper into his jacket.

He turned into a side road and took out his phone, on the pretence of consulting it for directions. He looked up and down the road; nobody around, nobody sitting in a car.

He walked down the rakish path of a modest detached house and gave three taps on the yellow wooden door.

Two bolts slid away behind, and the door creaked open.

Sawyer held up his warrant card.

The figure in the unlit hallway hung back. 'Fuck me twice. I spent two months chasing you around, and now you pitch up at my home.'

'I come in peace. Just a quick chat.'

Terry Barker stepped aside, flicked on a pale light and swept a welcoming arm towards the open door of a small sitting room.

Sawyer walked through; an ageing Labrador padded out and greeted him, tail flapping.

'Go straight in,' said Barker. 'He's as soft as you like.'

The sitting room was low-ceilinged, uncluttered. Brown leather sofa and matching chair; bookcase; turntable and speakers. The room smelt salty; the coffee table in front of the TV was littered with takeaway leftovers in foil trays. A dog bowl by the side of the chair had been licked clean.

Barker followed him in. 'Sit down. You've caught me indulging in a late-night Chinese.'

Sawyer sat at the television end of the sofa. 'All that MSG before bedtime. You won't sleep.'

Barker shrugged. 'I was planning on staying up for a while, actually. I'm watching Netflix. *I Am A Killer.* Documentary about death row inmates.' He eased his bulk down into the chair, groaning with the effort. He wore black jogging bottoms and a large white *A Clockwork Orange* T-shirt that only just covered his stomach.

Sawyer looked round the room, up at the ceiling. Six recessed spotlights, one bulb out. 'This your place?'

'Parents' old house. Came back here when I left Wakefield. Well, when I had to leave Wakefield.'

'I heard.'

'I'm sure you did. We all make our mistakes. I do know what it's like to be *persona non grata*, Sawyer. You seem to have made quite a habit out of it.'

Sawyer smirked. 'You had a look round Lanzarote.'

'That was Keating's fault. Dead end, but it wasn't exactly a hardship. Had some nice seafood in Punta Mujeres.' He reached over, topped up a glass of beer. 'Drink?'

'I'm okay. Like I say, not stopping.'

'Did you walk from the village? I didn't see a car.'

The dog parked itself next to Sawyer; he petted it.

190

'Exercising discretion, yes. Although I'm no longer a wanted man.'

'Yes. Good work with that. Took you long enough.'

'I had to get away for a bit.'

Barker took a swig of beer. 'Decompress?'

'More of a recalibration.'

'So why the discretion?'

'I'm here to warn you about a possible entanglement. There's a chance you might have become a loose end for some bad people.'

Barker laughed. 'An entanglement?'

Sawyer took out his phone and held up a picture of Barker's blue Volvo taken by the motion capture camera. 'You came to the house in the Lakes.' A wry smile. 'Good work with that. But you were too slow in flushing me out, and I got the jump on you. Unfortunately, it looks like your collaborator got impatient and passed details of my whereabouts to the bad people.'

'You mean Dale Strickland?'

Sawyer raised his eyebrows. 'Yes, I do. The worst type of bad people. A small-timer with access to big-time resources.'

'How did you get the pic of my car?'

'Motion capture camera on a tree at the end of the lane. It's a basic model. Takes a picture, sends an alert to either a phone or a separate device. You can get versions that take live video. But, y'know. Lake District. Internet.'

Barker took his own phone from a side table and navigated to an image. 'A big rule of private detectives, Sawyer. Know your client. DCI Farrell hired me off the books to find you. I'm sure you know this. I did my own surveillance.'

He handed the phone to Sawyer, who swiped through several long-lens camera shots of Strickland entering and leaving the GMP headquarters in central Manchester with two men Sawyer had never seen before. The final shot showed Farrell leaving the building soon after.

'Don't recognise these two,' said Sawyer.

'I'm looking into it.'

Sawyer gave the phone back. 'Strickland has a beef with me. I'll need all night to explain it. But I know that he's already moved on to violence to try and get me to bite. Farrell has been humiliated by my return. Strickland has shown his hand too early. Now Farrell's association with you will come under investigation. He won't want that. They're both powerful men with a shared interest in seeing you—'

'Removed from the board? I've known Robin for a long time, Sawyer. We used to work together. He's not going to have me bumped off.'

'I can try to make Strickland regret his recent action, but we could do with knowing the identity of his new friends. Strickland's friends are rarely good news for anyone with a shred of empathy. I imagine he hired them to do this. It's the ex-husband of a close friend of mine.'

Sawyer held up an image of Justin, badly beaten by the aqueduct wall.

Barker winced. 'Don't worry. I'm a big boy. I've put away worse people than Strickland. I'll see if I can find out who his pals are. And I'll make good use of anonymous audio-visual tech.' He finished the beer. 'So did you come away from your exile awash with new self-knowledge? Your walkabout. Your time in the wilderness.'

Sawyer stood up. 'As Socrates said, "the unexamined life is not worth living".'

Barker nodded. 'Self-knowledge is power.'

'Of course. Fucking hard work, though.' He grinned. 'But all play and no work makes Jake a dull boy.'

35

In the morning, Sawyer dusted down the wooden man dummy in his bedroom and worked through a standard routine of grappling and forearm strengthening, pivoting around the imagined centreline, thrusting his arms into the spaces between the struts. Despite the rigorous strength and cardio conditioning at the Lakes cottage, his movement was stiffer than usual; it would take time and patience to re-awaken the muscle memories.

Bruce entered, and wound himself around Sawyer's legs, purring.

'Feeling entitled already, big man?'

He fed the cat and sat down at the coffee table with a generous latte: more coffee-flavoured hot milk than caffeine.

Eyes closed, take a sip of the foam.

Morning birdsong.

Bruce chomping his food.

Bubbles in the foam, cracking and settling.

'I liked that other place.'

He opened his eyes. Jessica stood in the kitchen, by the side door, standing over Bruce. The morning was overcast, and the light from the window was only enough to render her in silhouette.

He took a breath. 'It was too small.'

'Do you still want to know more?'

'About what?'

She crouched down; Bruce didn't flinch.

'About me.'

'Of course I do.'

'Remember what your dad said. "There is nothing in darkness that will not be disclosed."'

'Yes. "Nothing concealed that will not be brought to light."' He opened his laptop. 'To be fair, I think that was Matthew.'

'Luke,' said Jessica.

Sawyer opened Skype and logged in.

'You said not to look back.'

'"The past is a foreign country."'

'*The Go-Between*. Opening line.'

She stood up. 'Yes. I was reading that book when I started at Pioneer.'

'I remember the cover. I remember looking through the books in your study. I liked the cover. A young boy carrying an envelope, walking away from a house. Looking back.'

'It's about a boy who feels too much, my darling.'

The Skype ringtone played on the laptop.

'It's all about time,' said Sawyer. 'The past. Being alienated from the past, yet not free of it.'

He glanced at the screen and accepted the call, looked back up to the door. Bruce had finished his food and was pouring himself through the cat flap. No Jessica.

'Hello, Jake.'

The face in the video window was too close, too bright.

Wrinkled smile. Light scarf: grey. Buttoned cardigan: beige.

Alex Goldman's grey hair was normally blow-dried and static, but she had tamed it into a thin fringe, tucked back at the sides. She sat before a backdrop of books, in a room Sawyer didn't recognise.

'I can understand you wanting to keep your distance.'

She smiled. 'It seems you've been doing something similar.'

'I'm back now. I couldn't bear the lack of human contact any longer.'

She sipped from a teacup, then replaced it on a saucer. 'I've thought about you a lot. My husband and I did some travelling.'

A dog barked on Alex's side.

'Still got Molly?'

'Oh, yes. I think she recognises your voice. Maggie has told me all about your recent adventures. I'm interested in the hallucinations. Of your mother.'

Sawyer rubbed his eyes. 'Maybe they're not hallucinations.'

'People talk to the dead all the time, Jake. It's part of the grieving process. But it's curious that you should *raise* the dead, imagine your mother as a physical presence. That tells me that you're trying to make her real, flesh her out. Define her as more than just a traumatic memory.' She shifted in place, leaned back from the screen. 'It sounds like you've moved into another phase of the grieving process. Turning your mother into something tangible, seeing her as a person in her own right. Someone who isn't just representative. She's someone you can say hello to.'

'And goodbye to.'

Alex took another sip of tea. 'Absolutely. How about your brother? I'm sorry to hear about his recent troubles.'

'He's a lot better since he tried to kill himself. Somehow the experience seems to have made him stronger. More lucid. He's moved out of the care facility, he's working. He also seems to be less affected by what happened to Mum.'

'And are you jealous of that? Resentful, even?'

He smiled. 'No, not really. I've had a few memory glitches of my own, lately. Neurosurgeon thinks I have something rare, called Urbach-Wiethe disease. Relates to amygdala damage. Can cause skin problems, and issues with episodic memory. It could also explain the other thing.'

'With not feeling fear?'

Sawyer nodded.

His phone rang. Walker. He screened it.

'So where did you go on your travels?'

Alex brushed her hair out of her eyes. 'You might think you're swerving away from the subject, but that's actually related. We travelled around India, choosing our destinations carefully, avoiding ice cubes. It's a magnificent country, Jake. Such a rich civilisation. We stayed in a guest house in Nepal. The owner told us about a place in the Himalayas, called Roopkund. It's a high-altitude lake, surrounded by glaciers and mountains. In 1942, a ranger discovered human bones in the lake. More than three hundred people. They believe they died as the result of a hailstorm. But there's a metaphor there, isn't there? The mysteries of the past. Like a deep dark lake. Unfathomable, unknowable. Standing water, unchanging, unchangeable. You can spend your whole life searching it, dredging it, and find nothing that makes sense.' The image glitched for a second as Alex leaned forward. 'An obsession with the past is in one sense an excuse for refusal to accept change.'

'And change is the constant,' said Sawyer.

'Exactly. You're locked in a toxic relationship with your past, your pain. Your loss. Remember Scrooge, in *A Christmas Carol*? Obsessed with his ledger. Ultimately, Scrooge doesn't change because he's frightened of the ghosts. He changes because they highlight the way he's trying to live a life without loss. It's a delusion. He can't redo his past, nor can he be certain of his future. And his epiphany comes when he realises that he can only change his present, that change can only take place in the here and now. This is what you haven't accepted. As you allow yourself to grieve, then you'll repair your relationship to your loss, and you can begin to come to life yourself. That's why the hallucinations of your mother are a good thing. You're seeing her as a person in her own right, outside her role as your mother. You were just one part of her own rich life.' Alex shifted forward again, closer to the screen. 'This is what will let you come to life, Jake. To let go and not look back.'

Sawyer lowered his head. 'I can't forget her.'

'You wouldn't be forgetting. You would be fulfilling her dying wish. To run, to go forward with your life and to not keep looking back at the time when you were a part of hers.'

'Maggie said to stop carrying a mountain when I could just learn to climb it.' He laughed. 'All these elemental metaphors.'

'They work because they relate to issues that are bigger than us. The unknowable, the elemental. Jake, you have a double horror. Post-traumatic stress disorder, from what you saw. Also, you haven't allowed yourself to grieve. You're Scrooge, refusing to accept the very idea of loss. There's a wonderful book called *The Year of Magical Thinking*, by Joan Didion. It's an account of her life in the twelve months following her husband's death. A memoir of mourning. She talks about how the Japanese believe the dead have simply passed through something called a *shoji* screen, and that we can still see them if we look hard enough. We can think hard about them, and magic them back to life in our memories. You need to build a vivid picture of Jessica Sawyer as Jessica Sawyer, not just as your mother. Then turn to this picture as comfort, and consolidate the fact that she can never be part of your present or future.'

Sawyer gulped back a breath. 'I'm sorry about what happened with Fletcher, about putting you in danger.'

Alex smiled. 'That's also in the past. We can keep it there.' She sipped from her cup and saucer. 'I've rambled on a bit today, but I hope some of this is useful. And you should really take that call you screened, Jake. It might be important for your future.'

———

Sawyer ended the Skype call and stepped out onto the back porch. He filled his lungs with the pure morning air, and called Walker.

'Sir.'

'Anything new on Yates?'

'What I don't know about him truly isn't worth knowing.'

He sat on the picnic bench. 'I'm the same with the life and works of Bruce Lee.'

'Pretty short life compared to Yates.'

'Thirty-two.'

'So, Yates was born near Salisbury. He started teaching in the mid-1960s at a place down in Dorset, but moved up to Derbyshire in the early 1970s when he got the job at Pioneer Primary.'

'My mum started there in 1974, as a teaching assistant.'

Walker paused. 'I know. I looked into the ex-staff. She completed her teacher training in 1973. Full-time teacher in 1976. Your dad visited the school as a police officer later that year, to do a talk. Evils of being led astray, that kind of thing.'

'And the rest is history.'

'Indeed. Since Yates retired in 1999, it seems he was the main carer for his wife, Penny, who suffered from MS. Local vicar says he attended church regularly when Penny was alive but dropped off when he was by himself. Holy Trinity in Ashford-on-the-Water.'

Sawyer cast his eyes up to the slopes of Kinder Scout. A red kite wheeled above the birch trees, patrolling the entrance to the Pennine Way. 'And that's when he started walking?'

'According to his old walking group, he was active in the community walks back when his wife was still alive. Used to bring her along on a few in her wheelchair. He still attended regularly after her death, though.'

'Tell me about his medal, his father.'

'Arthur Yates. World War II infantry. Awarded the George VI Cross. It's mainly a civilian honour, but it was given to servicemen for actions away from the enemy. He was stationed in Egypt. Tanks. The main story is that this particular medal really isn't worth much.'

'But the killer, or stabber, wouldn't necessarily know that. If you're going to rifle through the drawers, you'd surely take the medal, just in case.'

'And those Royal Doulton figures are probably worth a few quid.'

The kite flapped and hovered, flapped and hovered, spiralling up on a thermal.

'It's not a burglary,' said Sawyer. 'But the intruder wanted us to think it was. But by trying to divert our attention, he's attracted our attention. Tell me more about Pioneer. The ex-staff.'

'Closed in the late 1990s. It's now a car park. Many of

the ex-staff are now elderly or dead.' Walker paused again. 'Sir. I'm sorry—'

'Don't worry. Carry on.'

'Shepherd and I spoke to the ex-governor, Esther Murphy. The only other staff who are still around are the ex-teachers and an admin assistant who now lives in Canada. It was a small, close-knit place. The only other connection was the caretaker, Gordon Kilton, who retired in the mid-1990s. Died a few years ago.'

The bird sank out of sight, pouncing.

'Tell me about the ex-teachers.'

'Graham Butcher, seventy-seven. I spoke to him. Doesn't deserve his wife, despite her old-school sandwich fillings. He was a form tutor, taught English. Headmaster was Norman Welch, eighty-two. He's still going. Lives up in Monyash, close to the old school site.' Walker paused, checking. 'There's also an art teacher, Miss Briscoe. Late seventies, lives down near Thorpe Cloud. Then there's Charles Yates, and a music teacher, Felix Parks. Died recently. Padwick Farm Care Home near Leek.'

Bruce hopped up on the seat next to Sawyer and curled into a ball, hitched against his leg.

'How recently?'

'Three days ago.'

36

'Can I get you a tea? Coffee?'

'We're fine, thanks.' Shepherd settled into one of the cushioned seats facing the desk.

'Are we?' Sawyer stayed on his feet, and leaned in to a framed photo on the back wall of the modest office that overlooked the reception area.

The woman looked up from the desk, frowning.

Sawyer turned. 'No. That's fine. Thank you.'

He studied the photo. A newspaper cutting of a group of elderly people in paper Christmas hats, most smiling, gathered around a tableclothed dining table. Some held crackers across the table, captured mid-pull.

'That's odd,' he said.

The woman smiled. 'What's that?'

'This photo. Everyone is wearing the paper hats you get from crackers, but they haven't pulled the crackers yet.'

She glanced at Shepherd, who gave an indulgent smile.

'I think...' The woman stumbled. 'They were from an earlier batch.'

Sawyer turned, satisfied. He took a seat. 'Was that taken last Christmas?'

'A few years ago, I think.'

'From the *Derbyshire Times*?'

'Yes.'

Sawyer nodded. He picked up the weighty Toblerone-shaped name tag from the desk, and turned it around in his fingers.

CLARA CAMPBELL
Front of House Manager

'You're not in the photo.'

'Ah, no. I've only been here for a couple of years.'

'They spelt the name wrong.'

She laughed. 'I know. Patwick instead of Padwick.'

A beat of silence as Sawyer studied the name tag.

Shepherd spoke up. 'Are the residents free to come and go as they please, Clara?'

'Yes. There's no curfew or anything.' She clasped her hands together on the desk, gave a nervous smile. Clara was welcoming, breezy, unburdened; impossibly young to oversee the treacherously old. She had rich black skin and wore tortoiseshell glasses with teardrop-shaped lenses. Ironic retro, maybe as a subtle signal of trust to her charges.

'Do they have routines?' said Sawyer.

Clara laughed. 'Oh, yes. They stick to their ways. Some residents prefer to get ready for bed by 8pm, and some prefer to sit in the lounge and watch TV with snacks until late. There's no lights-off time. If a resident wanted to sit up all evening then that's fine. When they're ready for bed, they can ask for help or make their way into their room by themselves.'

Sawyer took a seat. 'Do you have night staff?'

'Yes. Generally, three or four members of staff work overnight between ten and eight. They complete two-hourly checks on each resident, quietly popping their head around their bedroom door to check they're asleep and not in need of support.'

Shepherd made a few notes. 'And that's how you discovered Felix Parks?'

Clara glanced at Sawyer. 'Yes. I think Natalie was on duty. She said she checked on him around 2am, and spotted a piece of birthday cake on the floor. We'd had a small party for our head housekeeper. Natalie cleaned up the cake quietly but then noticed that Mr Parks was lying in an unusual position, on his back. She checked closer, and, well...'

'What's the procedure for a death, Clara?' Sawyer took out a boiled sweet, unwrapped it.

'Firstly, we call the family. Then, when they've had time with their loved one, we call the on-call doctor to confirm the death, and then our funeral director will collect the body.'

Sawyer slipped the sweet into his mouth. 'And which doctor do you call?'

'Normally, their GP, as listed on the resident's file. We also have a couple of doctors we can contact in emergencies.'

'Are there any external staff who visit regularly?' said Shepherd.

'Regional director Helen Marsh visits a couple of times a month, and we have a GP who does a regular round every Tuesday, visiting each resident one by one for a weekly update. She's familiar with the staff. Apart from the standard service and cleaning professionals, there's nobody else. I can get you all their details.' Clara frowned. 'Do you mind if I ask you what this is regarding?'

'We're looking into a connection with Mr Parks and

one of his ex-colleagues,' said Shepherd, 'whom I'm sorry to say was found dead in suspicious circumstances.'

'Oh dear. Felix wasn't in a good way, physically. He couldn't possibly—'

'He's not a suspect, Clara,' said Sawyer. 'At this stage, it's just a link. To the past.'

'We get a lot of that here.'

'A lot of what?'

'The past. Talk of the old days. It's what keeps a place like this going, really. Nobody here is under any illusion that they have much life left to live, so they do tend to revisit their better days. We urge them not to dwell on regrets, though. Focus on the positives, and try to enjoy the time they have left. Care homes are often seen as depressing, but they're not hospitals, or prisons. You'd be surprised at how much laughter there is.'

'What was Mr Parks's cause of death?' said Shepherd, pen poised over his notepad.

'Same as most in here, I'm afraid. Natural causes.'

'An excess of the past,' said Sawyer.

37

Sawyer slid a tray onto the tabletop and sat down opposite Shepherd.

'This is very you,' said Shepherd, nodding to the surroundings: the High Peak Bookstore, a converted warehouse and café on the edge of Sterndale Moor. The place was busy, mostly young mothers and babies.

'I like to take my coffee under the cold, hard stare of books.'

'As opposed to motivational plaques.'

Sawyer nodded to the wall of the partition that divided the bookshop from the café; a framed sketch of a steaming coffee cup beneath a slogan rendered in an opulent recursive script.

LIFE IS GOOD WHEN THE COFFEE IS STRONG

Shepherd smiled and sipped his tea. 'Can't get away from it.'

'Homilies, platitudes.'

'I suppose it's harmless. Whatever helps.'

Sawyer sliced into his cake.

'Is that Battenberg?'

Sawyer smiled, nodded. 'Haven't had it for years.' He tried a chunk. 'Fuck. That is sweet.'

'Even for you?'

He chased the cake with a slug of latte. 'So. Dead end?'

'Parks? I think so.'

'Do some more cross-checking of the people Clara mentioned. Or get Moran on it. All the external visitors, anyone who comes in and out of the home regularly. See if there's the slightest sliver of a link to Yates or Pioneer School.'

Shepherd replaced his cup on the saucer; he struggled a little to settle it in place.

'Your hand is still shaky,' said Sawyer.

'Still?'

'I saw it in the care home office.'

Shepherd nodded, took another drink.

'"Whatever helps". So what's helping you?'

Shepherd sloshed his tea around. 'I see someone. It helps settle things. A sort of debrief. Disinterested.'

Sawyer mock-choked on his cake. 'I don't think I've ever heard someone use that word correctly.'

'I'm seeing a counsellor, sir, not an etymologist.'

'Remind me not to play Scrabble with you, Shepherd.'

'Can we get back to Buxton soon? Appointment.'

Sawyer nodded, took another slurp of latte. 'And it's helping?'

'It is. But remember the panic attacks? From when we first worked together? They came back, with all the stress late last year. I'm starting to recognise the onset now. But I have to work hard to let them pass.'

'Pointless to try and fight it.'

'Yes. Chest tightness, shallow breathing.'

'Do you know what triggers them?'

Shepherd studied the table's wood pattern. 'Not really. It varies. Usually high stress.'

'Does Keating know?'

'He'll just push me onto a TRiM. I'm not quite in his bad books after joining you for the Bowman raid, but he's definitely in a sulk.' He sighed. 'Set me back a few years for the DI track.'

'You won't make DI with untreated mental health issues. I hear there was a complaint over dangerous driving? You and Walker, few days ago?'

Shepherd shook his head. 'That was nothing. Just one of those moments. We all have them. Didn't see the bloke coming. Tree shadows.'

They shared a silence.

Sawyer's phone buzzed with a call.

He stood up, swished his coat around his head and shrugged it over his shoulders. 'Drink up. I'll drop you at Buxton. I've got an appointment, too. Just need to take this.'

Sawyer stepped outside into the car park and walked away from the building, to the roadside verge. He connected the call.

'DI Sawyer,' said Terry Barker.

'Staying healthy?'

Barker laughed. 'Always. Got IDs on Strickland's new best friends. The black lad with the wolf tat is Curtis Mavers. Fresh from a stretch in HMP Manchester. GBH, this time, but he's also got a sheet for theft, assault, weapons, burglary. Younger sister Jayne OD'd a couple of years ago, so he's not a fan of drug dealers. He put her connection in hospital. Kneecapped him with a cricket bat.

Hasn't walked since. He got two years, served eighteen months. No Section 18. Must have had a decent brief.'

'Or a senile judge.'

Sawyer watched a heavily laden hay truck judder around a corner and join a track leading across the moor.

'And who's the thin white duke?'

'Nasty fucker. Levi Wilmot. A wine dealer, no less. That's in his family, at least. Probably a front. He's quite a charmer. Served time in Manchester, too. He's been out longer than Mavers, though. Animal cruelty, burglary with violence, common assault. He was accused of rape but the charge was dropped. Whispers of witness intimidation. He used to be an enforcer for a shark in Sheffield somewhere. Earned him a nickname.'

Sawyer turned; Shepherd had exited the bookshop and walked over to the Mini. 'Go on.'

'The Smiler. Y'know. The Glasgow smile. He had a speciality of using a straight razor to slit his victim from the corner of one mouth up to the ear. And if that didn't get what he wanted, he did the other ear, too. Combined with a kicking to make sure the victim screams and opens the wounds, to leave a deeper scar.'

Sawyer headed back to the Mini. 'I hope this has convinced you to keep your head down. I know you've known Farrell for a long time, but he doesn't strike me as the type to respect old acquaintances when his own head might be on the block.'

Barker scoffed. 'Jokers like this don't scare me, Sawyer.'

'No, but Strickland and Farrell make a gruesome twosome, and it would make their lives a lot tidier if you stopped breathing. Get away for a while. Wait for Strickland to find another toy.'

'I'm fine where I am, thanks. You back on a case?'

'Charles Yates. Tricky one.'

'Call me if you need any help getting back up to speed. I imagine you're a bit rusty after five months chopping logs.'

'I'll bear it in mind.' Sawyer used the transponder to unlock the Mini; Shepherd climbed in. 'Might need more than three days to solve this one, though.'

38

'I thought I might stay up at Irene's for a few days.'

Dorothy Butcher ran a wet cloth over the kitchen surface; her husband stood by the conservatory door, stirring a cup of milky instant coffee.

'Who's Irene?'

Dot tutted. 'I used to work with her. Husband passed away last year.'

Graham slid his feet into a pair of brown leather slippers and shuffled out to his wicker chair. 'The one with the cats?'

'She hasn't got so many now. She can't look after them.'

Dot tidied the kitchen, settling everything back in its designated resting place. Chopping board, knife block, rolling pin. She dropped a used baking tray into the sink and squirted it with washing-up liquid. 'That was a nice steak and kidney. I'll make that again, shall I?'

Graham grunted and flopped into the chair. 'What am I going to do for dinner?'

'When I'm at Irene's?'

He sighed and reached for his copy of the *Daily Mail*. 'Yes, when you're at Irene's.'

'I'll do the fish pie, freeze it.'

The doorbell rang.

Dot walked down the hall. Her gait had become more stooped lately, and she bobbed from side to side with each step, taking a second to make sure each movement was secure before attempting the next.

She opened the door.

A middle-aged woman—slight, with unstyled shoulder-length blonde hair—smiled and raised an ID card for Dot to read. 'Mrs Butcher? I'm a GP at Youlgreave Health Centre. I'm not your personal GP, but I'm just doing the local rounds to survey registered patients in your age group. We want to make sure we're meeting all their needs.'

Dot squinted at the card. It showed a blue-and-white NHS logo and a headshot of the woman standing before her, smiling into camera, wearing a pale pink blouse, with a stethoscope around her neck.

The woman smiled. 'It won't take long.'

'Of course, my dear. Come through.'

Dot led her down the hall.

'Is it just you here?'

'No,' said Dot. 'Me and my husband, Graham. Will you be asking him questions, too? Only he can be a bit tricky.'

'Tricky?'

'Well. Downright rude sometimes, actually.' They stopped in the kitchen. 'I'll get the kettle on.'

'Is it dementia?'

'Oh, I don't know. They say it might be mild cognitive impairment. I don't know what to do with him sometimes, I really don't. Would you like coffee or tea?'

'A tea would be nice. Thank you, Mrs Butcher.'

'We've only got bags.'

'That's fine.'

With difficulty, Dot opened a tin tea caddy and lifted

out a teabag. She reached up to a wall cupboard and took down a squat white mug. 'We don't really need any medical help, Doctor.' She lowered her voice. 'Although I could do with someone looking after him from time to time. Give me a bit of freedom.' She gestured out to Graham, in his garden chair, absorbed in the newspaper.

The woman nodded. 'Of course. How's your own health, Mrs Butcher?'

Dot filled the old-fashioned whistle kettle and set it on the stove. 'Oh, mustn't complain. Nobody would listen if I did.'

The woman took the rolling pin from its place on the kitchen surface and brought it down with full force on the back of Dot's head.

There was a wet crunch, and a spatter of blood across the white surface. Dot lurched forward, jolted by the blow. Her forehead banged into the side of the unit, and she stumbled to the floor, flailing, bringing a tea towel and wall hook down with her.

The woman reached forward to the dividing door between the kitchen and sitting room, and slid it closed.

'Oh dear... Oh dear...'

Dot lay on her front. She gripped the tea towel with both hands and tried to turn.

The woman crouched, lifted the rolling pin high and hit her on the side of her face. Twice, three times.

Dot spasmed for a few seconds, then went still, face down in a slurry of blood and bone, the side and back of her skull collapsed.

The woman gave a gasp, and sprang to her feet. She backed away, holding the dripping rolling pin, staring at Dot's body.

She took a moment to steady her breathing, then slid a heavy chopping knife out of the block.

The kettle began to whistle.

'You making tea, love?'

Graham's voice from the garden.

The woman slid the door aside and strode out to the conservatory.

Graham heard the movement and raised his head from the newspaper, too late.

The woman gripped the knife handle with both hands and buried the blade deep into the side of Graham's neck.

He barked in shock and listed over, falling out of the chair onto the decking, causing the woman to let go of the knife.

Graham's glasses came off, as he groaned and clawed at the air, blood surging from the wound and cascading down his shoulder, spilling over the edge of the decking.

He looked up at his attacker and tried to cry out, but he was drowning, and could only gurgle and retch, spraying blood with each attempt to vocalise.

The woman reached down and yanked out the knife, prompting a rush of blood to burst from the stab wound and puddle in front of her feet.

She stepped back and crouched, watching him in silence, fascinated by the folds of skin on the back of his bloodied hands.

Graham thrashed his feet, and tried to clamp his hands over the wound, which was now leaking heavily, releasing steady eruptions of blood as his panicking heart accelerated, struggling to pump the liquid around his ageing veins, desperately rushing the oxygen to his adrenalised brain.

But the knife had broken the circuit, and his grappling waned, and faded to stillness.

His breathing: a wet rasp.

His yellow cardigan: sopping red, sinking into the gaps between the decking.

And yet, something still burned behind his eyes, fixed on his killer.

The woman leaned in close. 'You know who I am, don't you? Sir.'

39

Sawyer rang the doorbell and turned away from the bungalow front door, surveying the showroom-fresh cars, all diligently slotted into the driveways. In the immaculate garden of the house opposite, a thickset man in bright orange gardening gloves crouched over his flowerbed, prodding the soil with a trowel. Sawyer caught his eye and nodded, but he dropped his gaze, focusing on the flowers.

The door opened and Sawyer turned around.

Justin Perkins stood back from the door, arms folded. He was wearing a blazer and light blue shirt, and had a large towelling plaster over his nose. His cheek was bruised and swollen.

'That your Merc?' said Sawyer, nodding to the green car parked in the drive, now blocked in by Sawyer's orange-and-black Mini.

'What do you want?'

'Sorry to cramp your style with my choice of vehicle.' He smiled. 'Five minutes.'

Justin turned and led Sawyer down the hall into the sitting room. He walked with difficulty, favouring his left leg. Inside, he eased himself down onto the granite-coloured sofa.

Sawyer remained standing. 'I'm sorry about what happened to you,' he said. 'Any word on—'

'Who it was? No.' Justin kept his eyes on Sawyer as he browsed a stack of framed original film posters, leaning against the wall. *Blow Up, The Ipcress File, Quadrophenia.* 'And you're not curious?'

Justin glared at him. 'Of course I am. Why, do you think you can help? I assume you've spoken to Maggie.'

Sawyer nodded.

'Dare I ask where you've been for the past five months?'

'Saving the taxpayer money.'

'How?'

'By avoiding a pointless trial brought about by the death of a man not even a mother could mourn.'

Justin took out a cigarette and lit it with a slim silver lighter. 'So have you popped in with a few hot leads?'

Sawyer took out his phone and navigated to one of Barker's images of Wilmot and Mavers outside the GMP headquarters. He gave the phone to Justin.

'I need to be careful not to ask you leading questions, of course. But, take a look at the men in this picture. What do you see?'

Justin pinch-zoomed the photo, swiped it around.

'Dale Strickland. Deputy Mayor, isn't he?'

'Amazingly, yes. And the other two?'

Justin squinted at the screen, then lowered his gaze for a second. He shook his head and handed the phone back. 'Never seen them before.'

'Maggie said that one of your attackers took off his mask.'

Justin scoffed. 'They beat the shit out of me, Sawyer. I was hardly in a state to take a mental picture for an e-fit.'

'Did they say why they did it? Did they ask for anything? Warn you?'

Justin shook his head, puffed on the cigarette, tapped the ash into a crystal ashtray. 'You know, Sawyer. I thought it was us.'

'Us?'

'Maggie and me. We started out well. Freddy and Mia came along. Our jobs kept us connected but not under each other's feet. But then I started to work criminal cases, and it was like... we'd crossed the streams. Talking shop all the time, differences of opinion. Unhealthy debate. Raised voices. Sex droughts. And all the while, I thought it was us. I thought I'd encroached on her territory, and so I went back to family law, advocacy. But it didn't get better. And I realised it wasn't about us at all.'

'This isn't fair, Justin.'

He puffed out some smoke. 'It was about you, Sawyer. Everything changed when you resurfaced, like a ghost from the fucking past.' He shifted position on the sofa, winced. 'You see, the thing about Maggie... She's one of those people who likes to refine, correct, steer, make good. She likes to save. She's a rescuer. A heart the size of a bus, but not a lot of room in there for anyone she can't fix, tinker with, put right. I suppose it's a trait in everyone who wants to be a therapist. So, in my criminal work, I got to people when it was too late, when the cause was lost. I helped to put them away.'

'Didn't you defend, too?'

'Yes, a few cases. The point is, Maggie is more about reform, reshaping.'

Sawyer looked out of the bay window. The man with the orange gloves was still busy with his soil.

'I see the disconnect, yes.'

Justin gave a dark laugh. 'Ever since you've been back

on the scene, Sawyer, it's all gone to shit for us. Mia, taken by that lunatic. Maggie attacked. Now me. My own son encouraged to punch me in the face.'

'And you think this is all down to my being in the vicinity?'

'Don't be coy.' Justin mashed out the cigarette, prematurely. 'Working in criminal law I came to realise some people just attracted trouble. Many of them even liked it. The drama. It helped them with the idea that they're the centre of the universe.'

'Solipsism.'

He shook his head. 'Narcissism. But the thing with these people is, they always get away with it. They pull the buildings down around them, and they walk out of the fucking rubble without a scratch. Meanwhile the people closest to them suffer. Wives, children, parents.'

'You're angry,' said Sawyer.

'Of course I'm fucking angry. But you wouldn't understand, would you? Because you've been running away all your life, leaving other people to bear the pain.'

'I'll go, Justin.' Sawyer turned, walked to the door. 'I'm sorry you're suffering. I thought I could help.'

———

Justin watched Sawyer climb into the Mini, reverse into the road, and screech away.

He raised his hands up in front of his face; both were shaking.

He walked into the kitchen, grinding his teeth at the sharp pains in his leg and chest, and poured himself a near-full glass of chilled Cloudy Bay. He sipped the wine and gazed out of the kitchen window. Next door's children bounced on their trampoline, their heads bobbing up and down behind the low wooden fence. Their squeals and shouts of joy rang hollow, evoking painful nostalgia. Freddy and Mia and Maggie. A garden picnic. Moment-to-moment living.

Justin set down the wine glass and scrolled through his phone contacts. His hands were settling, but his heart thumped against his aching ribs as he found the number and connected the call.

A voice at the other end. Sonorous, with a Caribbean lilt.

'Who dis?'

'Justin. Justin Perkins. Hello, Glenroy.'

A laugh, loud enough to rattle the plaster. '*Fucking hell*. Bredren Perkins. Long time. Yuh good?'

'Not that long, Glenroy. Not even a year.'

The laugh again. 'True. Don't get too many, I s'pose. Years.'

Justin took a gulp of wine. 'You said to call. If I... needed anything.'

'Brother. I'm a free man 'cause of you. You can name it. Is it paper?'

'Money?'

Another laugh. 'Yeah, yeah. Money.'

'No, I have that.' More wine. 'There's this guy. From a case I worked a while back. I don't think he remembers.'

'This sounds like trouble, my friend. I'm good for trouble, if that's your need.'

'His name is Levi Wilmot.'

A big laugh. 'This boy sounds old-school. You on your regular phone?'

'What? Oh. Yes.'

'Tell you what. Get yourself a burner, call me back. Whatever the gig, I'll consider it a pleasure. Paid in full.'

40

Sawyer pulled the Mini into the expansive car park of the roadside Yondermann Café. He sat there for a while with the windows down, listening, braced by the spectral winds that swooped in over the fields.

Whinnying lambs and admonishing ewes; keening curlews. The whirr of a distant drone.

He got out, walked past the ancient Three Stags' Heads Inn, and climbed the steep track that curved through his home village of Wardlow. As he reached the mini estate of grey-stone semis that lined the road, his thighs strained against the gradient, dropping him back into the past, stirring the muscle memory of a thousand childhood trudges up the same hill.

He passed the footpath that led to the shortcut between his old house and old school, past the grass verge where his mother had taken her final breath, beneath a searing afternoon sun.

Sawyer had expected the horror to engulf him, as it usually did, raking him with its abysmal surrealism. His life and loves collapsing around him; the green, green grass showered in shining red blood, bludgeoned from the body that had once housed and nurtured him.

But today, there was nothing but the unhurried progress of the surroundings; nature busy with its preparations for summer. As complex as necessary, and no more.

He opened the old gate; the same one Jessica stood by in the photo in his wallet. It was freshly painted, but structurally unchanged.

The front door was new, and the sight of the unfamiliar woman who stood in the doorway stirred something close to anger, which faded to despair. In another life, she would have been Jessica, now in her sixties. And they would embrace. And his father would rise from the sofa and greet him with that crunching handshake, and offer his opinion on the Yates case. His mother would have aged elegantly, and Harold would be lumbering but still strong, like a hardy bison.

'Are you Jake?' The woman smiled.

'Yes. Kate?'

She nodded. Mid-fifties. Dark jeans, white fleece. 'I'm glad you got the koala bear. You're a bit old for it now, though.'

'This is the tough exterior. My inner child still runs the show.'

Kate laughed. 'You sound a lot like my husband. He's out in the back garden. He's a National Park ranger.'

'No need to disturb him. I'll be ten minutes. Like I said in my message, I'd just like to take a quick look around. I haven't been here since I started training.'

Sawyer held up his warrant card; the woman leaned in and studied it. Her greying blonde hair had been tugged into a loose ponytail, with two curtains hanging down over her cheeks.

She stepped aside and he walked in, wiping his feet on the *WELCOME* mat.

'I'll be in the kitchen. Just bagging up a few old things for the dump. I'm so very sorry for your loss, Mr Sawyer.'

'Which one?'

'Your father. I sent the package, and your brother told me—'

'Ah. Yes. Thank you.' He put a hand on the carved sphere at the end of the banister rail; it felt tiny in his adult hands. 'Do you mind if I go upstairs? My old room...'

Kate turned and walked towards the kitchen at the rear. 'No problem at all. Take your time. You might be investigated by a curious cat called Ozzy, but he's harmless.'

Sawyer smiled and climbed the stairs in a daze, slipping further back into the past.

The house had been extensively redecorated, but the fittings remained familiar. The patterned, Moroccan-style carpet—loved by his mother, hated by his father—had been replaced by exposed oak floorboards, suspiciously distressed.

He peered around the door of his parents' old room. Double bed, made to military precision. White bedding, blue pillows. New sliding-door wardrobe, ochre rug. Harold and Jessica preferred the headboard beneath the window, but Kate and her husband had moved theirs into the centre of the adjacent wall.

He walked across the landing and entered his old bedroom. It was now clearly being used as a spare, with a cheap-looking bedside table, functional lamp, grey mattress cover, no bedding or pillows.

Could buildings be changed by the emotion experienced by those who lived in them? Tainted by their suffering. Sentimental nonsense, of course, but the memories still rose in him, dredging up the pain.

The tears he had spilled in here. The impotent rage.

He walked to the far end of the landing and entered his mother's old study. It had been refitted as a contemporary office room. Upcycled wooden desk, iMac, printer. A vast bookcase covered the wall to the right of the door, with a shorter unit pushed up against the left, stuffed with box files, more books.

Sawyer studied the wall above the smaller bookcase. It had been repainted in clear white, but a tiny blemish still sat in the centre where the bracket for his mother's mirror had been fixed. The bookcase had been slotted in over the top of the old fireplace, and the shelf above the hearth was scattered with knick-knacks and bits of stationery.

He listened.

Clattering pans in the kitchen, cupboard doors opening and closing.

Sawyer took out a pair of latex gloves and snapped them onto his hands.

He crouched and gently eased the bookcase forward, disturbing a puff of dust. The fireplace was a small arch, built into the original masonry, with a sliding metal tray beneath the hearth for collecting ash. The grill above the tray was crusted with rust, and although the chimney had been blocked long ago, the flue retained the faint metallic whiff of old soot, preserved by condensation.

Sawyer ducked down, rolled up his sleeves and reached up into the hearth, feeling around the back wall of the flue. He crawled his fingers around to the front wall and his hand brushed against a shelf-like protrusion, thick with powdery grime.

He probed further, and his hand fell on something smooth and yielding. Vinyl. Maybe polythene.

He eased the object away from the shelf and pinched it

between his fingers, bringing it down and out of the opening.

It was a clear plastic folder, with a series of press-studs down the length. Sawyer wiped the dust away into the fireplace, opened the bag and took out a small hardback notebook with a dark orange cover and a white label, neatly handwritten.

Jessica Mary Sawyer
My life and thoughts

He stared at the words, holding his breath, as if to exhale might erase them.

A male voice downstairs. More noise from the kitchen.

Sawyer steadied his breathing and opened the book. Age had warped the edges of the paper, but the bag had kept it structurally preserved.

Instinct nagged him to tuck the book away, out of sight, to study later. But he couldn't wait; he had to catch a glimpse now, reclaim the marks his mother had made for herself.

He turned the pages at random. The book was a diary of sorts, with some pages dated, some entries timed. Some corners had doodles, sweeping curves, calligraphic elaborations of a central image; usually a simple heart shape, occasionally a five-pointed star with curled edges.

For the first thirty or so pages, dated 1974 to 1983, the entries were strictly sequential and written in rich, thoughtful prose, but as the dates moved deeper into the 1980s, they became erratic, more note form.

Sawyer replaced the bookcase and sat cross-legged on the floor, browsing the diary at random. As he read, his mother transformed in his mind, blooming from a source of torment—a figurehead of unfathomable loss—into something separate, independently alive, brimming with ambition and desire, buffeted by confusion, contradiction, yearning.

She had noted all the major waypoints: the completion of her teacher training in 1974 and her starting work at Pioneer Primary; her promotion from assistant to full-time teacher in 1976; marrying Harold in 1977; Michael's birth in 1980.

And in 1982...

Michael 'helped' me to change his new baby brother... I am still so tired and pulled all over the place by the birth and I can't believe I have made two beautiful boys. It blows my mind. They didn't exist and now they do exist... Mikey was never a good sleeper but little Jake is so good. He goes down so nicely. He sometimes lies awake for a while, staring at me with those gorgeous green eyes, kicking his little legs like he's running. But then I sing to him, and he settles.

Sawyer flipped forward, to the last entry, around two thirds of the way into the notebook: a drawing of a heart, surrounded by an expanding array of curlicued tendrils, reaching up and out, entwining back around the central heart shape.

The male voice again, downstairs.

'...kids up at Peter's Stone. Third time we've been up there this week.'

The voice moved further to the front of the house, and the door opened and closed.

In 1976, Jessica wrote about the long, hot summer: a solstice mini festival up at Nine Ladies Circle on Stanton Moor; a Slade concert at Sheffield University; a holiday with Harold to Brittany; heatwave grass fires, drought, wedding plans.

Early in the summer term, she began to write about her passion for children's welfare, fuelled by her outrage at the mistreatment and manslaughter of a seven-year-old girl, Maria Colwell, by her stepfather.

Her work-related entries showed further concern for child protection, particularly the methods of corporal punishment at Pioneer, and she began a campaign for reform that appeared to have received little support from her fellow teachers.

Sawyer browsed this section.

Miss Briscoe is wonderful, but nobody else seems to care...

Mr Welch's Friday caning sessions at Assembly seem like something from Victorian times. The looks on those poor children's faces when they know they're next in line...

And it's not just Friday. I see plenty of them going up to Mr Welch's office in the week. Steven Frain, Gary Latham. They're regulars up in the 'lair', as we call it. And little Michelle. She's being called up there a lot lately. It worries me the way Mr Welch closes the blind on his office when he's punishing the children. Someone should complain and put a stop to it.

'How are you getting on, Mr Sawyer?' Kate called from downstairs.

'Very good, thank you,' he shouted back. 'That was really helpful.'

41

Sawyer strode into the packed MIT briefing room and took his seat at the head of the table. He nodded at Shepherd, sitting next to him.

Shepherd activated the multiscreen system and navigated to a preloaded gallery of images. All the attendants' screens lit up with the hero shot: a gauzy photo of a dark-brick building set below street level, behind a line of slender railings.

'What's this?' said Sally, browsing the accompanying images: a vast playground with flat-roofed equipment huts; an assembly hall with a window above a tall stage; a gatepost with a mottled red-and-white plaque: *PIONEER PRIMARY SCHOOL.*

'This,' said Sawyer, 'is the new main focus of our enquiry into the Yates case. Pioneer Primary, Wardlow. Opened in 1922, closed in 1996. Yates taught there from the late 1960s until his retirement in 1999.'

Shepherd activated another gallery: a grid of headshots, four men and two women. 'Ex-staff and teachers. Charles Yates, Maths. Felix Parks, Music. Both deceased. Graham Butcher, English. Norman Welch, head teacher. The women are Anita Birch, an admin assistant who now lives in Canada, and Carol Briscoe, Art. She's still alive, and local.'

Moran sighed. 'This is all fascinating, but what does it mean?'

Sawyer tapped his screen. 'This man, Felix Parks. He died in a care home outside Leek three days ago. Natural causes, but I've asked Frazer Drummond to conduct an urgent PM.'

'Why?' said Myers, frowning at the screen.

'Because I think someone wants these people dead, and I'd like to know why. It's too late for two of them, but I want to look deeper into the culture of the school and try to establish a deeper link between the two deceased men, which might extend to the others. Then, apprehend this person before they get to the other four.'

'Sawyer...' Moran took off his wire-framed glasses and rubbed at his eyes. 'I thought we were supposed to be elite detectives investigating major crimes. I'm still not seeing any actual crimes.'

Sawyer forced a smile. 'Moran, as an elite detective, I'd be shocked if you weren't at least a little bit curious about an intruder who feels the need to stab a dead body in the throat and eyes. As I've said before, I think this person arrived at Yates's place with intent to murder. They found his body, recently deceased, and, frustrated that they couldn't do the job themself, stabbed in anger, then tried to make it look like a burglary. Possibly to buy time.'

Walker looked up from his screen. 'Why now?'

'How do you mean?' said Shepherd.

'If somebody connected to the school wants the ex-teachers dead for whatever reason, they've had a long time to do it.'

'Half a century,' said Myers.

'Yes. So why wait until they're all approaching the end of their lives?'

'I've received information that the school had a closed culture. Unhealthy. Possibly even secretive. Discipline was reinforced with brutal corporal punishment. The headmaster, Welch, had a ritual where he would carry out canings in front of the school at Friday morning assembly. I want to know more about it. There are secrets here, and we need to focus and work smarter to shake them out. DC Myers, DC Moran. Call all the junior detectives away from their other work and put them onto victimology for the ex-teachers. Find out as much about them as possible. Walker, go back and see the charming Mr Butcher. More robust questioning.'

Walker ran a palm across his forehead. 'He'll love that.'

'DS Shepherd. Go and see Norman Welch, the head. I know that corporal punishment was legal until the mid-1980s, but I'd like to find out Welch's views on it. Confront him with the Friday morning ritual. Maybe we're looking for a parent or pupil with a grudge. I'll call in on the art teacher, Carol Briscoe.' Sawyer sprang to his feet.

'Can I ask, sir,' said Moran, 'where you've received this information on the school's culture?'

'You just did,' said Sawyer, heading for the door.

―――――

Back in his office, Sawyer closed the blinds that looked out on the MIT office, and did the same for the blind covering the window that looked down on the street.

He scrolled through the contact list on his phone and tapped Maggie's name. The call rang for a while; no answer.

Mid-morning sunlight filtered in around the edges. Sawyer sat back in his chair, basking in the golden gloom.

He took his mother's book out of the desk drawer and turned the brittle pages with great care.

'I tried to write in it every day,' said Jessica, sitting in shade at the circular table in the far corner of the office. 'But I don't think my life was interesting enough to sustain that.'

Sawyer looked up. His mother's long dark hair cascaded over her left shoulder, onto the tabletop. She swished it back and forth across the surface.

He could see the whites of her eyes, her gaze fixed on him.

'Plenty of people would trade thrills for stability.'

She smiled. 'I'm not here, Jake. You know that. I'm you.'

'I know. I wish I could ask you questions, though.'

'You're close. With the school. It was a nasty place. When Marcus started there, it made things more bearable for me.'

'You know this because I know this.'

'I don't know anything anymore. I'm not here, remember?' Jessica toyed with the blanket of hair. 'I had my time, as we all do. A tiny blip in the history of the universe. Your time will be up one day, too. Unlike me, you can shape your journey towards that moment. But not if you keep looking back, dredging the lake. I'm part of your old story, Jake. You have to let that go and start your own. Focus on what you can control, on what you can change. *You*. Narrate a new story. Start a new chapter. That's the problem with always looking back. You can't see where you're going.'

Sawyer smiled. 'I like that. Did I just make that up or is it a quote from somewhere?'

'Don't waste your adulthood trying to reclaim the love you feel was denied in childhood. Find someone who can help you write that new story. Someone who doesn't represent a version of what's gone. Like me.' Jessica closed her eyes. 'No, I'm not here. And I never will be again. I might not be able to tell you in person anymore, but there's something that will always be true. I will always love you.'

His phone buzzed.

Maggie.

He tapped the call accept button, looked up to the table in the corner.

No Jessica.

'Hi,' said Maggie. 'Sorry. Just finished with a client. What's up?'

Sawyer pushed himself upright and walked to the window. 'I saw Justin.'

'He said. I'm not sure there's a lot to be gained—'

'I showed him some pictures. The men I think attacked him. Dale Strickland was in the pictures. He knew Strickland, but there were another two in the shots. I could tell that Justin recognised them, or one of them.' He re-opened the blind, squinting into the light.

'Okay…'

'It's even more worrying that he didn't want me to know about the one he recognised. He's angry. Humiliated.'

'Of course he is.'

'You should talk to him.'

'Should I?'

'You should make sure he doesn't do anything stupid.'

42

Terry Barker slid the bolts away, opened his front door and smiled.

'Bright and early, Robin.'

Farrell stepped into the hallway and closed the door behind him. Barker's old Labrador waddled through, wagging its tail; Farrell ignored it and walked past, into the sitting room.

'Why don't you come in? Can I get you a coffee?'

Farrell shook his head; Barker followed him inside.

'How busy are you?' said Farrell.

'Well, as you can see, it's a hive of activity—'

'Can you get away for a while?'

Barker laughed and crashed down into the brown leather sofa. 'Robin. I'm not scared of Dale Strickland.'

Farrell steadied himself. 'Please listen. This is messy. People like Strickland don't like mess. But in his world, he's a general. He doesn't like to get his hands dirty. And he has two keen new foot soldiers.'

'I've seen them. I've already been warned about them.'

Farrell sat down. 'What?'

'Look. Sawyer outmanoeuvred everybody, practically by default. We should have been bolder. Sent in a team. You should have been bolder, Robin. We showed him too much respect. We held off. It's the chess analogy. We had an advantage, but we didn't capitalise. We've let him set the tempo. And now he's back, and we move on. And if you think I'm in Strickland's sights because of Sawyer, then you are, too.'

Farrell held his head in his hands. 'No, no. Strickland wants me to help him with something. That's the point. That's why I'm here. I'm useful to him. Mutually assured destruction. You can only be a problem for him. And, no disrespect, Terry, but your demise wouldn't register too far up front in the *Manchester Evening News*.'

The dog came over to Barker; he patted it. 'Unless my demise linked me to further revelations about our time at Wakefield.'

Farrell leaned forward. 'I helped you. That was your private...' He snorted. 'Your weakness.'

'And yours, too.'

Farrell lowered his voice. 'It would have been much worse for you if I hadn't eased your exit.'

'Yes, but you kept your position, your standing, while I was cast out. Robin, I get the feeling that you're more here to save yourself than to protect me.'

A knock at the door.

They eyed each other.

'Expecting anyone?' said Farrell.

'Maybe some post.' Barker got up. He settled the dog and walked to the door.

Farrell stood at the sound of a familiar voice.

'Terence Barker.'

He closed the sitting room door quietly, looked around. No obvious alternative exit. The only other way out was down the hall to the back door, but the visitors would see that.

A different voice, also familiar.

'Can we come in for a few minutes?'

The dog fussed against the door, thrashing its tail against the floor.

Heavy footsteps in the hall.

A crash. Something heavy falling.

The dog barked and scratched.

Voices, consternation.

The front door closed.

Farrell stepped back, putting the dog between himself and the sitting room door as it flew open.

Curtis Mavers stepped through and grabbed the dog by its collar. It snarled and yelped, as he dragged it out of the sitting room, down the hall into the kitchen, closing the door behind it.

Levi Wilmot shoved Barker through into the sitting room and forced him down onto the armchair. Barker's nose was bloodied.

'Ah! A vinyl man.' Mavers reappeared. He walked past Farrell and browsed through the shelf of records beneath the turntable and speakers. 'It's all a bit *white*, Terry. Black people make good music, too, you know. Don't get me wrong. I love ELO—'

'You followed me,' said Farrell.

Mavers grinned. 'Old-school.'

'We appreciate you making the introduction, DCI Farrell,' said Wilmot. 'But this is a private conversation.' He twirled his finger in the air. 'So, if you wouldn't mind... You know. Fucking off.'

Barker leapt to his feet; Wilmot shoved him back into the chair and hit him with a full-force right cross. He leapt away, dancing in place, holding his fist.

'*Fuck!* Caught him on the jawbone.'

The dog scrabbled and yelped in the kitchen.

Farrell stumbled towards the sitting room door.

Mavers stood in his way. 'DCI Farrell. Let's be clever, yes? We weren't here. Neither were you.'

Wilmot tucked his fist into his armpit, wincing. 'I mean, you can stick around and help us out, if you like. For jollies.' He looked around. 'This is a delightful abode, but I've no desire to hang around any longer than necessary. Many hands, and all that.'

Barker lunged off the armchair and reached under the shelving unit, feeling for something. Wilmot pulled out a length of cord and wrapped it around his neck, dragging him back, up into the chair. Mavers held Barker, as Wilmot crouched and reached beneath the unit.

Wilmot pulled out a cricket bat and held it aloft, laughing. 'Howzat?' He smiled at Barker who watched from the chair, panting. 'Thanks, Terence. This should come in handy. We might use it to put that lump of lard in the kitchen out of its misery. Once we've trimmed the main bit of fat, of course.' He crouched down at the side of the chair, close to Barker's face. 'Don't feel too bad. You had your fun, didn't you? Some of it might be viewed as a little problematic, these days. But you probably gave as much as you took. And you got plenty of worse people off the streets.'

Barker pulled out a handkerchief and mopped at his nose. He stared at Wilmot, glassy eyed, pale with fear. 'Okay. I'll go.' He glanced up at Farrell. 'I'll go away. I won't be a problem.' Eyes back to Wilmot. '*Please.*'

'Don't,' said Mavers. 'Don't beg. He likes that.'

The dog whined and scratched.

Wilmot held the bat with both hands, striking at the air; a practice swing. 'A silly young slut once told me to stop.

Pleaded with me. She said she was a virgin.' He laughed, shrill and cruel. 'As if that wasn't an incentive.'

Mavers stepped aside, nodded to Farrell.

Farrell caught Barker's eye for a second, then turned and hurried out to the front door.

43

Sawyer strode across the MIT floor and stopped at the small windowless office in the far corner. He tapped three times and opened the door without waiting for a response.

Sally O'Callaghan sat with her back to the door, gaze fixed on one of the monitors lined across the back wall. 'No need to show off on my account, Sawyer.'

'Sorry?'

She turned, smiled. 'The dramatic arrival. Knock and enter. You could have caught me in a compromising situation.'

He took a seat. 'I think that's just a basic lack of office etiquette. And I wasn't expecting the occupant to be wearing a fitted white rollneck underneath a scarlet blazer from...' He waggled his head. 'Karen Millen?'

She sat back. 'Ralph Lauren. Sorry to disappoint. I'm sure you prefer to fantasise about me in my Tyvek chic.'

'It's the lack of moustache that really threw me.'

'Rhodes and I share this office now. I occasionally have to tweezer an apple core out of the bin, but it works.'

'I was going to check in on passive data. Phone mast

pings at a care home near Leek. Cross-ref with the Yates scene. Same for ANPR.'

Sally made a note. 'On it. Rhodes is in later. I'll pass it on. Once he's relieved me of his latest offering.' She nodded at a crumpled tissue beside the CCTV analysis monitor.

Sawyer winced. 'Surely that's not—'

'Christ al-fucking-mighty, Sawyer. I hadn't even considered that. I assumed he'd blown his nose.'

'The shoe print. From the Yates scene. Depending on what we get from passive, I might need you to do a sweep of the care home. Surroundings, inside a specific room.'

'Your wish is my command. As long as it's legal, of course.'

A knock on the door. Shepherd.

'Sir. Thought I saw you come in. Keating for you. On video, in the conference room.'

Sally smiled. 'You can have one of my weighty forensics books to stuff down the back of your trousers if you like.'

'Sally, you have a lovely way of making an offer sound like a threat.'

Sawyer got up and walked through to the central conference room.

'DI Sawyer.' Keating's voice greeted him as he entered and closed the door.

'Sir.' He sat down, at one of the central console chairs with active camera and mic.

On the main screen, Keating glowered into the camera. He sat at the front of a generic hotel room, with a made bed in the background, beneath a vast and insipid watercolour.

'How's the conference, sir?'

'Ghastly. Recruitment and retention, diversity and public engagement. I have a session this afternoon called The Workforce Well-Being Agenda.' He took a sip from a teacup. 'Drummond called me, wanted to set this up. He's joining us soon.'

'So, does this make Drummond Mum?'

'How do you mean?'

'You've clearly told him to keep an eye on me while you're away. Channel any crucial outcomes through you.'

Keating sighed.

Sawyer smiled. 'I'd do the same, sir.'

'Would you now? Well, it's good to know that our brilliant minds are in sync. While we wait, I got a call from the Met Homicide and Serious Crime Command. Your old gaffer.'

'DCI Hatfield?'

'Yes. They have to run eighteen regional MITs down there, these days. Hatfield's team, MIT 7, have been assigned a diabolical case. Quadruple murder, Hammersmith. Hatfield's team is under the cosh and they're looking for a brilliant detective to take a temporary transfer.'

Sawyer smiled. 'And while they do that, they've asked if I'm available.'

A blank window in the corner of the conference screen opened to show the sombre, underlit face of Frazer Drummond.

'Obviously, you and I could do with a debrief,' Keating continued. 'But it'll have to wait.'

Sawyer gaped in mock surprise. 'Oh. So I've already had a think about it?'

'You have. And I'm pleased to report that you've agreed. I take it that suits your current domestic situation?'

Sawyer nodded.

'You can regain some brownie points after the Bowman mess. And I'm considering a bump for Shepherd.'

'DI?'

'Yes. A shuffle up the ladder. In normal circumstances, I'd say you should make a push for DCI. But I think we need a cooling-off period. See how this Hatfield transfer goes, too.'

Drummond waved at his screen, mouthing something.

Keating pointed to the bottom right corner. 'You're on mute, Frazer.'

Drummond crackled into life. '...bastard fucking...'

'There he is,' said Sawyer.

'Oh. Thank fuck.' Drummond tipped his head back. 'Are we three private here?'

'We are,' said Keating. 'Let's crack on. I have a seminar on the future of the force in fifteen minutes.'

'Robots?' said Drummond. 'Hope so. Let them do all the work while we run out the clock in Bermuda.' He took a breath and looked down, off camera, browsing something. 'Sawyer. This hurts, but it can't be denied. Whatever kind of consciousness-expanding retreat you've been on for the past five months, it hasn't blunted your brilliant mind.'

Sawyer sat up. 'Go on.'

'Felix Parks. The least natural case of natural causes I've ever encountered. He was carrying a shit-ton of diamorphine. I once saw a stomach-churning leg break back in medical school. A middle-aged Dutch vicar who went cross country skiing and suffered a horrific open fracture of the femur. He was a big lad, around seventeen stone, and he only got 15mg diamorphine, over a five-minute period. Parks was eighty years old, nine stone soaking wet, and some kind soul loaded him with, I'd say, 35mg. It would have knocked him out instantly, and he would have stopped breathing soon after. And, as we know, more than three minutes of not breathing isn't good for your health.'

'Could it be self-administered?' said Sawyer.

'Kudos for the belt and braces, Sawyer. But not in this

case. Bruising around the jaw indicates he was held down. Two injection points in his right shoulder. First jab to sedate him, second to give him the good news. Now, I know what you're both thinking.'

'Shipman,' said Keating.

'Indeed. The upstanding Dr Shipman violated his Hippocratic oath in a similar way, doing a lot of harm to at least fifteen victims.'

'They estimate he could have killed over two hundred,' said Keating.

'Birthday cake,' said Sawyer.

Drummond frowned. 'Sorry?'

'The care home manager said the member of staff who found him saw that Parks had knocked a piece of birthday cake to the floor. Probably in the struggle. So. No initial PM because of no apparent suspicious circumstances. On-call doctor attends, funeral director collects the body... It was their regular GP who attended, right? Did they register the death?'

Drummond looked down again, off-screen.

'Yes. Dr Michelle Hawkins.'

44

Norman Welch peered into the pilot light window of his ageing boiler. He pounded the ignition button a few times and the blue flame flared.

He grunted in approval and exited the outhouse, returning to the narrow, boxy kitchen. Welch was hunched and rotund, but not ponderous. He moved with short, rapid steps; something close to a scuttle. The years had warped his features into a wrinkled permascowl, gathered around a vast, pock-marked nose, flushed red by his appetite for daytime beer and night-time gin and Martini.

He yanked open the wall cupboard and took a packet of Senior Service from an imported stash, then scurried into the sitting room, muttering to himself.

Yelps and squeals filtered in from the street through his net-curtained window. Children, heading home from the Monyash village school. Welch blinked at the flashes of primary colour from their bags, uniforms, hair. He edged closer to the window and indulged in his daily ritual of disapproval: peering out through the gap in the curtain, watching the children as they frolicked and wrestled, swinging their shoulder bags, jostling for each other's attention.

He took a sour kind of solace in scripture, which often drifted into his mind as he stared.

Man that is born of a woman hath but a short time to live, and is full of misery.

He took down the heavy, flat-based vintage table lighter from his single shelf of books, and jerked his thumb along the sparking dial once, twice.

Nothing. Out of gas.

He turned and headed back to the kitchen.

In the midst of life we are in death.

The doorbell rang. Welch cursed, changing course, back across the sitting room to the front door.

He pressed his nose into the space beneath the peephole and saw a fish-eye image of a middle-aged woman with shoulder-length blonde hair. She was formally dressed in a light blue blouse and black jacket, carrying a small leather bag.

Welch opened the door, his bulk filling the frame.

'Mr Welch?' The woman smiled.

'Depends.'

'I'm sorry?'

'Why don't you tell me who you are first? Then I'll let you know who I am.'

Another smile, broader. 'Ah. Of course. I'm the community doctor from the Youlgreave Medical Centre.' She held up the ID card with headshot and blue-and-white NHS logo. Welch poked his head forward, close to the card. He studied it for a few seconds then stood back.

'And what do you want?'

'Well, I'm not your regular GP, but I'm doing the rounds to survey registered patients in your age group. We want to make sure we're providing an optimum service.'

Welch looked at the card, then at the woman. 'I think I've seen you at the centre. You seem familiar.'

She smiled again. 'I'm sure you have. Do you mind if I pop inside? It'll only take a few minutes.'

Welch indulged in a deep, deep breath. 'Yes. Yes, I do mind. I'm resting. I try not to commit to anything in the latter part of the day.'

'Oh. It really wouldn't take up too much time.'

Welch retreated. 'I'll tell you exactly how much time it will take. None. Nil. You can't just turn up and walk into my house. There's been no letter about this. Nothing.'

'Honestly. It'll be quick and painless, I assure you. Once I'm gone, you'll never see me again.'

She took a tentative step forward, but Welch eased the door shut, speaking through the gap as it closed.

'Give me a bit of notice and I might let you in next time.'

He closed the door, latched the chain into its groove, and hurried back into the house, heading for the kitchen.

———

Michelle Hawkins sighed and turned away from the front door. She walked to the end of the path opposite the small village green, and looked back at Welch's house.

Two storeys, stone-built, set behind a drystone wall.

Behind, a car swished through the afternoon drizzle towards Bakewell.

She walked down the side road and turned into the entryway that ran along the back of Welch's house, with low gates opening onto the back of his and four other properties.

Michelle found the corresponding gate—numbered 14,

like the front door—and turned the black metal latch ring, taking care not to make unnecessary noise.

The latch raised, and she slipped into a well-tended back garden, with a crazy paving pathway and a neat set of steps that led down to the sunken back door.

She stepped into the shade behind a ramshackle shed, and watched Welch through the kitchen window, searching through drawers. It looked like the sitting room was adjacent to the kitchen, which would make it difficult to get inside undetected, even if the back door was unlocked.

Through the window of the shed, Michelle could see an extendable ladder, slid along the back of a work bench.

She looked up to the first floor window.

Vertical sash, open a few inches.

It was too risky to do anything in daylight, and there was still some time to go until dusk.

She would wait.

She could cope with a couple more hours.

She had already waited forty-six years.

45

Levi Wilmot browsed the bottles in the rack on top of the fridge. Lagavulin, Glenmorangie, a selection of high-end reds.

'Strickland keeping you in good supply, then.'

Curtis Mavers leaned back on the sofa. 'Fill your boots. We're men of leisure until next week.'

Wilmot walked into the sitting room. 'What's happening next week?'

'New gig, up in Sale. Bigger fish, this time. I might be forced to secure your mask with gaffer tape.'

Wilmot stood over Mavers and swept his arm around the room. 'So is this all yours now, then? Home sweet home in an upper middle-class part of Didsbury. Sparsely furnished. A little show home-like, but with excellent transport links to the city centre. I mean, do you *live* here, Curtis?'

Mavers smiled and sipped from his glass, rattled the ice cubes. 'We've come a long way from B Wing. That was hell on Earth for a sophisticated man like me, having to share with a brute like you.'

Wilmot laughed. 'Fuck off. You're the snorer. Took me

three weeks to get earplugs into that place.' He rubbed a hand over his knuckles. 'How's your medicine cabinet?'

Mavers stood up, drained his glass. 'Has he bruised his ickle knuckles on the chin of the bad man? Kitchen drawer. I'm off for a slash.'

He disappeared into the bathroom at the end of a long corridor adjacent to the sitting room. Wilmot rummaged in a kitchen drawer and pulled out a roll of bandages.

Two knocks on the front door. Not cautious. *Boom, boom.*

Wilmot walked back across the sitting room and opened the door.

Heavy hands shoved him backwards, sending him sprawling against the edge of the sofa.

Two men, tall and wide, stepped in. Both were black, one in a white muscle-fit T-shirt with a chin-strap beard and teardrop tattoo, the other more formally dressed: grey waistcoat, fingers loaded with bulky rings, close-cropped hair dyed blond on top.

The blond one closed the door behind them.

Wilmot scrambled to his feet and pulled out his cut-throat razor.

The bearded man recoiled in mock shock, sniggering. 'Gonna give us a shave, boss?'

The other one held up his hand, palm out. 'Put it down.'

Wilmot kept the razor out. 'And who the fuck might you be?'

The blond man took a stroll to the window; Mavers's flat was five floors up, but he closed the blind anyway. 'Friends of someone you shouldn't have fucked with.'

'And who might that be?'

The blond man turned. 'Where's Mavers?'

'Out.'

'Can you be more specific?'

Wilmot shrugged. 'I'm not his keeper.'

The bearded man rushed Wilmot, gripped the arm holding the cut-throat razor.

Wilmot managed to swipe the blade across the man's cheek. Blood splashed over his white T-shirt.

The man drilled a punch into Wilmot's stomach, doubling him over, forcing him to drop the razor. Wilmot rose up, tried a headbutt, but the man was ready: he swayed backwards, out of Wilmot's range, and pivoted forward, swinging a hook punch around and into Wilmot's face, dropping him onto the floor.

He held a hand to his cheek. Blood oozed from a short slash wound.

Wilmot crouched on the floor, laughing. 'You're welcome. That'll come up nicely.'

The man hit him again and he crawled away, out of range.

The blond man raised his hand. He nodded to the bearded man, who walked into the kitchen.

'Okay. Here's the deal. Tell us where Mavers is, and I'll let you keep your teeth. Keep this shit up, and it'll be elbows first, then your knees.' He pulled a heavy-looking lump hammer from a bag.

Wilmot scowled. 'And what about the screaming? This is a residential area.'

The man laughed. 'We'll take a trip to our lock-up first. Nice and padded. Middle of nowhere.'

The bearded man emerged from the kitchen with a strip of bloodied bandage tied awkwardly around his cheek.

Wilmot laughed again. 'That's not a good look, my friend. Might start a new gay trend, though.'

The bearded man grabbed Wilmot under his chin and lifted him up until his legs scurried in place, a few inches above the wooden floor. He squeezed Wilmot's neck, making his face flush.

The blond one hustled Wilmot's arms behind his back and tied his wrists together with cord. His friend pushed Wilmot face-first over the coffee table, holding him firm.

The blond man held Wilmot's wrists and crouched to the side, wielding the lump hammer. He lightly tapped the metal head of the hammer on Wilmot's elbows a couple of times. 'I hope you owe this Mavers boy big. Last chance. Where is he?'

Wilmot's breathing was quick and ragged. He squeezed his eyes shut, as if bracing, then cried out, shrill and desperate. *'Curtis!'*

A movement at the end of the corridor. Both men turned.

Mavers stood a few feet away, pointing the Glock, with a silencer fitted. 'Who's this friend who you're willing to risk your fucking lives for?'

The men stood off Wilmot.

The blond one lowered his head and glared at Mavers. 'Y'think that's a good plan?'

Mavers nodded, calm. 'I shoot you, bury your bodies. Seems solid.'

The blond man hissed a laugh through his teeth. 'Our boys know we're here. We don't come back, they send more.'

'I'll shoot them, too. Got plenty of bullets.'

The bearded man spoke up. 'You don't want to do this.'

Mavers took a couple of steps towards them, jabbing the gun forward. He raised his voice, close to a shout. 'Oh! You *know* me, then? You know what I want to do?' He held the gun on the bearded man, but spoke to the other. 'So, go on. Give me a clue. Who okayed this? Who's paying for your little hammer and your stupid barnet?' Mavers moved in and dug the barrel of the gun under the chin of the blond man. 'Who's pulling your strings, soft lad?' He pushed the gun in harder, causing the man to tilt his head back. 'And is he really worth dying for?'

Mavers paused for a few seconds, holding the moment. He backed away, then pointed the gun at the bearded man's shoulder and squeezed the trigger.

A muffled thud as the gun discharged. The man jerked to the side and crashed into the wall, howling in pain. He crouched, back to the door, holding his shoulder.

Mavers trained the gun on the blond man. 'The same is coming to you, Paul Pogba. Unless you can answer my question.' He took a step closer. 'I'll give you one go. I know who it is. You know that I know. So if your answer doesn't match the name in my head, I'm going to do some damage.'

The blond man looked down at his colleague, then turned his raging gaze to Mavers. 'Mr Valance.'

Mavers nodded. 'Glenroy Valance? Yardie drug scum. Never had problems with him, though.' He aimed the gun between the blond man's legs. 'So, I'm wondering what's motivated him to send you two clowns to rough us up.' He smiled. 'I think you know, soft lad. So, let's have one more name, yeah? You can either give it to me now, or you can give it to me after I've put a bullet in your bollocks. Penetrating trauma.' He sucked in a breath. 'Not good. I saw a lad with that once. Shotgun spray. No more sex. No hard-ons, see? What's left of it was just hanging there, like a limp balloon. They had to cut a hole into his bladder to make a permanent catheter. That can't be much fun, can it?'

The blond man blinked, his expression wavering.

Mavers stepped forward, keeping the gun aimed between the blond man's legs. 'So, can I trouble you for that name? I promise I won't tell your boss. And then you can fuck off out of my house, and you won't have to piss through a plastic tube for the rest of your life.'

The blond man lowered his gaze. 'Some guy called Justin.'

46

Sawyer tapped on his touchscreen. The image of a middle-aged blonde woman appeared on the consoles of the detectives gathered in the MIT conference room.

'Michelle Hawkins. Fifty-five. GP. Based at Youlgreave Medical Centre. Recently signed off, stress-related. Lives alone in the nearby village. There's nobody at her house, but it does look lived in. We have an unmarked car observing.' He swiped the screen, revealing the image of Pioneer Primary School with inset photos of the ex-staff.

Shepherd picked up. 'The man bottom-left, Felix Parks, died three days ago at Padwick Farm Care Home. Initially registered as natural causes, but a subsequent PM has revealed a massive dose of diamorphine. Hawkins was the attending GP and she registered the death.'

Walker sucked in a breath. 'Could it be an accidental OD?'

'Not at that dosage,' said Sawyer.

'This is like Harold Shipman,' said Myers. 'I thought there were extra checks in place for this kind of thing, these days. Safeguarding against malpractice.'

'There are,' said Shepherd. 'All deaths are now referred

to a medical examiner for approval. In Parks's case, the ME concluded that there was no need for a PM. The decision is based on family records, family requirements. Parks had multiple conditions, so the ME was happy with Hawkins's death certificate.'

Moran sat forward. 'So, what's this got to do with the school?'

'Victimology,' said Sawyer. 'Also, potential motive. Yates was a teacher there, as was Parks. As mentioned at the last briefing, we have three more ex-Pioneer teachers still alive and living relatively local. Norman Welch, Carol Briscoe, Graham Butcher...'

'Heading back to Butcher's after this,' said Walker.

Shepherd nodded. 'Same, for Welch.'

'Michelle Hawkins was a pupil at the school from 1973 to 1977,' said Sawyer. 'When we gain access to her, we can cross-reference her footwear to see if it's a match for the shoeprint found at Yates's place. But we need more on motive. The Yates stabbing suggests frustration and anger at finding him already dead, which implies that Michelle had some kind of personal issue with him. She went to a lot of trouble getting a private encounter with Felix Parks, to administer the diamorphine. We'll look more closely now we have the diamorphine info, but I imagine she found her way into his room through the side doors that lead out onto a communal veranda.'

Shepherd swiped through a few more photos of Michelle: various social media images, a formal shot of her with a patient, taken from the medical centre website. 'We have an arrest warrant for Michelle, for the murder of Felix Parks, and it's crucial that we co-ordinate and apprehend her as soon as possible.'

Sawyer stood up. 'Myers, Moran, get all the teams on finding Michelle. Phone data, social media, talk to her managers at the medical centre, parents, family. Let's get her in, focus on the Parks case, connect up with the Yates situation later. I'll go to see Carol Briscoe. We need more clarity on motive, but for now, we have to assume the worst. I want Osmans issued to Briscoe, Butcher and Welch. Moran, talk to Anita Birch, the ex-admin assistant at Pioneer when Canada wakes up. All aboard for a good old-fashioned womanhunt.'

47

Mia and Freddy tumbled from the back seats of the olive-green Mercedes. Freddy stomped across the gravel path towards Maggie, waiting at the open front door. Mia hurried past him, gave her mother a squeeze and shedded her padded jacket onto the floor, beneath an enormous Kandinsky reprint.

Maggie snatched up the jacket and tucked it over a chair. 'Mia...'

'Sorry, Mum. Need the toilet.' She charged upstairs and closed the bathroom door behind her.

Maggie swept Freddy up into a hug. He tolerated the moment, turning his head to the side as she planted a few kisses on his cheek, then wriggled away and followed Mia up the stairs.

Justin hovered in the hallway, outside hugging range. He left the door open.

Maggie smiled. 'Tea?'

He shook his head. 'Can't stay long. Need a smoke.'

'How was it?' said Maggie.

'Like all the other Marvel movies, to my mind. Lots of

people in silly costumes. I hate all that jokey wisecracking dialogue. Everything's so bloody ironic, these days. I think Freddy enjoyed it more than Mia.'

She eyed the plaster over his nose. 'You don't look too bad.'

He scoffed, with affection. 'Is that a compliment?'

She stepped closer. 'Your cheek is swollen.'

'Unlike my ego.'

'Who has your case?'

He lowered his head, pinched at his forehead, ruffling the skin. 'GMP. They're checking on the car they used.'

'My ears are burning.'

Justin and Maggie turned to the front door.

Curtis Mavers stood on the porch, gun raised at hip height.

Levi Wilmot stepped around him. He had a bright-red bruise around his left eye, and a cut around his jaw. He nodded at Maggie. 'Sorry to intrude, Ms Spark. Now. Let's keep nice and quiet. Nice and calm.'

Maggie turned to Justin. 'Are these...'

He nodded.

She faced Wilmot. 'Who are you? What's this—'

'Nice...' Mavers stepped in and closed the door behind him. '...and quiet.' He held Justin's eye. 'Hello again. No ballies this time. I thought we'd go for a more personal touch. And you know who we are, anyway.'

Wilmot waltzed past Maggie and turned into the sitting room. 'A fine domicile.' He beckoned with his head. 'Come and join us.'

Mavers shepherded Maggie and Justin into the sitting room. He prodded the gun towards the chocolate brown futon; they both walked over and sat down, side by side.

'Kids?' said Wilmot.

Maggie rocked in place. She held her hands to her face, cupping her mouth. Justin stayed silent, glaring at Mavers.

'We know they're both here,' said Mavers. 'Saw them come in. So where are they now? I'm not a big fan of surprises.'

Wilmot walked to the window, looked out into the dusk. 'A panoramic vista. Is this where you do your head-shrinking, Ms Spark? If I'd known your consulting premises were so salubrious, I'd have booked in a few sessions myself.' He turned. 'How old is your little girl?'

Maggie scowled up at him. 'Mia is thirteen.'

Wilmot closed his eyes and gave a slow nod. A smile crept over his lips. '*Ripe*.'

Justin shuffled in his seat. 'If you touch her...'

'Then what?' said Mavers. 'You gonna get your big mates on us again?' He pushed the gun barrel into Justin's cheek. 'That didn't work out too well for them.' He pushed his head close to Justin's. 'And now here I am, asking politely, for the last time, where are the kids?'

———

Upstairs, Mia crept into Freddy's room and closed the door quietly.

Freddy looked up from his Xbox. 'What?'

Mia stood with her back to the door. 'Those guys. They're *here*.'

The colour drained from Freddy's cheeks. 'The same ones?'

She nodded. 'I heard their voices.'

'Is Dad still there?'

'Yeah.'

Freddy flopped back on the bed. 'What do they want? Why can't they leave us alone?'

She held up a hand, shushing him. 'We need to call Uncle Jake. He gave me his number.'

Freddy sat forward. 'Do it! Quick!'

She closed her eyes, shook her head.

'What?' said Freddy.

'Phone is in my jacket pocket. Downstairs.'

48

'I hope I'm not disturbing your evening,' said Sawyer, stepping into the sitting room.

He stood to the side, as Carol Briscoe inched her way across the floor, supported by a wheeled walking frame. Carol was small and shrivelled—childlike, in stature if not agility—with a modest mane of lacquered white hair.

'Don't be silly, my love. It's nice to have a visitor.'

She huffed and puffed as she made it to a wooden-framed chair in the corner. Sawyer stepped forward to help, but she waved him away and slowly pivoted around, preparing to sit.

She brushed down her dress—blue, with a dense speckle of white daisy heads—and sank into the seat.

'Now, you mustn't judge me for wearing these...' She nodded to her slippers; beige with black trim, fitted to her feet with Velcro straps. 'I won them at bingo, can you believe it? So I'm determined to get some wear out of them. Can't stand the bloody things.'

The room was small, on the edge of poky, and smelled of recently sprayed air freshener. Cushioned foot stool; dark wood mantelpiece loaded with faded, framed photos; old

TV topped with more framed photos; small fish tank; a couple of wilting pot plants. A display cabinet beneath the window held a collection of cheap-looking figurines, and an old pendulum clock hung on the wall behind Carol's chair. All the surfaces carried either floral prints or abstract floral patterns. The floor-length curtains had both.

Sawyer sat in an armchair and nodded to an easel propped in the corner by the TV. 'Are you a painter, Carol? You used to be an art teacher, didn't you?'

She waved a hand. 'That thing is a bloody ornament in itself. It has more artistic merit than any mark I could leave on it, I can tell you. Would you like a cup of tea? I've got some fruit cake, too.'

'It's tempting. But I'm in the middle of an important investigation. I don't really have time.'

'My grandnephew is called Jack. That's him there.' She nodded to a photo on the TV: a bearded twentysomething in a graduation gown, clutching a diploma.

He smiled. 'It's Jake.'

'Oh. Of course. I'm sorry.' Carol zoned out for a second. Her eyes bobbed behind the thick lenses of her half-frame glasses.

The clock pendulum clicked out a steady two-tone percussion.

Tick, tock.

Tick, tock.

'Do you have children of your own?' said Sawyer.

She puffed out a breath and shook her head, as if the notion was ridiculous. 'No, no. I never married. I like things the way I like them, do you know what I mean? I've got my two cats as companions. They're keeping a low profile, though—'

'Could I talk to you about Pioneer Primary School? You used to work there in the 1960s and 1970s.'

'Goodness me. That's going back a bit. I can't promise I'll remember much. Can I see your identification again, my love?'

Sawyer handed over his warrant card. Carol reached out to a side table and took a full minute to swap her glasses with a dark-framed pair. She squinted into the card.

'Sawyer...'

'My mum used to work at the school. Maybe you remember her?'

Carol looked up, eyes wide. 'Of course I do! Young Jess. Oh. She was lovely. Such a terrible, terrible thing that happened to her. I'm so sorry, my love.'

'Thank you. I found an old journal she kept while she worked at the school. She seemed disturbed by the culture, the methods of punishment.'

'Oh, dear. Yes. It all seemed quite severe, even back when that sort of thing was more accepted. Mr Welch, the headmaster. We used to call him Bighead. Everyone was scared of him, and not just the children.'

Sawyer took out the journal, opened it to a bookmarked page. 'Here, my mum mentions someone called Michelle. She says she's concerned because she's getting called up to Mr Welch's office a lot. She also says that he closes the blind on his window, when he's punishing the children. Carol, do you remember Michelle? We think this might be Michelle Hawkins, a local GP now.'

Carol's head dropped. She handed back the warrant card and swapped her glasses around again.

Tick, tock.

Tick, tock.

'Yes. Michelle was... She had problems. That's what we used to call it. She had some kind of condition. An abscess, on one of her legs. Oh, it was horrible. Used to be all red and leaky. You know. *Pus*. Poor girl. Oh, it made you heave,

261

the smell of it. And I don't think she had a lot of home support or treatment, and she always had unwashed hair, which made the smell worse. She's a *doctor* now?'

'Carol, was Michelle badly behaved?'

'Oh, no. She was just... unfortunate. I used to take her for a nature painting class and she was quite talented, always so polite and positive.'

'So why was she getting called up to see Mr Welch so often?'

Carol chewed her lip, looked across to the fish tank. 'There were some nasty rumours, about old Bighead and a few of the others.'

'What kind of rumours?'

She shook her head, grimaced. 'Like I said, it's a long time ago. It's like another world.'

He leaned forward. 'Carol. There's no shelf life here. Michelle is a suspect in some very serious crimes. I need to understand what might be motivating her. Was she singled out for punishment, for some reason? Was she abused, Carol?'

She took off her glasses, cleaned the lenses. 'I remember she started to wear a bit of perfume or something. It made her smell better. I suppose it covered up the other thing. I think that's when she started to get called up to Bighead's office more often.'

'You used to call it the lair, didn't you, Carol?'

Carol said nothing and finished cleaning the lenses, replacing her glasses.

Sawyer continued. 'Did you notice how long she spent up there?'

'Sometimes it was half an hour or so.'

Sawyer frowned. 'That's a long time, Carol.'

She snapped her head up, irritated. 'I know it is! Can't

you hear what I'm telling you? There was all sorts going on up there, so we heard.'

'All sorts?'

Tick, tock.

Tick, tock.

Carol shook her head, banishing something. 'I don't want to say, Mr Sawyer. I don't know. It's just things we heard.' She flapped at herself. 'Oh, I'm all flushed now.' She took a few steadying breaths, patted her forehead. 'It was Mr Welch.' She cast her gaze over at the fish tank again. 'We were all scared of him. We did what he wanted. He took a shine to Michelle. Once he got his hooks in, I don't remember him asking for anyone else.'

49

Mia eased open the door to Freddy's room, and listened.

Voices, downstairs. Mostly one of the men, the bigger one. Sometimes her mum, dad. And the other taller man; she shuddered at his clipped, sing-song voice.

She turned to Freddy, still sitting on the bed, and whispered. 'They're in the sitting room.'

He jumped up. 'I'll get your phone.'

'Don't be stupid.'

'They'll come up and find us soon.' He pushed past her, out onto the landing. 'We've got to be quick, Mia.'

She lunged for him. But he was gone, heading for the top of the stairs. Quiet, shoeless.

'Freddy! Get back here.' A whispered shout.

He waved her away without turning, and crept down the stairs, out of sight.

Mia strained to listen to what the voices were saying, but they were too vague and muffled.

She looked around the room. At a push, she could use Freddy's desk chair as a weapon. She opened his wardrobe. Clothes, trainers, football gear.

Back to the door.

Waiting, waiting.

Mia couldn't hold on. She crept out of the room, keeping low, and headed for the landing. Freddy was scampering back up the stairs, holding her phone.

'Got it!' he said, too loud.

The sitting room door flew open, and Wilmot charged out. He gripped the head of the banister and launched himself around the corner, pushing up the stairs.

Mia backed off as Freddy reached the top.

He cried out, as Wilmot grabbed him, pulling him back.

Freddy reached up and slid the phone across the landing carpet, towards Mia. It stopped short, and she had to edge forward to swipe it up and retreat back into Freddy's room, easing the door closed behind her.

She crouched at the far side of the bed and, with trembling hands, navigated to the contacts list.

Outside, Freddy's screams and shouts.

Her father, protesting. Her mother, shouting, in distress.

The bigger man's voice, angry and insistent.

Mia tapped out a message, her thumbs swift and practised.

Footsteps on the landing.

She dropped, flat on her belly, out of sight.

The door opened, slow and silent, light seeping in under the bed. Mia glanced up and saw Wilmot's legs striding in, pausing, then hurrying around the foot of the bed, heading for her position.

She jammed the phone under the mattress, as he loomed, smiling down at her.

'Game over, little girl.'

50

Sawyer parked the Mini in the usual spot at the foot of Ecton Hill, near the old Manifold railway line that had been converted to a walking trail. A trip up to Thor's Cave in the dark wasn't ideal, but the path was clear, and the crag wouldn't be loaded with tourists.

He walked down to the trail, glancing up at the turquoise steeple of Ratcliffe's Folly, poking up through the top of the trees. It had been close to half a year since he'd visited his favourite spot for calm and contemplation. But this was its appeal: it would be unchanged, impassive. It didn't depend on him. It wouldn't have missed him.

Sawyer joined the trail and walked towards Wetton Mill, deeper into the valley, on the edge of a mobile service blind spot.

He stopped, cast his gaze along the track where it disappeared beneath a thick canopy of ash trees. The lure of the cave was strong, but this really wasn't a good idea.

Sawyer took out the bag of heroin he'd retrieved from the loose brick around the back of his house, and scattered it onto the verge beside the path, watching it disperse in the light breeze.

He took out his phone and made a call; the ringtone was fragmented and he took a few steps back in the direction of civilisation.

The call connected.

'Myers.'

'I saw Carol Briscoe,' said Sawyer, squinting up at the moon. 'Send an officer to watch her house this evening. We'll review tomorrow. I don't think she's in any danger. But it's a precaution, given that she's ex-Pioneer staff.'

'Will do. And sir...'

The phone vibrated with a message alert as he listened.

'Go on.'

'Keating has cut short his conference. He's heading back.'

Sawyer's stomach flipped. 'New victim?'

'New case. Ex-copper found at home. Adlington. Battered to death. Sally's there now.'

Sawyer closed his eyes, dropped his head. 'Terry Barker.'

Myers paused. 'Yeah. Did you know already? Neighbour called the plod. His dog wouldn't stop barking.'

He turned, hurried back toward the car. 'I'll go. Get that officer round to Carol Briscoe's. Anything from Walker or Shepherd?'

'Not yet.'

Sawyer disconnected, and clambered up the bank, towards the Mini.

He got in, sat there for a moment, waiting for the internal light to power down.

Rear-view mirror. Nothing.

His phone rang again.

Walker.

'Sir. On scene at Butcher's house.' He was agitated, out of breath. 'No answer but a neighbour let us in. Two vics. Elderly man and woman. I assume it's Butcher and his

267

wife.' He caught his breath. 'The man has been stabbed, in the neck. Looks like the woman was—'

'Slow it down, Matt,' said Sawyer. 'They won't be any less dead if you rush.'

'She was battered, sir. Her head is... Jesus, there's so much blood. I could smell it through the letterbox.'

Sawyer gunned the engine and reversed the Mini onto the road. 'I'll be there soon. Heading to Welch's place. It's not far.'

He disconnected, and pulled away, holding the phone in one hand as he drove, navigating to his text messages.

51

'Norman Welch?'

Welch flicked on the hall light, and peered out. 'Now, you don't look like a doctor.'

Shepherd showed his warrant card. 'Sorry?'

'Nothing. Hold on a second.' Welch studied the warrant card. 'What can I do for you, Detective Sergeant?'

'Apologies for the relatively late hour, but I'd like to ask you a few questions relating to your time at Pioneer Primary School.'

Welch spluttered, laughed. 'Bloody hell. Talk about ancient history. Do I have to let you in?'

Shepherd managed a smile. 'Technically, no. But it's a murder enquiry, and we think you might be able to help. I also need to inform you that you're currently subject to something we call an Osman warning.'

'And what might that be?'

Shepherd's smile wavered. 'If I could just step inside, Mr Welch. I promise I won't keep you for long.'

Welch turned and walked away. 'Come on, then. Let's get on with it.'

Shepherd followed him down a short hallway into an

airless sitting room that stank of unwashed socks and tobacco smoke. Welch settled himself into a shabby armchair and retrieved a lit cigarette from a crystal ashtray on the arm.

'What did you mean when you said I don't look like a doctor?' said Shepherd.

Welch took a puff of the cigarette and waved his arm. 'Let's just... What's this warning business all about?'

Shepherd perched on the edge of a footstool.

Welch laughed, spewing smoke. 'You're a bit big for that. Sorry. Only got the one chair. I don't do a lot of entertaining.'

'An Osman is the legal term for a police warning about a potential threat to life.'

Welch's watery eyes widened. 'A death threat?'

'Yes. Not necessarily something clear and direct. It might just be based on intelligence we consider serious enough to trigger the warning. It's a protective measure.'

Welch sucked on his cigarette. 'Right. And what do I do about this warning? Do I get special protection? Bodyguards? Can I get women bodyguards?'

He coughed out a lascivious chuckle; Shepherd didn't indulge him.

'We sometimes station protective officers, yes. We just advise the recipient to change their schedule, look out for suspicious, out-of-place activity. Sometimes we might suggest temporarily moving home. In this case, we're keen to station an officer here or close by until we consider the threat passed. I want to make it clear, though. The Osman doesn't entitle you to retaliate in the event of someone carrying out a threat.'

Welch flapped away a wisp of smoke. 'Like Tony Martin.'

'Well. He acted in the moment, when his house was

burgled. It's different. And he was ultimately convicted of using excessive force.'

'Can I ask about the nature of this threat? I'm wondering what an eighty-two-year-old man might have done to make someone want to hurt him?'

Shepherd took out his notepad. 'So are we, Mr Welch. We're investigating the deaths of two of your colleagues from the school. Felix Parks and Charles Yates. In particular, how they might relate to an ex-pupil, Michelle Hawkins.'

Welch held Shepherd's gaze, took another drag. 'Sorry to hear that Charlie's gone. Parks isn't much of a loss, though.'

'He is to his family.'

Welch exploded into a wheezy laugh. 'I heard they dumped him in that care home. I bet they're over it already.'

Shepherd fidgeted on the footstool.

Welch scowled at him. 'Are you okay, officer?'

'Detective Sergeant. Yes. It's just a little warm in here.' He turned to a page in his notepad. 'We believe that Felix Parks was murdered, Mr Welch. And there's a strong suspicion of foul play involved in Charles Yates's death.'

'And what does little Michelle have to do with any of this?'

'You remember her?'

Welch took a long draw on the cigarette, then prodded it into the corner of the ashtray. 'I watch the children from the local school. Going home, past the window. They're so different to the kids at Pioneer. These days, they're all treated like young adults. And if you brush against them, somebody calls you a paedo. My kids were given strong boundaries, and when they stepped over the line, they were punished. That gave them respect for the boundaries, and for the punishers. They didn't run to mummy when somebody raised their voice.'

'Did they have respect,' said Shepherd, 'or fear?'

Welch didn't miss a beat. 'I know. It seems like another world to your generation. But it was perfectly normal back then.'

'Things change, Mr Welch. Often for the better.'

Welch was impassive. 'That all depends on your scale of measurement. Geological change, fashion trends, scenery going past the window of a car. Everything is moving, moving, moving. Changing, changing, changing. Forging into the future. It's this... hunger for anything but now. And in the meantime, the past just piles up behind us, pushing at our backs. We spend our youth wanting to be older, and our old age wishing we were young again, pining to be back there, in the olden days, when things were simpler.'

Shepherd closed his notepad. 'Maybe that's because we want to take another go at something. Correct our mistakes. Right our wrongs.'

Welch winced, dismissive. 'I sometimes think it would be better if dementia kicked in for everyone sooner. A bit of a clear-out after thirty or forty years. Wipe those memories. A fresh start. Then we could stay there in the present, in a state of bliss. With the fog both ahead and behind, and at a time when your body is physically more able, less decrepit.'

A thud upstairs.

Shepherd looked up at the ceiling.

'That's my cat. Fat little bastard wants its second dinner.'

Shepherd swiped his forehead. 'Do you mind if I use your bathroom, Mr Welch?'

Welch laughed again. 'The bog's upstairs, yes. No bath. First on the right.'

Shepherd pulled himself upright. He headed out into the hall and scaled the steep stairs, feeling vague and unsteady.

He turned right at the landing and shoved open a wobbly door, revealing a minuscule room with a tiny sink, hand towel and wooden-seat toilet.

He pulled a cord which clinked on a retina-searing overhead light from a shadeless bulb.

He faced the mirror, leaning into the familiar sense of rising alarm, seeping up through his core, constricting his breathing.

Deep, slow, five-second inhale through the nose.

Long, slow, five-second exhale through the mouth.

And again, eyes closed now.

And again, conscious of the prickles of nausea, turning into waves. Riding them.

Shepherd leaned forward and splashed cold water on his face, mopped it away with the towel.

His phone vibrated with a call.

Sawyer.

He stepped out of the room and headed back down the stairs, connecting the call, trying to steady his breaths. 'Sir.'

A pause. 'Everything okay?'

'I'm fine. Just been going up stairs.'

He dabbed at his forehead. Cold, clammy.

Revving engine at Sawyer's end.

'Have you been to Carol Briscoe's place, sir?'

'Yes. Just left. I'll be there as soon as I can. Are you at Welch's?'

The walls and ceiling throbbed and warped. Shepherd reached out a hand and steadied himself on the banister. 'Yes.'

'What does it smell like?'

'Sorry?'

Engine rev. 'Is it pleasant? Musty? Sweet? Sour?'

Shepherd's nose twitched. 'I wouldn't call it pleasant.' He inhaled through his nose. 'There is a kind of sweet, perfumey smell, yes.'

'And Welch is definitely alone?'

Shepherd reached the bottom of the stairs, his breathing quickening. He opened his mouth wider, trying to take in more oxygen.

Sweat trickled through his beard, over his lips.

His legs buckled. The hallway pulsed in the half light.

Now his inhales were rasping gasps.

His mouth gaped, desperate for air.

'Shepherd...'

Sawyer's voice, receding.

'Walker found Butcher. Dead. Stabbed in the neck. His wife was battered to death.'

Shepherd's hand slumped down; the phone slid through his fingers and fell to the carpet.

His lips were cracked and brittle. He swept his tongue over them, but they instantly dried again.

His heart boomed against his ribcage.

He was on his knees, in Welch's hallway.

He gripped the banister support with both hands and tried to hoist himself upright.

Fingers closed around his wrist, squeezing for his pulse.

Shepherd dropped to the floor again. He was a shell, scooped hollow.

The owner of the fingers stepped back and looked down at him.

A woman's voice, patient and calm.

'Hold each breath for longer. Your body has the oxygen it needs. You just have to slow down your breathing. Focus on the banister. The texture of the wood. The shape.

Accept what's happening to your body, and take your mind away.'

Shepherd looked up, through a haze of fear.

Michelle Hawkins smiled. 'You're having a panic attack, Detective Sergeant. It'll be over soon.'

52

Wilmot shoved Mia into the sitting room. Mavers sat at Maggie's consulting desk, holding the gun on Maggie and Justin, still side by side on the futon, with Freddy squeezed between them.

'Where was she?' said Mavers.

Mia ran over to Maggie and squeezed her hand.

Wilmot nodded to Freddy. 'In the boy's room.'

Mavers angled his head from side to side. 'So, the boy comes down the stairs, you spot him. He hurries back up and you catch him. But the girl stays in his room, and doesn't help her brother.' He turned to Freddy. 'Have you got your own phone, son?'

Freddy glanced at Maggie and Justin, then gave an urgent shake of his head.

Mavers jabbed the gun towards Mia. 'I know you have, though, darling. We saw you with it at your dad's house.' He smiled, gestured to Wilmot. 'You think he's an idiot, don't you? There's not many who'd disagree with you. He didn't think to check if you'd hidden your phone in the room, did he?' Mavers glared at Wilmot. 'Get back up there and find it. Take her with you.'

'Mum!' Mia leaned in to her mother. Maggie wrapped her arms around her.

'Let her stay here with me,' said Maggie. 'Please.'

Wilmot grabbed Mia by the arm and tried to wrestle her away from Maggie.

Mavers moved in and pushed the barrel of the gun into Justin's cheek. 'See, if your dad had just taken his beating like a man, instead of going running to his ex-clients, none of this would be happening.'

Mia let go of Maggie and Wilmot hustled her away.

He glanced at Mavers, nodded toward the stairs, raised his eyebrows in question; Mavers shrugged.

Maggie leaned forward on the futon. 'Don't hurt my girl. *Please.*'

Wilmot smiled. 'Don't worry. I'll be gentle. I'm known for being a considerate lover.'

'You *fucking*—'

Justin convulsed with rage; Mavers grabbed his hair and pulled back his head, digging the gun barrel harder into Justin's cheek.

'I'll be honest with you, Justin. Your little stunt with the Yardies has put you top of my shitlist. But you've caught me in a playful mood. Tonight's games probably won't be your idea of fun. Everyone here is going to suffer, and it'll all be down to you. But at least you'll have grown a bit by the end of it. You'll have learned a personal lesson, and I promise you that you'll all still be alive at the end.'

Justin turned his eyes to Maggie. Tears ran down his cheeks. 'I'm sorry, I'm sorry...'

Maggie held on to Freddy, cradling him, burying his head in her chest. She kept her gaze away from Mavers, her whole body trembling with fear and fury.

Wilmot pulled Mia out of the room and shoved her up the stairs ahead of him.

She glared over her shoulder. 'If you try to touch me, I'll rip off your balls.'

Wilmot bayed with laughter. 'Wonderful, Mia. We were made for each other. Overly compliant partners don't really do it for me.'

He forced her back into Freddy's room. She swept her hair back over one ear, then stood by the TV. She turned and stared at Wilmot, head high. 'I can see why you wore a mask. Should have kept it on.'

'Where's your phone, little girl?'

She forced a smile. 'Being repaired.'

Wilmot closed the door behind him. He stepped around the bed, to where he'd discovered her, lying face down. He crouched and looked under the bed, lifted the pillows and duvet.

'You're very mature for a thirteen-year-old, Mia. Have you had boyfriends? I bet they were much older, yes?'

Wilmot dug his hand underneath the mattress. He jerked his head up over the edge of the bed and shot Mia a psychotic grin. He held up the phone, then placed it on the bedside table.

'Let's not worry about that for now.' He moved around the bed and stood close to Mia, speaking in a half whisper. 'You smell delightful. That's the thing about youth. Even the cheapest body spray can make your head spin. It's the way it mingles with those freshly stirring hormones.' He moved his mouth close to her neck, inhaling. 'There's nothing sullied in there. It's all so clean and untouched. Pure potential, untainted by the past. It makes me think of a fresh fall of virgin snow. The way you just want to step in it. Feel that crunch. Savour that violation, the end of its innocence.'

Mia slapped Wilmot across the cheek, and he took a step back, reeling, more in shock than pain.

He grinned again. 'You know what, Mia? I think your loved ones need to be a part of the moment where you transform. From a girl into a woman. It seems like a bit of a waste to keep things private up here.'

He swiped up the phone and grabbed Mia's arm, hustling her back out onto the landing.

'Let's move Mummy and Daddy off that expensive velvety futon and give them a show they'll never forget.'

Mia writhed and jerked as he dragged her down the stairs. 'You won't do anything to me. You won't get near me.'

'No, no. You're going to be a good girl, Mia. Because every time you lash out or resist, I'll take my razor and I'll make a little cut into your brother's face. And if you keep resisting, I'll cut off his eyelids.' He stopped on the stairs and pushed his face close to Mia's; she twisted her head away. 'I did that to a man once. He'd stolen money from my employer. We left him tied up and gagged in his own garage. He was still alive when they found him, three days later. His corneas had perforated, and his eyeballs were just two rotting bags of pus.'

Wilmot dragged Mia to the bottom of the stairs, back into the sitting room.

'Mia!' Maggie moved to get up, but Mavers raised the gun, barrel pointed upwards, and shook his head. Wilmot held her firm.

'What's the score?' said Mavers.

Wilmot held up the phone. Mia broke away and ran to Maggie. She curled up on the edge of the futon, embracing her mother.

Mavers held his hands up, palms out. 'And?'

'I haven't checked it yet.'

Out in the hall, the front door opened, then closed.

Mavers and Wilmot froze, stared at each other.

Mavers gave a sharp nod.

Wilmot exited the room, leaving the door ajar.

Maggie looked up at Mavers; he caught her eye and held a finger over his pursed lips.

The room hung in silence for a few seconds.

Wilmot crashed through the door, stumbling backwards. He tripped over a chair and fell onto his back.

Sawyer followed him in. He looked around, taking in the scene, then held up a front door key, waggling it towards Maggie. 'I'll have to give you this back one day.'

Wilmot scrambled to his feet and pulled out his cut-throat razor. He crouched, low, arms out at his side, stalking Sawyer, inching closer.

Sawyer looked down at him. 'Go on, Levi. Make me smile.'

Wilmot leapt at him, swinging the razor.

Sawyer stepped outside the arc and Wilmot swiped at air.

He tried again, forcing Sawyer back towards the door.

As Wilmot completed another swing, with his arm briefly stretched at full reach, Sawyer rushed him and drove his elbow down into the middle of his arm, snapping it at the elbow joint.

Wilmot roared in agony and fell to his knees, dropping the razor. He gripped the shoulder of his broken arm, gazing down in horror at the bent-back joint.

Sawyer pivoted on his left leg, and thrust his right knee up into the centre of Wilmot's face, drawing a loud crack and an upward spatter of blood. Wilmot dropped to the floor, like a shot animal, and lay motionless.

Mavers took a couple of steps forward, giving him sight of Wilmot. 'Did you just kill a man with two blows?'

Sawyer crouched by Wilmot, keeping his eyes on Mavers. He checked his pulse. 'He'll be fine. They'll reset his elbow, although they'll probably have to knock him out again for that. And I've definitely improved his looks.'

Mavers nodded. 'Detective Sawyer...' He wandered out in front of the futon, holding the gun out in front. 'I'm wondering who here you might care about the most, based on what I've read about you.'

Sawyer stood up. 'Been doing your homework?'

Mavers walked around the back of the futon and held the gun vertically above Maggie's head, pointing it down at the top of her skull. She closed her eyes tight, holding Mia and Freddy close.

Sawyer moved forward, but Mavers held up his other hand.

'Come on, now. Stay there. One false move. Blah, blah, blah. I need a second to think. You've ruined my plans for the evening.'

Sawyer took a seat at Maggie's desk. 'What happened, Curtis?'

Mavers frowned. 'Tonight?'

'You were on the books for Tranmere, weren't you? Promising centreback. And you've got a decent brain, good family. Lower middle-class parents. But now look at you. Hanging round with psychopaths, terrorising women and children. What would Jayne say if she could see you now?'

Mavers ran a hand across the top of his head, displaying his wolf tattoo. 'This isn't a good plan, Mr Sawyer. Appealing to my softer side. Bringing my sister into it.'

Sawyer leaned forward on his seat, resting his elbows on his knees. 'You're not a wild man, deep down, Curtis. You're not a wolf. You're a lapdog for a glorified drug dealer.'

'And how'd you work that out?'

'I don't know what he's fed you, but Dale Strickland ran a county lines drug operation exploiting vulnerable young men. I knew at least one who lost his life as a result. Strickland's no different from the people who took Jayne from promising medical student to homeless junkie.'

Mavers shook his head. 'He's made his mistakes, but that's not his business anymore. He's trying to stop all the crime related to drugs.'

'That's his front, yes. His new civic status makes it easy to keep himself outside the blast zone. But he's also an addict. Power is his fix, and you're just another pawn to be sacrificed in his latest play to bump himself up another level. Your sister was a victim of men like him, Curtis. And now you're another victim.'

Mavers raised the gun, aimed it at Sawyer. 'I've gotta say, Sawyer. I don't feel like a victim. Not with this in my hand.'

Engines outside.

Multiple vehicles. Crunching gravel.

Mavers jerked his head at the noise, held the gun back to Maggie's head.

'Thing is, Curtis, you've brought a pointed stick to a swordfight. I've called in a few colleagues who use Heckler & Koch submachine guns, Remingtons. If I were you, I'd abandon the idea of cold-blooded murder and save myself by leaving through the connecting door that leads to the kitchen, and then out of the back onto Blackshaw Moor. And I'd do it now, before my AFOs surround the house and you find yourself being processed at Manchester Prison, probably by the same screw who signed you out.'

Mavers stared at Sawyer, wide-eyed, breathing fast.

He wrenched himself away and charged across the room, shouldering through the kitchen door.

Mia sprang up and ran at Sawyer, embracing him.

Freddy clung to Justin, both wrapped in each other, sobbing.

'Armed police!'

Sawyer hugged Mia, held up his phone. 'This "well old" thing just saved your life.'

Footsteps in the hall.

Maggie made her way across to Sawyer, haunted and trembling. Mia stepped back, and Maggie fell into Sawyer's arms. Her grip was fierce, needful; he returned it, holding her head to his chest.

Running, in the hall. Bodies entering the room.

Sawyer held on to Maggie with one hand, and edged out his warrant card with the other. He held it up, facing the officers behind. 'One adult male, armed with Glock semi-automatic pistol. Exited the house through back door.'

'Sir.'

Shouts, orders.

More footsteps, hurrying out, along the hall, through the kitchen.

Sawyer prised Maggie away, looked into her eyes.

'Can't stay.'

53

The room swam into focus. Shepherd lay face up, his vision filled with the floral pattern on Welch's anaglypta ceiling.

He tried to roll over and raise himself, but found his wrists had been secured behind his back with his own handcuffs.

'We lost you for a while there.'

Michelle Hawkins knelt on the floor, crouched over the footstool, working on something she'd laid out beside her.

'Your heartrate was high, but it's come down now. I have some benzodiazepine in my bag if you feel you need it. But panic attacks tend to peak and fade fairly quickly. They rarely reoccur.' She smiled. 'You're safe now, Detective Sergeant. I'm sorry you've become involved in this.'

Shepherd managed to shuffle his body against the wall and sit upright, facing Michelle.

Norman Welch sat in his rancid old armchair, mouth covered by a strip of gaffer tape, eyes wide. His wrists had been fixed together with a tightly knotted bathrobe cord, with a further binding of gaffer tape wound around his forearms, keeping his elbows locked together.

'I know he doesn't look relaxed,' said Michelle, 'but I've

given him a big dose of midazolam. Intramuscular because I couldn't keep him still enough for intravenous, but it's taking effect now. I realise this must all be distressing for you, and I'm happy to give you a small dose to ease you back down. Things will seem calmer five minutes later.'

'Is he the last one?' said Shepherd, his voice faint and cracked. 'Did you kill Parks? Butcher? Butcher's wife? Did you try to kill Yates?'

She nodded. 'Yes, I did. And, yes. No more. Keep taking slow, deep breaths. Hold the inhales for a few seconds each time.' She waved a hand. 'But you know this. Have you suffered this before?'

Shepherd's eyelids drooped. The urge to submit, to sleep, tugged at him. 'Is that diamorphine?'

'Yes, it is.' Michelle held up a syringe, studying the contents. 'I was going to save the worst for last. Put an empty bubble into an artery, cause an air embolism. Watch him die a painful and distressing death. But...' She sighed. 'This is so much easier. And I'm not some kind of sadist.'

'So what are you, Michelle?'

Sawyer walked in slowly, stood over Shepherd.

Welch twisted in his seat, trying to see the new arrival.

Michelle stood up, holding the syringe at her side. 'I'm a killer. I accept that. But I'm not *diseased*, like this one.' She nodded to Welch, then held Sawyer's gaze. 'How did you get in?'

'You didn't bother to pull the ladder up.' He took out his warrant card. 'Detective Inspector Jake Sawyer. Let's put down the syringe.'

She laughed. 'I'm sure you've faced worse.'

'I'm sure you've saved more lives than you've taken, but I can't let you take another.'

Michelle leaned forward, studying the warrant card. 'Sawyer...' She stared at him. 'Oh my goodness.'

Sawyer nodded. 'She was my mum.'

Welch had managed to shift himself around in the seat. He stared up at Sawyer, imploring.

Michelle dropped her head. 'Miss Sawyer was kind to me. She was kind to all the children. She didn't deserve—'

'Does anyone?' said Sawyer.

She nodded. 'Yes. Any idiot can claim they regret what happened yesterday, say what their lawyer says they need to say. But there are too many who escape justice.'

'Is this justice? Isn't it more retribution?' He took a step closer. 'A personal debt. And what if I stand down and watch as you settle your debt? What then?'

She shrugged. 'You're right that I've helped save more people than I've hurt. But some human beings are... aberrations. The world is a better place without them.'

Sawyer gave a grim smile. 'We're a long way from "do no harm" here, Michelle. Why didn't you just pursue the abuse? Make an official allegation? Particularly in the post-Yewtree era. You could have come forward, sought justice for yourself and the others. Yes, there are people the human race won't miss, but it's not your decision to discriminate.'

'You discriminated, didn't you, Mr Sawyer? With that killer last year? I read all about that. And you must have hated the man who killed your mother. Well, hate never leaves you. It's like a constant ringing in your ears. Those teachers, they all colluded, feeding their desires, advancing their careers. Yates, Parks, Butcher.' She jabbed a finger at Welch. 'All in service of this piece of filth. All picking up brownie points by feeding his hunger.' Michelle looked at Shepherd, then Welch, as if momentarily dazed by the reality of the scene. 'Parks. He started it, with his private singing lessons. Then he procured, along with Butcher. They were both sometimes rewarded by Welch, allowed to take a slice for themselves. Yates was a watcher. Never got hands-on. He just stood there, staring.'

'How long had he been dead when you got into his house?'

Michelle held Sawyer's eye. 'He was nearly done. Mottled skin. Cold hands. Weak pulse. No muscle tension. Low blood pressure. Rapid breaths followed by periods of apnoea. He'd probably been on his way out for hours.'

'Did you watch him go?'

She gave a slow nod. 'His eyes were open, and I hope he recognised me. He'd seen me suffer, so many times. At least I got to do the same in his final moments.'

Sawyer took a step closer. 'But you waited too long, Michelle. You were too late.'

'Yes. And I was angry that he'd denied me the chance to have the last word.'

'Is that why you stabbed him in the eyes?'

She tipped back her head, smiled. 'I have to say, that felt good. Pushing that blade in, living out something I'd fantasised about for so long. Whatever happens to me, I'll never say that I regret it, or I was driven to it by what was done to me.' She raised her head. 'I'll stand in the dock, and I'll say it loud and clear. That I only wish I could have killed them twice.'

'And what about Butcher's wife? Why kill her? Collateral damage?'

She took a deep, slow breath. 'That's one way of putting it. I'm sorry to say, but... she was in the way. I couldn't risk her raising the alarm. I tried to make it quick. She wouldn't have known much about it.'

'You beat her to death, Michelle. She had no part in your pain. She just married the wrong man.' Sawyer moved in a little more. 'You can't correct the past with righteous wrongs. At some point, you have to see it as a double ruin. It's the effect the events have had on you personally, psychologically, and the way you've chosen to react, how that tears you down, poisons you. When you spend so much time looking back, you're just wasting your life. You lose sight of the way forward, and you deny yourself the room to believe in a brighter future.' He reached out, hand open. 'And so you get stuck in an eternal pause. Forever delayed. Unable to take another step forward.'

She looked down at Sawyer's hand, then lifted her eyes and held his gaze. 'It's an impossible grief, isn't it? We've both been grieving. For the childhoods that were taken away. For the love we were never given, and never got to give. When you lost your mother—'

Sawyer reared up, shouting in Michelle's face. '*I didn't lose my mother*. I know exactly where she is. She's in a box, under the ground, in the graveyard of Tideswell Cathedral. She's bones and teeth and dust. She has not passed. She has not been lost. She has not gone to a better place. She is not asleep. She is extinct. And no amount of fucking euphemisms or rhetoric or kind words will ever change that.'

He stood there a moment, shoulders heaving, then whipped out his other hand, gripped Michelle's arm, took the syringe and threw it to the floor.

'There is no comfort in soft words spoken at a safe distance,' said Shepherd. 'That's what my old college chaplain used to say.'

Sawyer stepped back. He took out a small key and unlocked Shepherd's cuffs.

Michelle reached out a steadying hand to the footstool, and lowered herself to the floor. 'I don't have many forward steps left, Mr Sawyer.' She winced as she settled into a sitting position. 'Breast cancer. Metastatic. Bones and brain.' She shook her head. 'I've seen enough patients go through it to know I have a year or two, at best.'

'So, this is why you acted now,' said Sawyer.

She raised her head. 'Before I meet my maker, yes. He will forgive me. I couldn't let the bastards outlive me. The past is all I have, and I wanted to... take control of it.'

'There will be an enquiry into the abuse at the school,' said Sawyer. 'I'll personally make sure it happens. I have a journal written by my mother that contains many observations that will back up your allegations, and I've spoken to another ex-teacher who I'm sure will support the claims. We'll also interview the school admin assistant, Anita Birch, and I would expect other ex-pupils to come forward. I don't know about forgiveness, but I hope you live long enough to get some justice.'

Sawyer stepped over to Welch, pinched the corner of the gaffer tape, and ripped it away from his mouth in one brisk motion. He crouched down beside him.

'You almost made it, didn't you?' Welch screwed his eyes shut. 'But the past caught up with you in the end. Over five decades, it stalked you, and it steered Michelle to this moment. And now your secret, your darkness, is going to be brought into the light.' He glanced at Michelle. 'And all shall be well.'

He stood up, nodded to Shepherd, and began to untie the cord around Welch's wrists.

Shepherd took a breath, and stepped forward. 'Michelle Hawkins. I'm arresting you on suspicion of the murders of Felix Parks, Graham Butcher, Dorothy Butcher, and the unlawful detention of Norman Welch.' He locked his cuffs around her wrists. 'You do not have to say anything...'

Sawyer walked out, down the hall, towards the front door.

He paused, studying a shape in a dark corner near the

entrance to the kitchen. But it was just a jacket hanging on a hook.

He looked across at the staircase, but Jessica wasn't sitting there, smiling.

Outside, he climbed into the Mini, held his eyes closed for a full minute, then looked up to the rear-view mirror.

The back seat was empty.

54

THREE DAYS LATER

Sawyer backed the Mini into a space in the main car park of Buxton's Cavendish Hospital. He killed the engine, but left the music playing. An earnest Northern Irish voice recounted tales of teenage exploits over a lo-fi ravey backdrop.

Maggie winced in the passenger seat. 'What's this again?'

'New band. For Those I Love. You don't like it.'

'I do. Just hard to tell what he's saying.'

Sawyer laughed. 'Music these days. It's all crash, crash, crash. And you can't hear the words. You're getting old.'

'I'm getting older. As is everyone.'

Sawyer switched the music. Now it was dubby, languid, with surging strings and an intoned voice with a Jamaican accent.

She smiled. 'The Aloof. Now this takes me back.'

'To the mid-1990s?'

'To your room at Keele. You had a lava lamp, for Christ's sake.'

'Don't judge me.' He reached over, rummaged in the glovebox, pulled out a brightly coloured bag of sweets. 'At least I didn't have a *Pulp Fiction* poster.'

Light rain scattered across the windscreen.

'I saw the piece in the *Derbyshire Times*. How the Hero Cop cleared his name. Is Dean Logan your official biographer now?'

'More or less. It pays to keep a few back channels open.'

She held his eye. 'I need to go in soon. My group starts in fifteen minutes, and they won't get far without the facilitator.'

Sawyer watched a family arriving and disembarking from a vast white people carrier. Two adults, two kids, one elderly woman in a wheelchair. 'How is everyone?'

Maggie sighed. 'Not great. It'll take time. Freddy wants to move, but Mia says that's giving in. Justin is paying for some extra security at the Roaches house. He's moving. I think he's met someone.' She tucked her hair behind her ear. 'I've booked a holiday. Crete. Get away with Freddy and Mia for a couple of weeks.'

She joined Sawyer in watching the family.

'Wilmot is in custody,' said Sawyer. 'We'll push for Section 18 ABH on Justin. Also, false imprisonment of you all. With a fair wind, we could sting him for twelve years.'

'You let Mavers go.'

'No choice. I had to get him to go in on himself, save his own skin, freak him out with a reality check.'

'Like the guy at the party. With the shotgun.'

Sawyer laughed. 'Fuck, I haven't thought about that for twenty years. We'll pick Mavers up soon. With the detail I gave him on Strickland's drug connections, there's always the chance that he'll turn on him. And I have an idea about something to help with your security. I'll come over later, after my virtual appointment with Alex.' He nodded to the hospital building. 'Get my brain looked at in there, then make a start on recalibrating my mind.' He took a sweet out of the bag, slipped it into his mouth.

Maggie snatched the bag away. 'Pear drops? Seriously?'

'They're nice! I used to get a quarter of them every Friday from the newsagent in Wardlow.' He rolled the sweet around his mouth.

Maggie turned to him. 'There could be room for one more in the Crete package.'

He smiled. 'Already spoken for. Keating's sending me back South, to help one of the Met MITs with a job.'

She turned back to the window. 'Your girlfriend wouldn't be too impressed, anyway.'

'I'm not sure she's my girlfriend anymore. A five-month gap between texts can play havoc with a relationship.'

Maggie pushed her nose to the window. The family had made it halfway up the path to the main doors. The elderly woman slumped forward in the wheelchair, a tartan blanket draped across her knees.

'Who do you think the courts will punish more? Michelle Hawkins or Norman Welch?'

'On paper, Hawkins. Three murders, false imprisonment. Probable perversion of justice for the assault on Yates's body.'

'Interfering with the scene.'

'Yeah. As for Welch, he's getting on a bit, but if enough ex-pupils come forward we can probably get him on legacy abuses. And my mum's journal will help.'

'Long time ago, Jake.'

'There's no shelf life to trauma. And he's a long way from the record for a paedophilia conviction. That guy Ralph Clarke went down for thirteen years in 2016. He was a hundred and one. Offences committed forty-odd years earlier.'

They got out of the car and walked through to reception, past the Costa outlet.

'What's the London job?' said Maggie.

'You don't want to know. I'm not sure I want to know.'

'Be careful, Jake. Your head's above the parapet now. You're a lot more than the anonymous rural type who earned his stripes in the big city.'

'I have a few more tools in my bag now.'

'Well, I'm just saying. You can't rely on being underestimated.'

They stopped by a sign, white on grey.

THE NUFFIELD HOSPITAL FOR NEUROLOGY & NEUROSURGERY

Sawyer turned to Maggie. 'I remember something you said once.'

'Just one thing?'

'About finding something bigger than yourself and dedicating your life to it. I've been doing that for most of my adult life.'

'Your mum.'

He nodded. 'And a lot of it was just hiding from the fact that I needed to move forward with my own life.'

'Find something else bigger than yourself. Something that's more about the future, less about the past.'

He laughed. 'We should probably get married first, before we start thinking about children.'

Kevin Tsong tapped his pen on the computer monitor. 'Here's our friend. Trigeminal schwannoma. It hasn't been long since the last MRI, but he looks pretty stable. No concerns there. Maybe another scan in a year or so.' He sat up, pushed his dense brown hair off his face. 'How have things been over the past few months?'

Sawyer laughed. 'I think that might be outside the scope of this appointment.'

'Any issues with memory? Dry skin? As we discussed last time, there's a possibility of Urbach-Wiethe disease. The genetic condition, often related to amygdala lesions.'

Sawyer shrugged. 'A few patches of dry skin, yes. One or two memory lapses.'

'Episodic memory?'

'I suppose so. More events. I don't really get the flashbacks anymore, of what happened when I was a child.'

Tsong smiled. 'Well, that's good news. I would like to do a few of those tests I mentioned, though. Galvanic skin response. It'll give us more clarity on the Urbach differential.'

'I may be in London for a while.'

'Ah. I'll look into options. I have several colleagues down there who come to mind. St Mary's, Cromwell. If we're on the right track, you might start to feel a little hoarse, maybe a few lesions on your eyelids. There's also the slight possibility of related epilepsy and other neuropsychiatric symptoms because of calcium build-up in the brain's blood vessels.'

Sawyer stared at the section of his brain, the unknowable matrix of channels and tributaries. 'If I do have this Urbach-Wiethe disease, you say it's genetic?'

'It tends to be, yes. Could be either side. In the few

cases I've seen, it does tend to affect episodic memory, as well as impacting on amygdala function. You might need to adapt a little, but it shouldn't cause you any life-changing issues. For the most part, it'll just make the past dimmer and more distant.'

55

Sawyer flashed his warrant card at the stationed officer and ducked under the crime tape.

'Sally all done?'

The man nodded. 'Sir. Delay with the PM so the cordon's stayed up. Word is it's getting lifted later today.'

He pushed open the yellow wooden door and walked through into the sitting room, already stripped of most of the furniture. It was a warm morning, but the house carried a musty chill, as if it had powered down, mothballed into the limbo between occupants.

Sawyer crouched, scanning the lower part of the room. Coffee table, empty dog bowl. Five of the six overhead spotlights lit up.

He turned off the switch and dragged the coffee table beneath the dud light, then stood on the table and shone his phone light up at the socket. Compared to the other bulbs, this one was smoother when unlit, less opaque. He reached up and eased his fingers around the edges, prising apart the holder clips and separating the glass from the fitting.

The lower part of the bulb had been cut away, and a small black cube fixed to the inside of the glass with thin strips of gaffer tape.

Sawyer lifted the cube away and studied it. Micro USB connection socket, small circular lens at the front.

56

'I don't believe in personality disorders, Jake. There's only bad training.'

Alex Goldman peered out of the video window, her skin luminous in the glare from her screen. Sawyer sat back on the sofa, laptop perched on the coffee table.

Bruce hopped onto Sawyer's lap.

Alex smiled. 'You look like Blofeld.'

'Funny you should say that. Bit of eye strain lately. I was considering a monocle.'

'Blofeld didn't have a monocle. It was a scar that looked like a monocle.'

He slurped on a can of Diet Coke. 'Anyway. What do you mean, bad training?'

'You've heard the old therapy axiom. You first have to admit you have a problem. But, I would say, you have to be able to define that problem effectively, to yourself. Only then can you explain it to a counsellor. If you can't do that, then you've spent your life training yourself to address the wrong problem. Or, to put it another way, when you focus on the actual behaviour, you can often see that there's no real underlying problem, just a solution that isn't working.'

'So... Self-medication. It might feel like a solution, but it can't work because it's toxic in itself.'

'Yes. You need to train yourself smarter. Find something that fills the hole but doesn't cause further issues. Think about smokers. They quit. Then, whatever cigarettes gave them, a release from anxiety perhaps, they try to get the same effect with, say, junk food. And that only redirects the anxiety to concern about weight gain, body image.'

Sawyer picked up the micro camera, rolled it around between thumb and forefinger. 'Something clicked. A sort of epiphany.'

'Go on.'

'For me, the problem is holding on, when I need to let go. I've been insisting that my mother is still with me. I've even been telling myself she's there, talking to me.'

Alex tipped her head back. 'And you know that's not true.'

'I saw Eva.'

'The woman who—'

'Reminds me of my mother, yes. We've been here before. I know I'd been away for a while, but I was shocked. It felt awkward. Something wasn't right.'

'We've talked about this before. The pattern.'

'How do you mean?'

Alex took an unhurried sip from a cup of tea. 'Seeking relationships with women who remind you of your mother. Jake... Listen.' She sat forward, wobbling the screen. 'When I was in India, I thought a lot about you. And, hearing you say this now, I have a question I want to put to you. I hope you won't find it too direct.'

'Okay. I'm braced. And you're safe behind the screen.'

'Do you resent the love you were denied from your mother? Do you blame her for getting into the affair that led to her death? Do you see it all as a betrayal of your father? Her love given to another man, and not him. Or you.'

Sawyer took another drink. 'That's more than one question. But, no. There's no resentment, there's no blame. Finding her journal showed me how her life may have been shorter than she would have hoped, but it made her real to me. Not an absence. A presence. Not an idea. A person. The journal gives her shape. It reveals her as a life lived, to be celebrated. So much more than a death to be regretted. My mother was someone who followed her heart, who was true to her own spirit. And so I'm going to work on doing the same. So, no. I don't feel any... deficit, of love. There's no loss. Only gain. From the life she gifted me and the love she gave me for the six years we shared the earth.'

Alex eased back in her chair. 'I'm calling this a breakthrough, Jake. We spoke of you being frozen, clinging to your teenage self. I think that's because as you matured, and your mature self was nagging you to accept that your mother had gone, you couldn't face it, and so you've worked hard to arrest much of your development, to hold yourself back in those teenage times, before your brain's frontal lobe became the inner adult, pushing you to acknowledge that she'd gone. The teenage part of you could cling to its short-sighted belief that Jessica was still with you, and you could wallow in a fantasy world where she might return some day, or where she could be watching over you.'

'And that's where the self-medication began.'

'Exactly. You found that process a struggle, and you sometimes needed to numb the edges, with substance abuse. But now, it seems, you've arrived at something. And this all connects to your experiences with women. We've talked before about how you've always sought out relationships that make it easy to emulate the drama you had with your mother. Because that's what women mean to you. It's deeply embedded in your learned experience as a child. An initial focus for love and comfort, and then a source of intense pain as they're taken away. And so, you take yourself away, before that can happen to you.'

Tyres on the drive. Sawyer looked out through the front window to see Shepherd's Range Rover slowing to a stop.

'What do you mean by "arrived at something"?'

'Like I said, I'm calling this a breakthrough, because it sounds a lot like acceptance, which, famously, is the final stage of grief.' She waved her arms in the air. 'And I think we've hit the nub of it all. The source of your behaviour, your trauma, your solution that isn't working. *Grief*, Jake. Good, old-fashioned grief.' Alex lowered her voice. 'You've found the courage to say goodbye to Jessica, to lay her to rest as part of the past. You've realised that there's nothing to be gained from sifting through her bones.'

'From dredging the lake.'

She clapped her hands together. 'Yes! And now you've accepted this, your recovery can begin.'

Car door closing.

'Jessica told you not to look back, didn't she? And now you've accepted that she's part of your past and not your present, there's no need to look back. I think you've suffered enough.'

'Nietzsche said that to live is to suffer, and to survive is to find meaning in the suffering.'

Alex grinned. 'Of course. I don't advise following Nietzsche on everything, but he's right on that. It also connects with your Stoic sensibility. Pain is inevitable, suffering is optional.'

Shepherd's plodding footsteps on the drive.

Sawyer exhaled. 'I think I'll always find it tough, this

idea of denying the past, always moving forward. Memory is what we are.'

'Yes, but you have to find a balance. There are two extremes to avoid. Being completely absorbed in your pain, and being so distracted by so many things that you stay away from the wound you need to heal.'

Shepherd's fist against the door; three loud thuds.

Alex leaned in to the screen. 'Jake. I think a big part of your apparent lack of fear comes from feeling that the worst thing has already happened to you, and so you feel invincible, because...' She hesitated. 'Because what could possibly be worse than seeing your own mother murdered in front of you as a child?'

Sawyer stood up, dislodging Bruce.

Tears formed in his eyes, but didn't fall.

57

They spent the first fifteen minutes of the drive in silence. Sawyer rested his head against the passenger window, gazing out as the desolate moorland blended into rippling farm fields, which receded to villages, outskirts.

Shepherd glanced over. 'Okay, now I'm worried.'

Sawyer lifted his head. 'About what?'

'We just passed a place called Broadbottom and you didn't comment.'

'That's because some of us are adults. Can I put something on?' He connected his phone to the car's Bluetooth audio.

'Let me guess. A bit of Coltrane?'

'Jazz makes me edgy.'

'Power pop? ABBA?'

Sawyer scoffed. 'Wasn't it you who told me you didn't like ABBA?'

Shepherd looked horrified. 'No. What kind of maniac doesn't like ABBA? It would be like hating chocolate. It's one of the things that makes live worth living.'

'If I wasn't so progressive, and this was twenty years ago—'

'You'd probably question my sexuality?'

The music started.

'This is an album called *We Will Always Love You*,' said Sawyer. 'By an Australian band called The Avalanches.'

'Do I look like a high court judge? I'm aware of their work. My wife has another thing by them. *Since I Left You*.'

Sawyer laughed. 'That was over twenty years ago. This one is more of a concept album.'

Shepherd rolled his eyes. 'Jesus. We're only going to Manchester, you know. Not Newcastle.'

'It's not that long. And it's a masterpiece. The band were inspired by audio recordings which were sent out to space on the Voyager probes in 1977. Summaries of life on Earth, music, greetings in fifty-five languages, animal sounds. It also contained the brain waves of the writer Ann Druyan, captured by her lover, Carl Sagan, after she'd accepted his proposal of marriage. It was his way of communicating the essence of human love, celebrating it.'

Shepherd nodded. 'Wow. Is this the bit where you embarrassingly declare your secret affections for me?'

Sawyer eyed him. 'It's pretty amazing, isn't it? A lot of the voices they sample are long dead, but their concept is about how human emotion and connection transcends the brief time we have together in person.'

'Yeah,' said Shepherd. 'We get so wrapped up in our own busy little worlds, we forget about all that.'

Sawyer rested his head against the window again. 'Your world is about to get a lot busier.'

Shepherd frowned. 'New case?'

'I'm recommending you for a bump. My Hawkins report makes it clear that she was your collar. Keating is sending me to London for a while, mainly because he wants to decompress. But when I return, I'd better return to Detective Inspector Ed Shepherd.'

305

Shepherd looked over, but Sawyer didn't turn. 'Don't you have concerns about—'

'You should take yes for an answer. And, of course I do. You suffer from anxiety. It doesn't detract from your professional abilities and instincts. But unless you want to be chaperoned on field work, you should take more serious steps to address the root causes, triggers. I can recommend someone who might be able to help more than your current counsellor. All I ask in repayment for my support is that you give her a try.'

'Thank you, sir.'

More silence, as they joined the motorway.

'The Yates shoeprint was a match for Hawkins,' said Sawyer. 'She isn't contesting the case. She's hoping the sentencing will be influenced by the abuse enquiry.'

'Strange that she stuck with the same perfume, after all that time.'

Sawyer opened a game on his phone. 'It wasn't perfume. Just the cream she used for her lifelong condition. Pungent, sickly. Probably loaded with something to make it vaguely palatable.'

'This is good,' said Shepherd, nodding at the music. 'This is like old-school trip-hop.'

'Don't let your son hear you say that when he's older.'

'When you were away, I did some work on the Darren Coleman case from last year. I looked through Walker's report. Lots of loose ends. Quite a few unsolved murders we'd connected to Scott Walton. The puppy mill guy, broiler farm owner, Duncan Hardwick, Mark Bishop, Milton Pope.'

'And Darren Coleman himself.'

'Well, yes. Walton's old boss, Sherratt, is still missing, too.' Shepherd carried another few seconds' silence. 'Walker did a good job, unearthing all of that. He answered a lot of questions about Walton's background and motivations, but there's still a big one left unanswered.'

Sawyer sat up. 'What's that?'

'We did a lot of work with GPR, gradiometers, searched a wide area of the grounds around the old abattoir. Sally's team made a few sweeps of the outbuildings. Most of them were filthy, impossible to extract any meaningful trace evidence from all the grime and comings and goings. Kids, rough sleepers. They did find a small filleting knife, covered with Walton's DNA. So, he was definitely there, not too long before we did the searches based on Virginia Mendez's movements, found Coleman and Pope in the woods nearby. So, Walton *was* there. The question is, where is he now?'

Sawyer turned back to the window. 'You've seen DI Pittman's old report. This is where you're leading to, right? I told you I'd been there with Pittman, back when I was a DC, investigating Pope's disappearance. So you're wondering if I went back, encountered Walton, buried him up near my Lake District hideaway.'

Shepherd laughed. 'That's quite a colourful—'

'Extrapolation? Well. That's not what happened, no. Good work following through your instincts, but you're way off. I didn't kill Scott Walton, and I don't know where he is.'

58

'Come!'

Sawyer entered the office, followed by Shepherd, who left the door ajar.

Farrell stayed in his seat, near the window, and smoothed down his tie. 'Gentlemen.' He rolled the chair over to his desk. 'What news from the wilds of Derbyshire?'

Sawyer took out his laptop and opened it on Farrell's desk. 'Sir. A professional courtesy.' He opened a video window. 'As we're all aware, you recently... collaborated with your ex-colleague Terry Barker, who was found dead in his home in Adlington three days ago.'

Farrell took his time opening his top drawer and peeling the seal off a fresh canister of breath mints. He shook one out onto his hand and flicked it into his mouth. 'Yes. Appalling. But nothing to do with me.'

'Barker was a capable detective in his day,' said Shepherd, 'but—'

'Yes, yes.' Farrell waved a hand. 'Alcohol abuse, underage prostitutes. This is all in his book.' He shrugged. 'Agreed, he wasn't the most salubrious character, but I did nothing illegal in seeking his assistance. He had a strong record of tracking down elusive criminals, and so I thought he'd help to find you, Sawyer. But then you pulled your little stunt with Stephanie and Jordan Burns.'

'And you're currently the subject of an IOPC investigation,' said Shepherd.

'I spoke to Terry Barker,' said Sawyer, 'not long before he was murdered. When I was away, I used a motion capture camera to give me advance warning of visitors. Terry was intrigued, and told me that he would have to step up his own surveillance game.' Sawyer took the micro camera out of his pocket and placed it on the desk. 'I found this in one of the light fittings in Barker's house. It had run out of charge, but not before capturing some very interesting high-def video. No sound, I'm afraid, but the pictures speak louder than words.' He pressed the space bar, and the video window showed a top-down view of Barker's sitting room, with a date and time stamp in the top corner.

Farrell shifted his chair to give himself a better view. He sucked on his mint, and glared up at Shepherd. 'Shut the door.'

Shepherd did so, and walked forward, for a better view of the laptop.

Sawyer smiled at Farrell, giving him the dimple. 'Sorry, sir, but I've forgotten the popcorn.'

The video jumped, and the three of them watched in silence.

Levi Wilmot, shoving a bloodied Barker into his armchair, browsing his vinyl records.

Farrell standing off in the corner, talking to Wilmot.

Barker standing, Wilmot pushing him back down into the armchair, punching him.

Curtis Mavers stepping into shot as Farrell moved to leave, discussing something with him.

Barker jumping up again, slipping out of the camera's

range. Wilmot pulling him back, with a cord around his neck.

Wilmot smiling, holding up a cricket bat.

Farrell turning, leaving the shot.

Sawyer tapped the space bar, freezing the image.

'They drag Terry away,' said Sawyer, 'mercifully off camera. You see a few flashes of Wilmot with the bat, which looks bloodied.'

Farrell raised his eyes to Sawyer, who held the moment.

'As I say, sir, a courtesy.'

'There's no implication that I'm involved in any crime here,' Farrell growled. 'I went to Mr Barker's house, these men arrived, said they had business with him alone.'

Sawyer leaned forward. 'And so you walked away, leaving him to their mercy, and it slipped your mind to call in support or report the incident.'

Farrell smiled. 'I'm not under arrest here, Sawyer. I'm not answering questions on this. I'm certainly not answering to you. I accept there's a possibility I might face disciplinary action for my association with Barker, but I see no evidence of my involvement in his murder.' He crunched on the mint. 'I expect I'll serve a suspension. Perhaps you could give me some tips on that, since you're quite the expert.'

'Well. Let's find out. I think a formal interview might be in order. I'm sorry to confirm that Adlington is a few miles outside your Greater Manchester jurisdiction. Barker's murder is being investigated by Buxton MIT, and your presence is respectfully requested at once.'

'I assume you've seen *Line of Duty*, Sawyer? A DI and a DS don't trump a DCI.'

'No, but a DSI outranks them all. Keating has been briefed and he's back at the station, eagerly awaiting your attendance.' He stood up. 'I'm afraid your carriage doesn't quite befit your status. But at least DS Shepherd's Range Rover is roomy, and anonymous. I could send for a squad car to pick you up out front if you prefer.'

Farrell swallowed, pursed his lips. 'Good work, Sawyer. But I still don't buy you. Your time will come. Someone, somewhere will take an interest in your loose ends. They'll pull at the threads and it will all unravel. I hope I'm still around to watch that happen.'

He stood. Shepherd opened the door.

'This is only partly my work, sir,' said Sawyer. 'Credit where it's due. You've got to hand it to Barker. It's quite a redemption. Potentially nicking a bent copper from beyond the grave.'

59

Sawyer lowered the rear windows of the Mini a few inches and turned off the engine. He stepped out, closed the door and turned to face the expanse of moorland, tinted purple by the late spring heather. He took out his phone and made a call, squinting through the warm morning sun across to the gritstone ridge and the pinpricks of colour, dotted beneath the prows and overhangs of Ramshaw Rocks. His father had called it 'the Roaches' ugly sister', and 'a crag with teeth'. But still the climbers blew in every year, regular as the seasonal shift.

'Dale Strickland.'

Sawyer walked a few paces from the Mini. 'Jake Sawyer.'

Strickland chuckled at the other end. 'Back from your travels. Or maybe travails.'

'Very good. Have you been watching *Countdown* in the downtime from your busy role as Mayoral Underling-in-Chief?'

'Let's keep it civil, Sawyer. To what do I owe the pleasure?'

'I'll be brief. Two things. First thing. I assume a learned man like yourself is aware of Dr Edmond Locard?'

Strickland sighed. 'Enlighten me.'

'French. Pretty much the grandfather of forensic science. He followed a basic principle. Every contact leaves a trace. The criminal always brings something to a scene, and they always leave with something. There's still a bit of work to connect everything to you, and clarify the motives, but your friends who murdered Terry Barker were most forthcoming with their trace evidence. I'd appreciate it if you'd keep yourself in the Greater Manchester area for the foreseeable future. Someone will be in touch soon.'

'Sawyer. Regardless of what you might think, I am a busy man. And this is all a bit cryptic. Are you really waiting for me to say I don't know what you're talking about?'

Sawyer walked around the high hedge at the corner of Maggie's house, and approached the front door, crunching over the gravel. 'Mr Wilmot is keeping tight-lipped, and his father's money has bought him a decent lawyer. But Mavers is still in circulation. This is a recurring theme with you, isn't it, Dale? You need to keep closer tabs on your employees' whereabouts.'

'Wilmot and Mavers,' said Strickland. 'Sounds like a firm of architects. I...' He affected an exaggerated tone of bemusement. 'I don't know what you're talking about, detective. So, what's the other thing?'

Sawyer stopped at the edge of the drive. 'You win, Dale. With Eva. I'm here to relieve you of your resentment, anger, jealousy, emasculation. Whatever it is that's keeping you fixated on me and my friends. It's up to her to decide on whether she keeps your company, but... Good luck. I'm out.'

Strickland laughed. 'Now that *is* interesting. You don't strike me as a man who makes concessions lightly, Sawyer.

What happened? Did Eva decide she needs a man who makes the news for the right reasons?'

Sawyer approached the front door. 'She's not my type.'

He hung up, knocked.

Freddy threw the door open and barrelled into him, hugging tight. 'Uncle Jake!'

Sawyer prised him away. 'Take it easy. I think I heard something crack.'

Mia and Maggie appeared behind. Sawyer handed Maggie the front door key.

'About time.' Maggie eyed him. 'You came all the way down here to give me a key?'

'Of course not. Step this way.' He turned and walked back, towards the Mini.

'All of us?' said Mia.

'All of you.'

They followed, at a wary distance.

As Maggie, Mia and Freddy rounded the corner, Sawyer had reached the Mini. He opened the back door.

Mia squealed with delight.

Two German Shepherd dogs leapt out of the Mini and bounded over, panting with excitement. Freddy and Mia petted them.

Mia looked up at Sawyer, twisting away from one as he tried to lap at her neck and cheeks. 'Are they yours?'

'No. They're yours.' He pointed to each. 'Rufus and Cain. I try not to do things in half measures. You wanted a dog. So I've brought you two.'

'What?' said Maggie. 'Where did you get them from?'

'They're my dad's old dogs. I had them rehomed last year, but the new owners are moving somewhere dog-unfriendly. It's either this or they have to go to a rescue centre. You wouldn't do that to them, would you?'

Maggie walked to Sawyer, away from Mia, Freddy and

the dogs. She stood in front of him, eyebrows raised, arms folded.

'This place is perfect for them,' said Sawyer. 'Mia and Freddy already love them, and they'll keep you safe. When I'm not around to dive in and save the day.'

Behind, the dogs lolloped around the house, towards the back garden, chased by Mia and Freddy.

'I'm sorry, Maggie.'

'What for?'

'Everything that's happened to you, to them, because of me. This isn't self-pity. It's an apology. All those wrongs. I'm trying to put them right.'

She looked past him, out to the distant rocks. '*Two* dogs, Jake.'

'They're well trained. And look at them. I'm serious. Nobody will come within five miles of this place. I did try to get you a dog who was left behind after the death of his owner. But he's an older boy. He's gone to a home that suits his needs more.'

Maggie took a step closer and smiled. 'I think I'll talk to you.'

'What?'

'The first words I ever said to you, Jake. Back at Uni. And the trouble they've caused me. This is a good start, but there's a lot of work ahead.'

He pushed a hand through his hair. 'Well. Like I said, I'm being posted to London for a while. Hopefully, it will help reset a few things. A bit of absence.'

'Makes the hearts grow fonder.'

Maggie stepped in.

The kiss was easy, unburdened, mutual.

60

Curtis Mavers crouched by the side of the bath.

'Really? Gold taps?'

'Turin. Brushed brass.'

'Amazes me why people give a shit about things like that. The water that comes out is the same for everyone.'

He aimed the gun at the bald man handcuffed to the radiator pipe, sprawled out, back against the wall. He was mid-forties, white designer T-shirt, fitted black jeans. 'We'll find you. You do realise? It won't be too hard. You're black, Liverpool accent, probably ex-con. And you wouldn't know to target me unless you had good connections. You might even be fucking dibble.'

Mavers smiled. 'Or I might have friends at GMP.'

The man raised his eyebrows, pointed. 'That's right. You might as well hand over your library card, save me a couple of days.' He rested his elbow on the toilet bowl. 'I've got a Polish lad in Ancoats. Loves taking teeth out. He told me he once kept a bloke in a shipping container for two weeks, pulling out his teeth with pliers, one every morning.' The man laughed, deep and dark. 'Apparently, he only spilled the name they needed on the twelfth day. They checked, and it was bullshit. So they came back and cut out his tongue.'

Mavers yawned, beneath his balaclava.

'Sorry,' said the man. 'Am I boring you?'

'Yes. I need two things, then I'll be on my way, and you can get busy tracking me down. The location of your personal safe, and the numbers I need to get into it. My contact tells me it's on the ground floor of this palatial crib. I just need a little more detail.'

'No problem. It's behind the Auerbach. If, as I assume, you're unfamiliar with his work, that's the big yellow and red picture in the sitting room. The safe is a modern Yale, in a recess behind the painting. Keypad combination. 12462481. Tell me. Are you a religious man, Mr—'

Mavers held up a finger. 'You cunning old fox. Nearly had me there. No. I'm not. Why?'

'Me neither. I believe we only get one chance at life, and our day of reckoning arrives, and then we're returned to the earth. So... Congratulations. Because you've just brought your day forward considerably. Wherever you think you're going to lie low after this, we'll find you. Whether it's a beach shack in the Bahamas, a bothy in Shetland or a cave in Shitfuckistan, you *are* going to suffer very, very badly for this.'

Mavers got to his feet, opened the bathroom door. 'Well. I'll just be taking those ill-gotten gains, and I'll be on my way. I'm not a barbarian. I'll let you keep your phone, in that funny little old-person wallet in your inside pocket. I'm afraid I'm going to have to put your lights out for a while, though. No permanent damage. I just don't want you calling any Polish torturers until I'm well on the way to Mexico.' He covered his mouth. 'Oops!' He stood over the bald man. 'When crime historians write about this, they'll talk about me, about how I cleaned up the dealers around

317

here, both the street thugs and the heartless puppet master scum. Like you.'

The man closed his eyes, bracing. 'And are you your own master, then? Is there anyone pulling your strings?'

'You wouldn't want to mess with my boss. Seriously. I don't care how many posh paintings you've got.'

'And who might your boss be, my friend?'

Mavers raised the butt of the gun.

'His name is Sawyer. Jake Sawyer.'

BOOK SEVEN IN THE **JAKE SAWYER** SERIES

JAKE SAWYER is in demand. With his profile raised after his successes in the Peak District, he's called to London to help the Met Murder Squad with a baffling case which has shocked the nation.

A family of four has been tortured and murdered in their Fulham home. The crime's disturbing details are kept private to deter copycats. But when the killer strikes again, so soon after the first attack, the pressure mounts to understand his motives before a third family faces his wrath.

As Sawyer struggles to settle in the big city, he follows a theory about the killer which leads him deep into an urban underworld where the lines between pleasure and pain are blurred.

https://books2read.com/crlsummer

JOIN MY MAILING LIST

I occasionally send an email newsletter with details on forthcoming releases and anything else I think my readers might care about.

Sign up and I'll send you **a Jake Sawyer prequel novella**.

THE LONG DARK is set in the summer before the events of CREEPY CRAWLY. It's FREE and totally exclusive to mailing list subscribers.

Go here to get the book:
http://andrewlowewriter.com/longdark

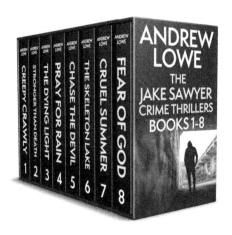

BOOKS 1-8 IN THE **JAKE SAWYER** SERIES

AVAILABLE IN EBOOK and PAPERBACK

READ NOW WITH **KINDLE UNLIMITED**

https://books2read.com/sawyerboxset4

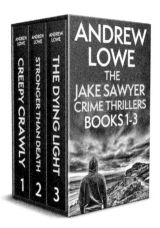

BOOKS 1-3 IN THE **JAKE SAWYER** SERIES

AVAILABLE IN EBOOK and PAPERBACK

READ NOW WITH **KINDLE UNLIMITED**

https://books2read.com/sawyerboxset1

BOOKS 4-6 IN THE **JAKE SAWYER** SERIES

AVAILABLE IN EBOOK and PAPERBACK
READ NOW WITH **KINDLE UNLIMITED**

https://books2read.com/sawyerboxset2

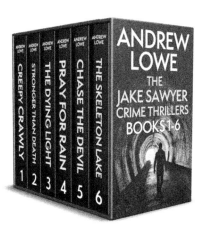

BOOKS 1-6 IN THE **JAKE SAWYER** SERIES

AVAILABLE IN EBOOK and PAPERBACK
READ NOW WITH **KINDLE UNLIMITED**

https://books2read.com/sawyerboxset3

ACKNOWLEDGMENTS

My infinite thanks to **DC Ralph King** and **DC Simon Albrow** for their wisdom on UK police terms and procedure, and **Andy Barrett** and **AJ Scudiere** for the unflinching advice on matters forensic and arterial.

I'm grateful to **Annie Hogg** from Launton Grange Care Home, for her extensive response to my vague query about security in residential care.

Bryony Sutherland was the all-seeing, all-knowing, ABBA-disliking editor.

Cover by **Book Cover Shop**

Special thanks to **Julia**, for listening to me go on about it all.

Andrew Lowe. London, 2021

PLEASE LEAVE A REVIEW

If you enjoyed **THE SKELETON LAKE**, please take a couple of minutes to leave a review or rating on the book's **Amazon** page.

Honest reviews of my books help bring them to the attention of others, and connecting with readers is the number one thing that keeps me writing.

Go here to leave your review:
https://books2read.com/theskeletonlake

THE JAKE SAWYER SERIES

THE LONG DARK
CREEPY CRAWLY
STRONGER THAN DEATH
THE DYING LIGHT
PRAY FOR RAIN
CHASE THE DEVIL
THE SKELETON LAKE
CRUEL SUMMER
FEAR OF GOD
TENDER IS THE NORTH
BLOOD NEVER SLEEPS (2025)

BOOKS 1-3 BOX SET
BOOKS 4-6 BOX SET
BOOKS 1-6 BOX SET
BOOKS 1-8 BOX SET

GLOSSARY

ACT – Acceptance and Commitment Therapy. A form of psychotherapy that uses acceptance and mindfulness strategies along with commitment to behaviour change.

AFO – Authorised Firearms Officer. A UK police officer who has received training, and is authorised to carry and use firearms.

ALF – Animal Liberation Front. A political and social resistance movement that promotes non-violent direct action in protest against incidents of animal cruelty.

ANPR – Automatic Number Plate Recognition. A camera technology for automatically reading vehicle number plates.

AWOL – Absent without leave. Acronym.

BSE – Bovine Spongiform Encephalopahy. Colloquially known as 'mad cow disease'. A neurodegenerative condition in cattle.

CCRC – Criminal Cases Review Commission. Independent body which investigates suspected miscarriages of justice in England, Wales and NI.

CI – Confidential Informant. An individual who passes information to the police on guarantee of anonymity.

CBT – Cognitive Behaviour Therapy. A form of psychotherapy based on principles from behavioural and cognitive psychology.

CID – Criminal Investigation Department. The branch of the UK police whose officers operate in plainclothes and specialise in serious crime.

COD – Cause of Death. Police acronym.

CPS – Crown Prosecution Service. The principle public agency for conducting criminal prosecutions in England and Wales.

CROP – Covert Rural Observation Post. A camouflaged surveillance operation, mostly used to detect or monitor criminal activity in rural areas.

CSI – Crime Scene Investigator. A professional responsible for collecting, cataloguing and preserving physical evidence from crime scenes.

CSO – Community Support Officer. Uniformed but non-warranted member of police staff in England & Wales. The role has limited police powers. Also known as PCSO.

D&D – Drunk & Disorderly. Minor public order offence in the UK (revised to 'Drunk and disorderly in a public place' in 2017).

Dibble – Manchester/Northern English slang. Police.

EMDR – Eye Movement Desensitisation and Reprocessing. An interactive psychotherapy technique used to relieve psychological stress, particularly trauma and post-traumatic stress disorder.

ETD – Estimated Time of Death. Police acronym.

FLO – Family Liaison Officer. A specially trained officer or police employee who provides emotional support to the families of crime victims and gathers evidence and information to assist the police enquiry.

FOA – First Officer Attending. The first officer to arrive at a crime scene.

FSI – Forensic Science Investigator. An employee of the Scientific Services Unit, usually deployed at a crime scene to gather forensic evidence.

GIS – General Intelligence Service (Egypt). Government agency responsible for national security intelligence, both domestically and internationally.

GMCA – Greater Manchester Combined Authority. Local government institution serving the ten metropolitan boroughs of the Greater Manchester area of the UK.

GMP – Greater Manchester Police. Territorial police force responsible for law enforcement within the county of Greater Manchester in North West England.

GPR – Ground Penetrating Radar. A non-intrusive geophysical method of surveying the sub-surface. Often used by police to investigate suspected buried remains.

HOLMES – Home Office Large Major Enquiry System. An IT database system used by UK police forces for the investigation of major incidents.

H&C – Hostage & Crisis Negotiator. Specially trained law enforcement officer or professional skilled in negotiation techniques to resolve high-stress situations such as hostage crises.

IED – Improvised Explosive Device. A bomb constructed and deployed in ways outside of conventional military standards.

IDENT1 – The UK's central national database for holding, searching and comparing biometric information on those who come into contact with the police as detainees after arrest.

IMSI – International Mobile Subscriber Identity. A number sent by a mobile device that uniquely identifies the user of a cellular network.

IOPC – Independent Office for Police Conduct.

Oversees the police complaints system in England and Wales.

ISC – Intelligence and Security Committee of Parliament. The committee of the UK Parliament responsible for oversight of the UK Intelligence Community.

MCT – Metacognitive Therapy. A form of psychotherapy focused on modifying beliefs that perpetuate states of worry, rumination and attention fixation.

MIT – Murder/Major Investigation Team. A specialised squad of detectives who investigate cases of murder, manslaughter, and attempted murder.

Misper – missing person. Police slang.

NCA – National Crime Agency. A UK law enforcement organisation. Sometimes dubbed the 'British FBI', the NCA fights organised crime that spans regional and international borders.

NCB – National Central Bureau. An agency within an INTERPOL member country that links its national law enforcement with similar agencies in other countries.

NDNAD – National DNA Database. Administered by the Home Office in the UK.

NHS – National Health Service. Umbrella term for the three publicly funded healthcare systems of the UK (NHS England, NHS Scotland, NHS Wales).

NHSBT – NHS Blood and Transplant. A division of the UK National Health Service, dedicated to blood, organ and tissue donation.

OCG – Organised Crime Group. A structured group of individuals who work together to engage in illegal activities.

OP – Observation Point. The officer/observer locations in a surveillance operation.

Osman Warning – An alert of a death threat or high risk of murder issued by UK police, usually when there is intelligence of the threat but an arrest can't yet be carried out or justified.

PACE – Police and Criminal Evidence Act. An act of the UK Parliament which instituted a legislative framework for the powers of police officers in England and Wales.

PAVA – Pelargonic Acid Vanillylamide. Key component in an incapacitant spray dispensed from a handheld canister. Causes eye closure and severe pain.

PAYG – Pay As You Go. A mobile phone handset with no contract or commitment. Often referred to as a 'burner' due to its disposable nature.

PM – Post Mortem. Police acronym.

PNC – Police National Computer. A database which allows law enforcement organisations across the UK to share intelligence on criminals.

PPE – Personal Protective Equipment designed to protect users against health or safety risks at work.

Presser – Press conference or media event.

RIPA – Regulation of Investigatory Powers Act. UK Act of Parliament which regulates the powers of public bodies to carry out surveillance and investigation. Introduced to take account of technological change such as the grown of the internet and data encryption.

SAP scale. A five-point scale, devised by the Sentencing Advisory Panel in the UK, to rate the severity of indecent images of children.

SIO – Senior Investigating Officer. The detective who heads an enquiry and is ultimately responsible for personnel management and tactical decisions.

SOCO – Scene of Crime Officer. Specialist forensic investigator who works with law enforcement agencies to collect and analyse evidence from crime scenes.

SSU – Scientific Services Unit. A police support team which collects and examines forensic evidence at the scene of a crime.

Tac-Med – Tactical Medic. Specially trained medical professional who provides advanced medical care and support during high-risk law enforcement operations.

TOD – Time of Death. Police acronym.

TRiM – Trauma Risk Management. Trauma-focused peer support system designed to assess and support employees who have experienced a traumatic, or potentially traumatic, event.

Urbex – urban exploration. Enthusiasts share images of man-made structures, usually abandoned buildings or hidden components of the man-made environment.

VPU – Vulnerable Prisoner Unit. The section of a UK prison which houses inmates who would be at risk of attack if kept in the mainstream prison population.

A WOMAN TO DIE FOR

AN EX WHO WOULD KILL TO GET HER BACK

Sam Bartley is living well. He's running his own personal trainer business, making progress in therapy, and he's planning to propose to his girlfriend, Amy.

When he sees a strange message on Amy's phone, Sam copies the number and sends an anonymous threat. But the sender replies, and Sam is sucked into a dangerous confrontation that will expose his steady, reliable life as a horrifying lie.

https://books2read.com/dontyouwantme

**WHAT IF THE HOLIDAY OF YOUR DREAMS
TURNED INTO YOUR WORST NIGHTMARE?**

Joel Pearce is an average suburban family man looking to shake up his routine. With four close friends, he travels to a remote tropical paradise for a 'desert island survival experience': three weeks of indulgence and self-discovery.

But after their supplies disappear and they lose contact with the mainland, the rookie castaways start to suspect that the island is far from deserted.

https://books2read.com/savages

ABOUT THE AUTHOR

Andrew Lowe was born in the north of England. He has written for *The Guardian* and *Sunday Times*, and contributed to numerous books and magazines on films, music, TV, videogames, sex and shin splints.

He lives in the south of England, where he writes, edits other people's writing, and shepherds his two young sons down the path of righteousness.

His online home is andrewlowewriter.com

Follow him via the social media links below.

Email him at andrew@andrewlowewriter.com

For Andrew's editing and writing coach services, email him at andylowe99@gmail.com

f facebook.com/andrewlowewriter

X x.com/andylowe99

○ instagram.com/andylowe99

♪ tiktok.com/@andrewlowewriter

BB bookbub.com/profile/andrew-lowe

a amazon.com/stores/Andrew-Lowe/author/B00UAJGZZU

Printed in Great Britain
by Amazon